King's Head Violin

Journey of a Paiute

Arvel Bird

And

Fred Rothert

ISBN: 979-8-9870671-0-9

DEDICATION

I want to dedicate this book to the hundreds of thousands of mixed-blood American Indian people in this country who felt like my Mother did. She neither felt accepted by the white society she grew up in, nor the Southern Paiute people who resisted her because she didn't grow up on the reservation. Back in the late 1800s, when my Grandmother was born in a teepee at the Indian village in Silver Reef, UT, there were no records kept. When she became an orphan as a toddler she was traded to a good Mormon family in St George, Utah, for a horse and buggy. She was assimilated into their culture and never got to know her Shivwit Paiute family. This was all part of the dominant culture's plan. This is what has made me who I am and I choose what part of my ancestry I wish to honor. I choose my Native American heritage and my Celtic culture.

I am Arvel Bird Celtic-Indian

Table of Contents

TABLE OF CONTENTS V

ACKNOWLEDGMENTS VII

CHAPTER ONE 1

CHAPTER TWO 17

CHAPTER THREE...31

CHAPTER FOUR 41

CHAPTER FIVE 53

CHAPTER SIX 67

CHAPTER SEVEN...77

CHAPTER EIGHT 85

CHAPTER NINE 105

CHAPTER TEN..117

CHAPTER ELEVEN...135

CHAPTER TWELVE..153

CHAPTER THIRTEEN 167

CHAPTER FOURTEEN..177

CHAPTER FIFTEEN 195

CHAPTER SIXTEEN..211

ABOUT THE AUTHORS 223

ACKNOWLEDGMENTS

Arvel Bird and Fred Rothert have been long-time friends and musical partners over the past 46 years. From once blazing a path through Fort Wayne, IN's late 70s and early 80s hot music scene, they have now shared their love of storytelling and novel writing. This is not like a documentary but more like a feature-length movie taking place during historical events.

I would like to acknowledge some of the violin teachers that have made a big difference in my life and in my violin playing. My first violin teacher in Salt Lake City, Mrs. Olea Kinke, who told me, "Arvel you don't have to be the best violinist or the fastest one in the world. As long as you play with a passion, that is what people will remember, that is what they want to hear." And Dr. Paul Roland of the University of Illinois at Champaign/Urbana. After struggling to play at my full potential for 10 years, he took me apart and built me back up from the ground floor basics to where I "knew" I knew how to play the violin and my performance level reached the top of my ladder and released that passion I was looking to deliver.

My Grandmother, Rhoda Carpenter Johnston, a full-blood Shivwit Southern Paiute, who gave my mother the violin I was destined to fall in love with and begin to play. Her warming love was what I needed at a time in my life when turbulence, anger, upset, and confusion were the norm in my household. To Mrs. Kenner, my third-grade teacher in Provo, UT, who gave a little boy, starving for love, a kiss on the cheek after school every day before I went home.

To the man, whose name I no longer remember, that told me at a workshop in Brevard, NC, that I had permission to let go of a humiliating experience, when I suffered a memory loss at a high-profile violin recital in Scottsdale, AZ. I was 15 years old. It was 15 years later when he told me, "You're no longer that 15-year-old boy now. You're somebody completely different now. Bless that boy who failed in the heat of the moment but got back up to journey on. He never gave up, he never gave in, and he learned how to win. Forgive him and don't beat yourself up anymore for his failure because that was just a step toward your own greatness."

To my dear friend Doris 'White Wolf' McFadden for her kindness, friendship, and the editing of this book.

To all the women in my life from relationships to marriages to mentors to Essence Twin Souls and daughters. Women have been the molders of my life and I have always strived to be, or become, the man they see in me. All my relationships have been an attempt to heal the Mother-Son relationship and I finally found that healing in myself with a woman named Karen Reedstrom who saw in me the man I was, and am becoming, the man I want to be. Her love and caring have been the healing and she has given me the safety to be myself without restraining or manipulating me. This is what I have always longed for. Karen Reedstrom has also been instrumental in the release of this book in all of its technical and publishing aspects. Without her, it would still be on my shelf waiting. —Arvel Bird

Chapter One

The calendar said April, but the cold wind offshore didn't carry any hint of spring with it. William Kennedy stood at the railing of the merchantman *Usher*, sailing from Liverpool, as she reached her destination – Baltimore.

It had been an uneventful journey; insofar as trans-Atlantic crossings of that era could be uneventful. It was cold and grey and very rough. William had spent several miserable days hunched over the railing, uncomfortable and bored, for the most part. The few good moments were the calm evenings when there was dancing to William's fiddle playing.

But now the voyage was ending, and William was facing a new life in a new world with a new slate. There hadn't been much future for him in Scotland, not for the third son of a small farmer. The New World had beckoned for as long as he could remember, and now, after much hard work and great sacrifice, he was here.

He turned to a man standing next to him as they watched the famous Fort McHenry glide by on their starboard. Just eight years ago it had withstood a memorable British bombardment. "Your first time here?" he asked the man, who looked to be in his early thirties, about ten years older than William.

Taking him in with a quick glance, the man replied, "No, I've been in Baltimore more times than I can count. I travel here on business quite regularly. And you?"

"My first journey anywhere outside Scotland," William answered with a diffident smile.

"Do you have people here?"

William shook his head as his gaze returned to the harbor. "Nae, I hae no friends nor relatives here, nor anywhere in America." The two stood in silence for a moment. Then William turned to his acquaintance and asked, "Since ye know the city, could ye recommend a good place to stay?"

The man chewed his lip and replied, "Well, I always take a room at Old Edna's, but I don't think she has any more vacancies. You might try The White Inn or Harbor Home." Glancing at the violin case in William's hand, he said, "I've heard you playing on board a few times. You do very well on that fiddle."

Before William could acknowledge the compliment, his companion went on. "I bet they'd love you at Curry's Saloon – maybe even let you live upstairs."

"Curry's?" William asked. "What kind of place is that?"

"Oh, it's not a bad old place. Pretty down-to-earth I'd say. I think I heard old Curry had fallen on some hard times though. Don't know. But I say, check the place out. It's just off Pratt after you cross Howard. Good luck to you, William."

The city spread out before him in the early spring morning – chilly and bare, with just a hint of yellow green in the trees. The church steeples poked up over the rambling city, and up away from the docks he could see some newly green pasture lands.

Once off the ship, William's legs felt odd, anticipating a list from side to side. He had to concentrate to avoid staggering for a few minutes before his land legs began to come back to him. The wharfs and markets were crowded with people, many of whom were black. They were everywhere doing every sort of job. William didn't know whether they were slaves or free blacks, but they were an oddity to him. He'd only seen a few people of color in his life.

He crossed Howard Street and up a little alley to his right he saw Curry's. It had seen better days, peeling paint and sagging porch a few inches off the bare dirt yard. It was open for business though, and at noon there was a boisterous mob eating and drinking with gusto. William decided to wait for the crowd to thin before going in and after a while open tables began to appear. Carrying his sea bag at his side and his fiddle in its case, he nervously entered. He walked to the bar and ordered a beer, gingerly fingering the few remaining coins in his pocket. He settled his bag to the floor and laid the fiddle case across his lap as the thin, sleepy-looking bartender pushed a foaming glass of beer his way.

The place was as seedy inside as out; a zinc bar across the far end of the room, mismatched tables and chairs scattered around the front space and dark wooden floor with wide beams and big cracks between. It was less than half full by now, and the cigar smoke was thick around the few remaining customers at tables. There were half a dozen men sitting at the bar, their eyes and attention focused on the drinks in front of them.

William sat sipping at his beer, wondering what he should do next. When his glass was nearly empty, the bartender came back and asked using his eyebrows if William wanted another one.

"Uh… ay, "he stammered, reluctant to waste his scanty funds on another beer, "I am a bit drouthy." The bartender shoved a frothy mug towards him with a bored expression and collected the nickel William had proffered. He summoned up his nerve and awkwardly blurted out, "Do'ye ever hae music here and Dancing, I mean? Fiddle music?"

The bartender raised his eyebrows skeptically. "Curry used to play here himself," he drawled, "but his hands're no good anymore. Since then, he does have somebody play once in a while. They've got to be good in this place, though. The customers don't put up with any second-raters." He leaned over the bar to look at the case on William's lap. "I'm guessin' you play – that's why you're asking?"

"Yes" he answered with some pride. "I had my share of good times in Edinburgh, and all across the Atlantic the passengers and crew danced to my fiddling."

"Oh… just off the boat, are you?" The bartender asked with a condescending grin.

William sensed the condescension and replied stridently, "Ay, and I'm looking for work and a place to stay, and a place to play my fiddle if I can find one that'll gie me a chance."

The bartender turned toward William in surprise and amusement. "All right friend, calm down. It's not as if it's my business, anyway," he shrugged. "You'll need to talk to Curry. He's the boss."

"Where might I find Mr. Curry?" William asked.

"Mister Curry? I wouldn't call him that. He doesn't care to be called 'Mister'." He looked around the room. "That's himself, sitting with those two other men. In the red corduroy jacket."

3

William followed the bartender's nod and saw three men swathed in smoke seated around a small table. They didn't seem particularly engaged at the moment, so he steeled himself to walk over and introduce himself.

He almost began, "Mister…" but he followed the bartender's advice. "Curry?" he asked hesitantly.

"And if it is?" Curry snarled without looking up.

"Well, my name is William Kennedy…"

"And if it is?" Curry barked again, turning toward him with angry dark eyes sunk in a bloated face.

"I'm sorry to bother you sir, but…"

"And you have bothered me, haven't you?" he roared. The few men in the saloon turned briefly to see what was going on and then returned to their concerns.

"I just wanted to ask if I could play the fiddle here!" William snapped in return. "I didna mean to disturb ye!" He stood awkwardly for a long moment, feeling foolish and furious.

"Well," drawled Curry, "you play the fiddle, do you? Where have you worked in town?"

"Why, I just arrived here from Scotland. I've had naw chance to open ma case yet. You're the first person I've approached."

Curry turned to his two friends with a gleam in his eye. "Should I not be honored by this, gentlemen?" he said. They smiled tolerantly; mildly interested to see where Curry was taking his encounter with this tenderfoot fresh off the boat. "That he has chosen my humble establishment". He gestured broadly around the now nearly empty room — "to make his debut in the New World! I marvel at my good fortune."

The three men laughed heartily while William's face turned red.

"D'ya want to hear me play, or d'ya just want to ridicule me for where I come from and how long I've been here?" William spit out.

The men laughed louder, and Curry beckoned, saying "Play! Play, indeed! Let us hear this Celtic minstrel!"

William, embarrassed and furious, was tempted to turn on his heel and give up this place as a lost cause. But, instead, he opened the case and tightened and rosined his bow. The fiddle he lifted from its case was an old one, with a rich dark finish from years of loving care. At its headstock was a curious carving of a king's head, complete with beard and crown. He tuned up the fiddle with a few deft twists of the pegs and began playing. "This one I learned just afore I left Scotland. I've been playing it a lot on the ship and fowk seem to like it. It's called 'Money Musk.'" And he began to play. He did not astound his audience. Curry had been a champion fiddler in his day and his friends knew their music as well; they weren't likely to be carried away even by a fine performance. But they could tell that he was good – good enough to play at Curry's, where the crowd didn't tolerate second raters.

When he was done with his first piece, Curry sat thoughtfully, chewing his lower lip. "Give us a waltz, if you have one," he said. William quickly launched into "Scots O'er the Border. ""All right," said Curry, "You've got a good touch on that fiddle. I won't say the greatest, but good enough for this lot of buggers and bums." His friends laughed appreciatively. "Here's my offer: you play from seven to eleven, and you can take a piss whenever you need to. You'll get a meal before you start and a bed after, so long as the customers like you. If they aren't satisfied, you're gone. That's all."

William didn't have to ponder long. He figured he would make some tip money, and a meal and a bed were the most important things on his mind for now. "There's a bargain struck, sir," he began, but he noticed the dark look crossing Curry's blotchy, fat face.

"I'm not sir – nor mister – I'm just Curry. Don't be putting on airs for me. I'm just a crippled-up fiddler and owner of this dive. And that's all I want to be."

"Well… Curry, then. I'll make a try. And I hope your customers will be satisfied."

"Lisbeth!" Curry called out to a light-skinned black girl working behind the bar. "Show this young man… What's your name again?"

"William Kennedy, si… I mean, Curry."

"Show William Kennedy to his room upstairs, Lisbeth. And get right back down here and finish your work."

Without a word, the young woman put down her towel and beckoned to William. She led him up a dark staircase to a musty-smelling room with one dirty window barely illuminating the place. There was a cot with a straw tick, a small table with a half-burned candle on it, and one chair with a missing rung.

He looked at it for a moment. It was rough quarters, but no worse than what he had had on the ship, or even the room in Edinburgh where he lived saving money for his passage. "Thank

5

you, Lisbeth," he shyly spoke. "How long hae you worked for Curry?"

She regarded him with an uncomprehending stare. "Well, I've been his slave all my life, if that's what you mean. He bought my mother before I was born."

William was shocked by the harsh reality of what it meant to be a slave. He had read about slavery and had heard about some of the agitation in Britain to end slavery in her colonies, but it was different to come face to face with an enslaved person, a girl somewhat younger than himself who had been born a slave and would likely remain so for her entire life. He didn't know how to respond.

"Oh, I see... well, you know, I'm from Scotland and we hae naw slaves there, so I didn't realize..."

Lisbeth knew better than to respond to a stranger's talk of slavery. That was a sure way to get a whipping. "You can get your dinner at six," she said. "Your chamber pot is under the bed. You can pitch it out the back window when it's full." She turned away and was gone before William could reply.

He dropped his sea bag on the floor, carefully placed his fiddle case on the table and stretched out on the bed. It had been an eventful day already. newly arrived in Baltimore, in America, and already settled in with a job and a room. More than he had expected. He dozed off feeling very pleased with himself.

Lisbeth shook him awake. He had no idea how long he had slept. He sat up with alarm. "What time is it? Am I late?" he asked anxiously.

"No, it's just six. Get yourself ready and come downstairs for your supper."

He busied himself with the chamber pot and tossed the waste out the window into the filthy back yard. There was a ewer and basin with cold water in it. He splashed his face to wash the sleep from his eyes, brushed back his black hair, tied a ribbon to make a thick, long ponytail, and headed downstairs with his fiddle under his arm.

He fed on steaming crab legs, oysters and potatoes, and good warm bread. And drank three mugs of frothy ale. Then he pulled out his fiddle and looked around the place. Over half full now and men still coming in. Women were there too – some likely proper wives with their husbands, others, ladies of the town. William stood in the corner where the bar met the outer wall and began tuning his fiddle.

The room was noisy, profane, and jolly. No one paid much attention as William began to drag his bow across the strings. No one seemed to mind, either, and that was something. On and on he played, sometimes provoking some dancers to step out in the middle of the floor, followed by applause for the dancers, yes... but, he realized, also for him.

Fresh glasses of beer continually appeared next to him as he played, and he downed them quickly between tunes. Requests were called out, and luckily, William knew many of them. When he played "To Anacreon in Heaven," he was puzzled to hear many of the customers breaking into song. They were singing lyrics he had never heard before. Someone told him the words were from a poem written at the siege of Fort McHenry during the last war. It was quite a popular piece in Baltimore. By the time he needed to take his first short break, the crowd was clapping along and heckling him for quitting. After a quick trip around the back to the stinking alley, he returned to continue with the music, song after song and drink after drink. When eleven o'clock came, the crowd hadn't thinned at all, and William gladly played on until there were only a few men left.

Curry hadn't been there most of the night, but he showed up around eleven o'clock, just in time for William's extended encore, and when he put away his fiddle, Curry approached him. "You play for the people, don't you? I like that. Not just by the hour, but for how long they want to listen. I think we'll get along just fine here." He paused and looked slyly at William. "Do you need a little company tonight?"

William was no virgin – he'd been with girls back on the farm in Scotland and in Edinburgh when he was working there. But it had been a long time since. "Aye," he nervously replied, "I wouldna mind."

Curry laughed a hoarse, smoky chuckle. "Yes, we'll get along just fine here. Sweet dreams." Through his ale-induced fog, William was pleased at this pleasantry from Curry. It was certainly an improvement from the gruff man he had first met earlier in the day.

He lurched upstairs to his tiny quarters, filled, and emptied the chamber pot, and sprawled out on the bed. He fought against the spinning room and in a few minutes, he drifted off to sleep. He awoke in the night, surprised to find a woman's body next to him. He got up, relieved himself in the pot, and slipped back into bed, reaching out for his bed companion. She turned toward him, and he felt her hot flesh press close to his. He leaned over to kiss her, but she turned her head away. Instead, she placed her hands on his cock, encouraging it to rise and harden. William moaned with pleasure and then she quickly pulled him on top of her. As he slipped inside her, she gasped and whispered, "Oh yes, yes!" at his size and hardness.

Afterwards, they lay side by side, panting. He turned to look at the profile of her face and recoiled in surprising shock.

"Lisbeth! He exclaimed. I'm so glad, but I didn't know it would be you."

Her stare was expressionless. Then her lips slowly broke into a smile. "I have to admit, this was the nicest order Curry ever has given me." She pulled him close to her and they fell asleep in each other's arms.

William awoke alone the next morning. He had no idea when Lisbeth had slipped from his bed. His head wasn't the clearest as he had drunk so much beer the night before…and he didn't know quite how he felt about what had happened with Lisbeth. It had been very pleasant, really wonderful in fact. It felt like a bonding, a deeper connection than just sex. But was it right to take advantage of an enslaved person? He wondered. Curry had ordered her to his bed. He probably ordered her into his own bed or those of other guests whenever he wanted. How did she feel about it? That was a question no southern American would ever ask, but he was a Scotsman, and he didn't believe that one person should be enslaved to another.

How did Lisbeth feel about sleeping with him? She had seemed pleased. She smiled. She took him into her arms and rocked him to sleep. Maybe she really liked it, maybe she would be his companion again.

He splashed cold water on his face and dressed. Downstairs he grabbed a warm roll and a mug of hot tea. Lisbeth was nowhere to be seen. He intended to walk the town today and get the lay of the land. Based on what happened last night, he thought he might be staying in Baltimore for quite some time.

The city looked very appealing in the morning light. It had turned warmer, and the harbor and bay gleamed a brilliant blue in the sun.

William walked down to the dock area and noted the many saloons, restaurants, warehouses, and stores clustered by the piers where ships lay moored, disgorging their cargoes. This was a big city, he thought. If it doesn't work out at Curry's, there were lots of places where he could gather a crowd and turn his fiddle playing into money.

He turned away from the harbor and hiked up the gentle slopes of the hills above the Chesapeake Bay. Here there were row houses, block after block with one wall abutting its neighbor. Everywhere he walked the streets bustled with crowds, black and white, wealthy, and poor. There was a feeling of prosperity and activity abroad, a city alive with commerce in a new nation on a new continent. Scotland seemed far away in time and mood as well as space.

He was back at Curry's in time for a rest and a meal. This time Lisbeth was working, and she gave him the slightest hint of a secret smile when she saw him. After he had eaten his fill, he pulled out his fiddle and began to play as the customers ate, argued, negotiated, celebrated, danced, and sang. William remembered some of the names and faces from the night before. He recognized the little flash of pleasure when he did a tune that someone had requested the night before, like "Money in Both Pockets," "Dusty Miller," and "Soldier's Joy," all favorites that the crowd loved. He joked with them all and worked the audience so that by the time eleven o'clock came around, the party again showed no sign of breaking up, and he played long after his quitting time. Curry sat through the whole night this time, occasionally giving William what might have seemed like an approving glance.

William held back a bit on the beer this time. He didn't want to make a habit out of overdoing it. When he climbed the stairs to his room, he didn't know what to expect. Would Curry send Lisbeth to him again tonight? Or someone else? Or no one? He stripped off his clothes and lay on the bed. The room wasn't spinning tonight. He stayed awake for a while, and before too long, his door swung slowly open. It was Lisbeth again. William realized that he had been hoping for this. He really didn't want another girl, and he would have felt almost... jealous if Lisbeth had been sent to another's quarters.

She saw that he was still awake and smiled shyly. "You didn't even know when I came in last night," she chided softly.

"I'm awake now," William answered, his voice thick with excitement.

She pushed the door shut tight and the room was suddenly dark. Only the crack of light from under the door illuminated her silhouette as she shrugged her dress off her shoulders and moved toward the bed. This time the lovemaking was much better. William was wide awake and fairly sober, and he knew who was in his bed.

Afterwards, he tried to talk, but she touched his lips with her finger. "Shh," she whispered and pillowed her head on his shoulder.

He felt wonderful and had no desire to break the mood, but he wanted to know more about her – her feelings and wishes. But a slave knows better than to trust a master, and Lisbeth wasn't about to open up to this young white man, even though he was very handsome and nice to her. This could only be what it was. A slave warming the bed of a customer at her owner's command. Desire or…surely, he wasn't thinking of love, had no place in her life. "That's what leads you to trouble," she thought as she and William drifted toward sleep.

He was alone again in the morning. Many feelings swirled in his mind, but it was all too complicated. Lisbeth was a slave, Curry's slave, and he would rather not follow that fact to its implications. After breakfast, he found a meadow not too far away where he could practice his fiddle in private. Couldn't do the same old tunes night after night. If he was going to keep the crowd at Curry's happy, he needed some new songs. "Bluebells of Scotland" was one he used to know. In a few minutes he had that one dusted off and ready to play. There'll be plenty of Scots in the crowd who will love that one, he thought.

The crowd was a little off that night – Thursday night. He didn't know why, but there weren't as many folks who came in, and the ones who did weren't too excited about his fiddling. Curry came up to him at the end of the night (no encores this time) and said, "Well, it's the way of things, William. No one has a full house every night. It's the devil's own business. I ought to know that as well as any. There'll always be nights like this one, and there'll be better days, too."

William waited in his bed with anticipation, but no one came in and he eventually fell asleep. When he woke to piss in the night, he was still alone. "Where was Lisbeth?" he wondered. Did Curry send her to another? Or was she in Curry's own bed pleasuring his fat old body? He couldn't stand to picture that! And then he couldn't really get back to sleep. It made no sense, but he wished she were with him instead of any other place.

The next afternoon, he sat in the corner awaiting his dinner. When she brought it over, he whispered, "I missed ye last night."

She looked shocked. "You mustn't talk that way or think that way. I'm not free. I can't make my choices. I just have to live as best I can. You're not from here – you can't understand what it's like for a slave in this country."

Before he could answer, she had vanished into the kitchen. He saw her carrying drinks and food that night, and it was a very good night, just as Curry had predicted, but she didn't come to his room later. As he tossed and turned, he found himself confronting a strange thought. Could he be falling in love with Lisbeth? A slave... a black woman? And if he was, what could come of it? She was right. He didn't know the ways of this country, and he could probably get himself, and her, into great trouble if he wasn't wise. But really, he did miss her in his bed.

There was no weekend for the working people of Baltimore in those years. Most people worked at least half a day on Saturday, and for many it was simply the last day of the work week. But no one worked on Sunday. By law, all businesses were closed. That meant that the saloons were at their peak on Saturday night. No one worked the next morning, and plenty of them would be happy to sleep through church. This Saturday night was a packed house at Curry's. William's name had travelled around town a bit, so there was some new trade. And the others who had heard him through the week liked what they heard and were returning.

He played the tunes that were popular with everyone and had gotten approval during the week and added new ones like "Paddy Snap," "Plough Boy," and "Rose Tree." There were more women than the other nights, and because of that, there was more dancing. Curry was as happy as William had yet seen him, greeting all his old regulars and dancing with the ladies. It was a good night for all, and when, long after eleven, the crowd had thinned to the point that William began to wipe down his fiddle and put it away, Curry drunkenly clapped him on the shoulder and said, "Yes, m'lad, I think we're going to get along just fine here. You have a gift... a gift!" His mind seemed to wander back to the days when he was the one leading the crowd through emotions and memories, happy and sad, jigs and waltzes. "We're going to do very well together, William. I'm going to add some money to your recompense. A dollar a night and you can keep whatever tips you may get."

William mumbled, "Thank you, Curry," but his mind was really on another favor he wanted to ask. "Uh, Curry?"

"Eh? What is it, lad?"

"I was wondering… tonight, could Lisbeth be my bed warmer again?"

Curry suddenly looked more sober for a moment and more suspicious. "Don't you know she's my bed warmer? I let you have her for your first couple of nights here, but you're going to have to find your own company for your bed. Look around this room! You surely would have no trouble getting one of these pretty young things to snuggle with you."

William felt humiliated and jealous. So, Lisbeth was his? Yes, he knew that she was Curry's slave, and that meant she was his. For now, he just had to get away. "Aye," he mumbled and headed toward the steps.

"Don't be upset. I'll send someone who will take your mind off her." Curry said.

William turned and Curry could see the angry flush in his face, "Dinna bother," he snarled, "I can find company masel!" He turned and climbed the rickety stairs to his room. Lisbeth, who was cleaning glasses behind the bar, saw and heard everything, but she didn't let on that she did. Instead, she just kept working with her head bowed.

Once in his room and in bed, William couldn't relax. He surely couldn't have fallen in love with a slave girl in such a short time, but it ate at him to picture her in Curry's bed, or in other men's beds. "Well, that was how it is here in America," he thought, "and I don't understand how it works. But I just wish Lisbeth were coming through the door with her arms reaching for me!" He turned over and tried to sleep. He dozed fitfully for some time when he was awakened to see the door slowly and cautiously open. A thin line of light grew as it swung back and there was Lisbeth. So, she had come after all!

Before he could express his joy, she put a finger to her lips and shut the door. But she wasn't smiling, and she didn't pull off her dress. "Be quiet and listen to me!" she whispered harshly. "I know this is all new to you, but you have to understand that you're putting me in great danger. Curry won't do anything to you, you're his new star. But me... he can whip me, beat me, sell me, anything he wants. And I don't want him to think I encouraged you to have feelings for me. I can't have any feelings! So please, forget about me. Enjoy some of the other girls, you'll see that I'm nothing special."

William stood up and faced her in the darkened room. He could just make out the details of her face and her pretty body under the thin shift. He took her shoulders in his hands and said, "I dinna know how I feel, Lisbeth. I've nae been around slavery and don't ken it. But I know how miserable I was before you came in and how happy I am now." He pulled her close and tried to kiss her, but she turned away.

"Please, William! Didn't you understand what I said? I'm in real danger if Curry finds out I'm here. I just came here to make you understand how things are and how they have to be."

At that moment, the door flew violently open. There was Curry in a loose robe, and a wicked-looking leather strap in his hand. He took in the scene and then slashed viciously at her back. She gasped in pain and then he struck her again, screaming, "So this is how you obey me! You stay with me until you think I'm sound asleep and then sneak off to be with this one!"

Lisbeth turned to face him, her voice pleading, "No, Curry. It's not what you think. I was just explaining to him how things are and..." He cut her short with another blow from his strap, this one to her breasts. She screamed in pain and William, stunned by what he was seeing, came to his senses and grabbed for Curry's strap. He swung it backhand and caught William across the right cheek, leaving an ugly welt that oozed blood.

The two men looked at each other in surprise and fury for a second. And then William smashed his powerful fist into Curry's bulbous nose, splattering blood all over the three of them. "You son of a bitch," the older man growled. "You're going to regret that!" He pulled his arm back to deliver another blow and William rushed at him, knocking him off his feet and through the flimsy railing guarding the second floor. Curry crashed heavily to the floor below and lay motionless, his head cocked at a queer angle.

There was a stunned silence and time seemed to stand still. Then, Lisbeth was running down the stairs. Reaching out to touch Curry's neck she turned to William with a terrified stare. "He's dead," she rasped. She looked desperately around the room. No one was there. No one lived in the place but Curry, Lisbeth, and William. "Oh, my God," she moaned, rocking back and forth on her heels as she crouched by the dead man's body. Then she fixed William with a cold stare. "Now listen to me," she said icily, "you have to do exactly as I say. I'm not in any trouble as long as no one knows I was with you tonight. I'm going back to my room and clean myself up, and I'll find his body in the morning, and you'll be gone. I'll say I never heard a thing. You must have robbed him and killed him sometime in the night."

"But what about ye?" he pleaded. "Come with me – we'll get away and start a new life. Please – come."

She shook her head. "No, I don't want to be an escaped slave running away with a murderer." She saw his shocked response to the harsh word. "No, I know you didn't mean to kill him, but that's what it will look like to everyone else." She stood up and faced him. "Curry showed me his will once. He told me that whenever he died, I would be free. If I just stay here, when all this is over, I'll be properly, legally free, and no one can question it. And that's what I'm going to do."

She felt the angry red spots where Curry had struck. "He didn't mark me," she said. "No one will know that he whipped me tonight. Now here's what you must do. Get your things together at once and take a few valuables from Curry's room. You've got to make it look like a robbery. Then you can take a horse and a pack mule and get out of town."

"But where could I go?" he asked plaintively. "I dinna ken anyone in the aw country."

"Curry was a man with friends, William. You can't go anywhere in the East. Someone would recognize you, especially if you get out your fiddle, and that would be the end. You're going to have to head west, far beyond the reach of the law."

"West," he mused. "What can I do in that wild country? I wanted to make a name for myself fiddling, maybe own my own place someday. I don't want to live the life of a wild animal, struggling to find a meal and a place to sleep."

"You have no choice," she sighed. "If you stay, you'll be tried for murder, and I might not be able to stay out of it. This is a chance for me to get my freedom. And I'm sorry for you, William. I really like you, but we are never going to see each other again. Get your things, take some valuables from Curry's room, and get out of this city and don't ever look back."

With that she turned and ran down the hallway in back of the kitchen to her little corner and slammed the door. William was in a daze. How could things have gone so wrong so quickly? But he looked down at the lifeless body of his former employer and realized that whatever he thought about it, he had no choice but to follow Lisbeth's instructions. He went to his room and stuffed his few possessions in his sea bag, took his fiddle case and went back downstairs. Curry had a fairly nice apartment on the other side of the bar room. The door was standing open as he had left it just a short while ago.

William entered the room. There was a sack with the day's receipts on the dresser. He dropped that into his bag and looked around some more. The only other thing that looked to be of value was Curry's old fiddle that hung on the wall. He put it there when his hands got too gnarled to play, and no one had gotten it down since. William pulled it from the wall and quickly looked it over. Dusty and marred, but still, it was a good instrument. "I can always use a spare, I guess," he mumbled with resignation. He wrapped it in an old blanket from the bed and pushed it down into his bag, pulled some clothes up over it and went out the front door. His brief stay at Curry's and his fleeting passion with Lisbeth were now a part of his past.

It was about four in the morning, and there would be no one about except the night watch. He swiftly made his way to the stables and picked out the likeliest-looking horse and a smaller pack mule. He strapped his bag and fiddle case onto the mule, saddled and mounted the horse, then softly snuck out into the night. He left the city behind and struck out on the newly completed National Road. He didn't know where it would lead him, but he knew it was the pathway to the West, and that was the direction of his future.

CHAPTER TWO

The morning promised another cold and clear day as William sat overlooking the marshy rivers in the small valley below. It was good to see green after so many days of relentless desert, punctuated only by sage and creosote bushes.

The sounds of morning in the camp wafted toward him as the mule drivers fed and watered their animals. The cook stirred up the pot of corn mush over the open fire, and the men emerged from their tents yawning and stretching.

It was cold but much more tolerable than the blazing heat that would engulf this land in the summer. That's why they had left Abiquiu in early November – better to wrap up in buffalo robes and brave the chill than to swelter day and night.

The expedition wouldn't be ready to pull out for another hour at least; enough time to get out his fiddle and play a greeting to the valley their guide called Las Vegas. "The meadows" in English. It was January 1, New Year's Day, 1830. He lifted the fiddle with the king's head carved on its scroll and drew his bow across the strings. A quick tuning and he was playing softly, not following any remembered melody, but allowing his fingers to move freely over the fingerboard.

He let his mind wander as he played, recalling the curious path his life had taken since he sailed from Scotland to this new land. He thought of Lisbeth, the beautiful slave girl he had fallen in love with in Baltimore, and Curry, the man he had killed in a fight over her.

When he left Baltimore in the dark of night after that deadly brawl, he had no idea what lay in his future. He knew that there was only one direction for him to go, west, away from civilization with its police and courts; away from Curry's friends who would seek revenge for their comrade's death.

William didn't know any geography – didn't have a clue what vast territories stretched out before him in the direction of the setting sun. The first few weeks of his flight had been relatively easy, compared to the truly rugged journeys he would later make west of the Mississippi. He followed the National Road, a well-graded track that had been in use and under construction for eleven years. There were good inns along the route, and William could afford to pay for his lodging using the money he had taken from Curry's room after the fight. While it was stealing, he knew Curry would have no use for it, and he would need some resources to make good his escape.

At first, he kept his fiddles hidden in his pack just in case word of Curry's death had spread this far. Curry had been a great fiddler in his day, and there was no point in risking being recognized as the young fiddler who had been so popular at Curry's Saloon.

He rode easily on the busy road, through the rich farms of Maryland, through the wild, green Cumberland Gap, and on to the Ohio River. The road continued through Ohio and into Indiana, but he had heard from fellow travelers that it petered out in western Indiana, fading into old Indian paths through swampy prairies. It was much better to take a flatboat down the Ohio to the Great Mississippi and upstream to Saint Louis, the thriving metropolis of the wilderness. He found a boat casting off for the West, paid his fare, and started floating down the "beautiful river", the meaning of its name in the Seneca language.

The trip from Wheeling, Virginia to St. Louis was a pleasant time. On the warm, early summer evenings, his fingers itched to bring out a fiddle and serenade the riverbanks and his fellow passengers, mostly families on their way to Kentucky and Indiana, and not a few with handsome young women who shyly glanced his way. But he worried that he was still not far enough away to be safe if people heard his fiddling and maybe made a connection to the killing back in Baltimore. Only when he disembarked on the riverfront of Saint Louis did he begin to feel he had safely escaped his past.

Saint Louis had a few things in common with Baltimore, the only other American city William had seen. It was bustling and ramshackle, and many slaves were visible working on the wharfs, driving wagons and providing service at the hotels and cafes. But it was smaller – about 5000 people, so he heard, and there was a feeling of newness and adventure that he hadn't experienced in the eastern city. It was the hub of the nation's newest state, Missouri, admitted just two years before amidst the national crisis over slavery that Jefferson had called a "fire bell in the night."

He found comfortable lodging and spent a few days wandering the raw, growing city that the locals called the Gateway to the West. He absorbed the mixture of Spanish, French, Indian, and American culture and read the bills posted in taverns and hostelries advertising for ventures to the distant, almost mythical Rocky Mountains.

One night, about a week after he had arrived, he decided to take his fiddle into The Golden West, a popular tavern near the waterfront. William wondered if the instrument might win him some notice here in St. Louis as it had in Baltimore. There, it had opened a door to a new life for him, but fate had closed that door after his fight with Curry. He hadn't played it in public for a long time, but now he knew his fiddle had been silent too long. He sat at a rough-hewn table and ordered some food and a drink. While he was enjoying his meal, a young man just about William's age stood up from the bar and strolled over to him. He was tall and muscular, with light hair worn long in a ponytail and had piercing blue eyes.

"I see you carry a fiddle," he said in a crisp yankee accent. "I assume you play… or are you looking to sell it?"

"Nae, I'm not parting with this," William laughed, patting the case that he always kept close at hand. "I do play a bit, though" he answered, expecting the stranger to ask for a sample.

And he wasn't wrong. "Can you give us a taste of it? We always like a good tune here at the Golden West."

William opened the case and pulled out his fiddle. The carved scroll caught the stranger's eye as soon as he saw it. "That's a beautiful instrument," he said. "Have you had it long?" He slid into a seat across the table from William.

William cradled the fiddle under his chin and replied, "Aw my life so far as I can remember. My pap gave it to me back in Scotland when I was sma. I ne'er let it out of my sight." With that he quickly tuned and launched into some of the favorite melodies he had played at Curry's back in Baltimore.

The crowd quieted and looked at the young man sawing away, pleased by the sounds filling the smoky tavern. They clapped and called for more, named some requests, tossed him some tips, and returned to their conversations. When he felt he was losing the crowd's attention he put away the instrument and turned to the stranger, who said, "That's fine playing, there. What do they call you?"

"My name's Kennedy – William Kennedy." He reached his hand across the table. "And you...?"

"Jedediah Smith," the young man answered, reaching to grasp William's hand in his.

"You make good use of that fiddle, William."

"Thanks. I feel a wee bit rusty – didn't get it out of the case on the trip out here."

Jedediah looked puzzled. "Why, I'd have thought you'd have played every step of the way, the flatboats, the taverns, you probably would have made a small fortune in tips. Why did you keep it hidden?"

William started, suddenly aware that he had said too much to this total stranger. "Well, I... uh, I dinna want to take a chance of harm coming to it," he explained awkwardly.

Jedediah nodded but took a skeptical glance at him. "Well, you're here from the East then... how long?"

"Oh, only about a week," replied William.

"That might explain why I haven't seen you in town. I thought I knew most of the bold young fellows around these parts."

"And you?" William asked, taking a quick pull at his ale. "What's yer line?"

"My line?" Jedediah smiled. "Well, I can say that I'm working on the greatest opportunity of my life – or anybody's life."

William's face was curious, but cautious. He'd heard a lot of such talk on the flatboat and on the streets of St. Louis. It was a time and place full of imperial ambitions. "That's a grand goal, Jedediah. Can ye tell me more about it?"

"I'll gladly tell you, William... and I have a feeling that you might be just the kind of man I want to talk to. What do you know about the Rocky Mountains?"

"I've heard of them," William said thoughtfully. "Read some handbills about expeditions there. I know they're high and impassable."

"Impassable?" Jed snorted. "Tell that to Lewis and Clark, Zebulon Pike, Donald Mackenzie or my boss, General Ashley. There's plenty of ways into those mountains, and fur traders have been going there for years to buy pelts from the Indians and bring them back here to St. Louis to sell. It's been a good trade, but a hard life and not many are getting rich. General Ashley's got a new idea. Gather a troop of outdoorsmen, good and true, and trap the critters direct! Cut out the Indian and get the whole profit for ourselves!"

He took a long drink from his mug and paused, wiping his thick mustache clean with the back of his hand.

William was intrigued, and it occurred to him that Jedediah Smith might be offering the very thing he needed. A way to totally escape the reach of society and its laws.

"How many men is your General Ashley taking with him?" he asked.

"He's advertising for a hundred. 'Ashley's Hundred' they call us. But I don't think we'll be all that many. I believe there were seventy signed on when last I looked."

The next day Jedediah took him to meet General Ashley and William signed on as one of Ashley's Hundred. He quickly made ready for a journey to a place of myth and legend, the Rockies!

He remembered the first glimpse they had of the towering peaks when they were still many days' journey away, and how he thrilled to see them grow every day as they were approached. They set up a base camp on the Green River, which the trappers called the Seedskeedee, at the foot of the Wind River Mountains. From there, they travelled in small groups, scattering throughout the Wind Rivers, the Big Horns, the Laramies, the Wyomings, and the Tetons, setting and tending their traps.

The beauty of the mountains thrilled William, and they often came upon steaming hot springs, enormous geysers, and bubbling sulfur pits. Fur-bearing animals abounded, especially the much sought-after beaver. They occasionally rubbed elbows with other trappers, men from Astor's American Fur Company, or with local Indians. These meetings were often tense and sometimes violent. William counted himself lucky that he was never involved in any deadly fights during those days.

The battle of 1823 was still fresh on everyone's minds when the Arikara Indians of South Dakota, facing encroachment of their fur trade, attacked members of the Rocky Mountain Fur Company, killing 15 trappers. Of course, the U. S. retaliated by burning and destroying the Arikara village. Most of their population was lost to the smallpox in 1830.

As the cool nights of autumn arrived, the company rendezvoused at their Seedskeedee base and packed the summer's harvest for transport to the markets of St. Louis. They reached the Mississippi River in November 1823 with full pockets, mighty thirsts, and powerful lusts for the beautiful women of St. Louis. Women of all nationalities and color were there. The winter in St. Louis proved so pleasurable that when the time came to return to the mountains, the members of Ashley's Hundred were all nearly broke.

On William's second journey, with his friend Jedediah Smith, South Pass was discovered, making possible for the flood of wagon trains to head west later in the century. The work with the traps was hard and unpleasant, and though it paid well, he found that he preferred the old way of trading with the Indians. Knives, mirrors, and trinkets for pelts, so he parted ways with Ashley's company and set out on his own. Many, like William relished the solitude and would live in the wilderness off of wild game for 2-3 years at a time. He did love the great natural beauty that surrounded him. He never thought anymore of killing Curry, the tavern owner, in Baltimore, though he never completely forgot Lisbeth and their brief love affair…so long ago.

After several years of making the long journey east each fall, he decided to seek quarters closer to the mountains, and he found a pleasant winter abode in the old Spanish capital of Santa Fe. In the winter of 1829, waiting out the weather, he heard of an expedition forming to seek a new connection to the Old Spanish Trail, which would be a way to avoid the long, grueling swing to the north in order to miss the impenetrable canyon lands. William had traversed this area often and knew many watering holes, many Indians, and many paths to avoid. He hired on with Antonio Armijo and helped him win his passage across the canyon and on to this spot where he now greeted the day with his music las vegas, which was discovered and named by a friend and fellow scout Rafael Rivera.

"Guillermo!" The cry broke William's reverie and brought him suddenly back to the present.

Walking toward him from the camp was their expedition's leader, Antonio Armijo. He was nearly five years younger than William, but he was a man who spoke with authority and acted with determination. No one on the Armijo expedition ever thought of challenging the leadership of this man.

"Serenading las vegas, are you? It is a great relief to see a bit of green in this stark land, isn't it?"

"Yes, though I love the canyons and desert aye," William replied. "And the mountains." He glanced off to the north with a faraway expression, pausing for a moment before telling Armijo of his decision to leave the expedition. "Now that we hae found this watering spot, Antonio, your journey to Los Angeles will not require a guide's services. I think it's time for me to return to the mountains and my fur trade."

Antonio looked solemnly at his friend. "Of course, I knew when you hired on that you would only come as far as your services were needed. Still, you've been much more to us than a guide. We value your friendship… and especially your music. You truly have the gift, William. We are glad you have shared it with us for this time." He took William's hand and drew him into a warm embrace. "Vaya con Dios, mi amigo. We're pulling out as soon as we are ready to move."

William had deeply mixed emotions as he watched the expedition fading into the southwest. He had made many friends, shared many hardships with those men. Would he ever see them again? Now they were going on and he was headed to a Nuwuvi village where he knew he could spend a few months until the snow melted in the passes.

The Nuwuvi Indians (the People) were hunter-gatherers who lived in small family clans in what is now called the Southern Great Basin or the Colorado Plateau.

He started out following the river his friend Jedidiah Smith had named the Adams River after President, John Quincy Adams. One of Smith's men, Thomas Virgin, had wanted to name the river after himself, but Smith insisted, and Adams was the name that stuck in William's mind. It traversed lands of stunning beauty. Canyons and mesas, mountains that grasped the grassy riverbanks with gnarled fingers of stone, and the stunning gorge where the river cut through a towering wall of rock, forcing William to lead his horse up the center of the river itself.

William was not a religious man, but at times he wondered to himself about the power it took to turn these rock layers on end and throw them crashing into each other, leaving tangled heaps of broken mountains. And how did these rivers cut their way through such mighty canyons, dwarfing the tiny humans who picked their fragile courses along the streams? Such mysteries were not in his power to resolve, though he didn't stop wondering.

All along the river, he passed small Nuwuvi villages. He was known among the Nuwuvi as a fur trader, one who dealt fairly with them when he exchanged trade goods for the valuable pelts they collected in the summers. After a few weeks of travel, he finally saw the settlement of Mukuntuweap at the foot of colossal canyon walls. Smoke drifted lazily over the village in the early evening sun. This was the largest one he had seen on the Adams River, and it had a more permanent look. As he rode by the first few pine bark teepees, children peeked out at him, hiding behind their mothers' robes. The village was busy, as usual, with women weaving baskets and making the Nuwuvi "biscuit," from grass seed flower as well as baking the agave plants to make yant, a sweet tasting dried food.

Many of the men were away from the village hunting, but the ones who saw him smiled and nodded. William had visited this village often during the winter months. He saw a familiar head poking out of a teepee. It was Jack Bobbee Qweets, the one he had come to see. He and Qweets had spent several summers in the cool mountains trading knives, axes, and mirrors for pelts collected by Shoshone and Cheyenne trappers, and they had shared many a winter evening around the smoldering fire in the cozy pine teepee.

"William!" he called happily as he looked up to see his friend riding slowly through the village.

"Qweets, my friend," William yelled. He leapt from his horse and the two embraced warmly.

"How have you been, old friend?" Qweets asked, holding William's shoulders, and gazing into his eyes. "Where have you been wandering in this cold season? We thought you would come to us in the autumn before the snows arrived."

"I was scouting with a Mexican expedition, looking for a path through the canyon lands. We found one and I left them back where this river meets the 'Hakhwata," using the Yavapai word for what the whites called the Colorado. "They are on their way to the mission at Los Angeles and won't need my services anymore, so I'm going to head back to the mountains and trade for pelts. But I need a place to wait out the spring thaw."

"You know this place is your home as much as it is mine," Qweets responded warmly. "Come in and have something to eat and drink."

He lifted the flap that covered the door to the pine teepee and stepped into the fragrant, dark interior. As William's eyes adjusted to the dark, he saw a form near the fire, stirring a pot. Her eyes flashed darkly in his direction. "Annie!" he exclaimed. "Is that you? I swear you've become a woman since last time I saw you in the spring."

Tsunnunk laughed shyly and stood up. "I'm told that is the way of nature, friend William. Little girls become women; just as little boys become men."

William took her hands and looked deeply at her. "And men become old men, I'm afraid," he said ruefully. Jack Bobbee smiled knowingly as he watched his old friend and his daughter renewing their acquaintance. His little girl had always had a crush on this handsome white man who had shared their home in winters past. This winter, she was disappointed that William hadn't stopped by their village. She talked of him often, and Jack could see that as she grew up, her feelings had grown apace.

"You must be hungry," Tsunnunk said. "Sit here by the fire and I'll get you something to eat." As he sat, she quickly produced some biscuit and rabbit meat and she happily watched William devour the meal.

"Annie," William sighed when he had had his fill, "that was a couthy supper – thank ye."

She smiled broadly at him. "It's no feast, but I'm glad you liked it. Now make yourself comfortable and tell us all your adventures since we last saw you."

William sat back and shared his experiences crossing the canyon lands in the winter with Antonio Armijo's expedition. As he talked, the weeks of riding in the cold desert began to lift from his shoulders and he soon became drowsy. His tales drifted into a murmur and his head nodded. Tsunnunk raised her eyebrows at her father in a silent question. His slight nod told her what she should do. She pulled a rabbit fur blanket over William's shoulders and eased him onto the soft pile of robes near the fire. He looked sleepily at her and tried to rise, but she gently pushed him back. "Sleep now, William," she whispered. He smiled weakly and allowed himself to drift into a deep, warm sleep, more comfortable than he had been in many months of living on the trail.

William happily settled into the life of Mukuntuweap as the winter passed away. He played his fiddle often, sometimes by himself while contemplating the unbelievable canyon walls, other times for his friends and neighbors in the Nuwuvi village. He had learned some of their tribal songs and incorporated them into his instrumental pieces. His listeners always broke out in a smile when they recognized a beloved melody coming from the white man's fiddle. Of course, he always played some of his repertoire of Scottish and American fiddle tunes, which were also popular with his audiences.

It was a relaxing time for William — welcome after the strenuous months of scouting through the cold and imperious canyon lands. He cheerfully pitched into the chores of the village and occasionally accompanied the men on their hunting trips in the nearby canyons. But most important to William were the many hours he spent with Tsunnunk, his "Annie." She had grown up to be a beautiful and graceful woman, but more importantly, she had become a mature, loving companion. She had a sharp mind and was curious about everything. She and William talked about his life in the faraway lands over the sea and in the vast stretches of the American prairies and mountains, the adventures he'd had and the famous people he'd traveled with. They talked about his plans to return to the fur trade in the spring with her father, Jack Bobbee Qweets and then their talk always turned to themselves and what they were beginning to feel for each other.

William thought the time had arrived to talk with his old friend and partner about his daughter. As the two men walked upstream along the river, idly looking for some game to shoot, William took a deep breath and plunged in.

"Qweets," he began awkwardly, "I suppose ye've noticed that Annie and I have become fond of each other?"

The older man turned to him with a look that might be surprise or anger or amusement. It threw William off from his carefully planned speech. "I mean, surely nothing out of line has happened, ye ken me better than that…"

Qweets stopped him with an upraised hand. "William," he said slowly and solemnly, "you surprise me."

"Surprise? Why surely ye've noticed that…?"

"You surprise me by waiting so long to approach me about this. Am I a blind old man who can't see what happens in his own teepee? You two have been mushing over each other since you arrived. And Tsunnunk was pining for you long before you came here. She was afraid you weren't coming to Mukuntuweap this winter since you hadn't arrived before the snows began to fall. She has loved you long, William and now that she is grown, she wants that love to be made real and permanent. She wants to marry you, my friend."

"Marry?" William searched Qweets's face for some clue as to how he felt about this development and found none. "How do you feel about that, old friend? Would you take me as a son-in-law?"

"William, you have been my trading partner who has always been honest and fair with me, unlike many who trade in these lands. You have also been my friend, one with whom I have shared many dangers and hard times. I think I know you and what kind of man you are. Tsunnunk is now of marriageable age, and she will have suitors from the village and from other men of nearby clans. She would have to choose from them." William's heart began to sink as he listened to her father's words. "But she would find no man who would be a better husband for her and a father to her children than you. You are a white man and not one of our people, but when you marry my daughter, you will become one of us and a member of our people…and I welcome that greatly."

The ceremony was complex. In fact, William wasn't quite sure at what point they became husband and wife but at the end of the happy celebration, they found themselves in a newly built pine bark teepee, alone and free to express their passion. There were a few times when young boys made rude noises near their love nest, but nothing could distract them from the infinite pleasures they had been so eagerly awaiting.

When the snows in the higher ranges began to melt and send the rich silt-laden water coursing down the gullies and dry stream beds, William, Qweets, and some other men of the village made ready to depart for their summer's enterprise. Even though the vast mountains seemed endless, and the population of animals appeared to be infinite, William had begun to notice that in the lower elevations, the otter, muskrat, bear, and most importantly, the beaver, which had been so numerous in the past, were becoming harder to find. He determined to trek deeper and higher into the mountains to find places where other trappers and traders hadn't yet penetrated. Often in the past, the whole village had moved to the cool, high meadows and helped with the preparation of pelts for shipment, but this year the men would travel alone. Their paths would likely be too difficult for the women and children to follow and would probably penetrate too far into the mountains for such an unwieldy group to keep up.

"Are you sure we can't go with you, William?" Tsunnunk asked. "I love the mountains in the summer, and we always have been a big help to the men bringing their pelts back to camp."

"And I would love to hae ye there, Annie. But we don't ken for sure where and how far we'll have to go. The beaver hasn't been plentiful in their old places. We must go where the trappers haven't yet reached. I wonder if in a few years the beaver will be hard to find anywhere in these mountains, though that doesn't seem possible right now. Surely there will always be streams and valleys in the mountains that men haven't yet found."

"And we must wait here for your safe return," she said glumly.

"We'll be safe," William laughed. "Your father and I have seen many a danger and lived to tell about it. I dinna think this year will be any different."

"When will you return?"

"That's hard to say – we don't know how far we must go to find the furs. But we nae will try to stay over the winter in the high country. Look for us when the days equal the nights, and we'll send messengers back to keep you informed of our fortunes."

"There is something else, William," she said seriously with her eyes downcast.

"What's that? Ye ken ye needn't worry about me mixing in with the camp women at the rendezvous, don't you?"

She gazed directly into his eyes. "No, of course not. I know you, my husband. But you should know something, too. Shortly after you return, we will have a little one added to our family."

William smiled broadly. "I can't say this is a big shock. We've surely been doing our best in the nights to get you in a family way. And I've seen you trying to hide your sickness in the morning. But it's bonnie news. I'll try to make a big fortune this summer so we can keep our wee one in high style." He grasped her close to him and kissed her. "If it's a girl, she'll be as lovely as her mother and if it's a boy, I'll teach him to fiddle like his da!"

"I can't say why, but I'm very sure it is a boy and he'll be a fiddler no doubt."

The men departed a few days later. As they expected, there were few traces of beaver or any other fur-bearing animals in the low reaches of the Rockies. The fur trade had grown and big firms from the East had followed Ashley's example and sent hundreds of trappers into the mountains. Most of them harvested pelts and sold them at the rendezvous on the Green River, but William and his Nuwuvi friends avoided the crowds and struck off by little-known trails for the high country.

Their lives settled into a comfortable pattern. William scouted ahead and found promising sites and Qweets and his friends set and tended the traps. In the evenings, they sat around their fires eating and smoking, listening to William's fiddle echo from the cliffs and forests. They found plenty of furs and sent loaded pack mules back to Mukuntuweap with a few men for escort. Tsunnunk and the other women were happy to see the riches their men were gathering and relieved to hear that all was going well in the mountains – and that all were safe. The men unloaded the mules and returned to their friends in the high country while in the village, the women prepared the pelts to be taken east for sale.

As the days grew shorter and the nights turned cooler on the banks of what William still called the Adams River, Tsunnunk remembered William's promise that they would return by the time the days and nights were of equal length and she began to search the horizon every day for signs of the men's return. She had grown quite heavy with her child and expected to deliver in about two more months.

The equinox passed without a sign of William or the others. Tsunnunk couldn't help but worry, though she was supremely confident in her father and her husband's ability to thrive in the wilderness. And she was elated, but not too surprised, to see a lone rider hurrying to the village late one afternoon in October. She shielded her eyes from the lowering sun and soon could recognize the tall form of her husband.

William galloped into the village, laughing, and waving at friends as he made his way to his own teepee where Tsunnunk was awaiting him. "Annie!" he shouted as he leapt off his horse. "Annie, how I've missed ye." He took her in his arms and kissed her and then held her at arm's length to gaze up and down at her very pregnant figure.

"Don't look at me!" she laughed and turned her head to the side. "I'm an old sow!"

"I never hae seen a more beautiful 'old sow' in my life!" he exclaimed. "How are ye? When will the baby come? I've so much to tell and so much I want to know."

"I'm fine. The baby's fine. And I expect he will be coming along in about six weeks. And I love you, William," she cried and buried her face in his chest. Her tears of joy mingled with his as they wordlessly embraced. William was home. They would have the long winter months to be together, to welcome their new child into the world. The next spring was too far away to think of – all that mattered was this moment, this joyful embrace.

CHAPTER THREE

The baby was born in December, a little later than Tsunnunk had expected. William paced endlessly outside the teepee while the women worked with her. She did her best to be stoic, but it was a long and hard labor, and William could hardly bear to hear the muffled cries from his wife. Finally, just as the cold sky was growing light, he heard a loud scream from Tsunnunk and then a few seconds later, the full-voiced wail of a newborn baby. He tried to lift the flap from the door, but Inola, one of the midwives, jerked the cloth from his hand and said, "You must wait, we will clean baby and tend to Tsunnunk , then you see them."

"But are they all right?" he asked desperately. "Is she… is she going to be OK?"

Inola smiled wearily. "She fine, it been hard labor. And your son," she paused and waited for his reaction, "seems healthy. He's big boy and got big voice too."

William shook his head to take it all in. "Your son," she had said. It was a boy, just as Tsunnunk had predicted. For the next few minutes, William paced as the day began to dawn cold and clear. He couldn't stop his thoughts from ranging over poor Annie, how she had suffered. And the boy, his son. How strange the words seemed in his mind. Would he be healthy? Strong? A man his people would look up to? William realized that some of those questions would have to be answered by him and by the things he would do for his newborn baby boy.

The flap of the teepee lifted and Inola wordlessly beckoned him to come inside. The air was hot and damp as he entered, and he couldn't make out where Annie and their new baby were in the dim light. As his eyes adjusted, he saw her lying on a pile of robes, tired, but smiling. And cradled to her breast was their son. William was so overcome with love and relief that he could only kneel at her side with tears streaming down his face. "Here is our little boy," she rasped hoarsely. "I think you're going to like him."

She gently held him out for William to hold. At first, he was afraid to take the tiny, vulnerable infant, but Tsunnunk said, "He won't break William. Let him meet his father." William cautiously took the baby from her hands and held him as gently as he could to his breast, staring at his face.

"A miracle," he whispered.

"Yes," Tsununk agreed, "our little miracle."

A thought suddenly occurred to William. "What will we name him?" he asked.

"I think we should call him Quaninch," she replied. "It means 'eagle' in our language. I think he will be a mighty one, a man who can fly above the others."

"Quaninch," he murmured. "The eagle... ay, that is a very good name. You've chosen well." He looked back at his wife, thinking she had never looked so beautiful as she did at that moment, weary though she was. A soft light glowed from her face, and he loved her more than ever.

That winter was an unusually cold one, but William and his little family were comfortable. Their teepee was well-made and kept the icy winds at bay. The summer season of trapping had been very successful, and they had plenty of food to eat as the snow drifted outside. William, Qweets and some of the other men hunted on days that the snow stopped, and as they ranged up the stunning canyon walls looking for game, William deeply felt the blessings of being alive, being a father, a husband, and a free man in this awesome land.

When the spring arrived, slowly with plenty of false starts, William began to plan for the summer's trading. He hated the thought of leaving Annie and their newborn alone again for a long season in the mountains, but he faced the same problem. They had to travel deep into the mountains to find abundant animals for their traps, and he didn't think Annie and Quaninch would be able to keep up with the strenuous journey.

"William," she said to him when they discussed this, "as you remember, I have traveled to the mountains many summers as a young girl. Surely, I can make this journey now, even with Quaninch." She glanced lovingly at her baby nestled in her arms. "He's not all that delicate," she laughed.

"But Annie, we have further to go than in the days when ye accompanied the village to the mountains. Then the men, or some of them, could return to the camp every night. With the way things are now, we would hae to leave you lasses and bairns alone in the camp for many days at a time. I think ye'd be safer here with aw the village around you."

"Who are we fearing, William? You say the wild animals are scarce where we would pitch our camp. We are at peace with the other tribes. What is the danger?"

"Annie, ye don't ken the kind of folk who walk in the wild in these times. Some of these trappers are nae more than bandits. They trade not, but prey on the ones who do by stealing their pelts and often as not, leave their bones bleaching in the mountains."

They sat in silence for a while as William thought over the problem. "Annie?" he asked quietly. She glanced at him resentfully. "Annie, I've got an idea, maybe. What if ye and Quaninch stay here in Mukuntuweap...?" She looked away in anger, but he pushed on. "Stay here, but when we send the pelts back, I'll come with'em. I can scout territory ahead to keep the others busy with their traps and get away for a few days. That way, we can spend some time together. Ye won't be so lonely, and I won't miss you so dearly."

"It's not what I want, William," she said. "But it's better than not seeing you from spring to winter. You'll come back two or three times, then?"

"Ay, I'm sure it won't be a problem. And I did miss you terribly last year. This will be so much better."

So, the pattern for the next few years of their lives was set. Winters in the secure and cozy village at the mouth of the beautiful canyon and summers spent apart with two or three short visits. During the winter months, as Quaninch grew and began to walk and talk, William played his fiddle, the one with the king's head carving, and little Quaninch would smile, and gurgle along and even clap his hands.

When Quaninch turned three, he began to reach for the fiddle when his father would play. William let him place his small hand over his own and draw the bow slowly across the strings, delighting the little boy and making him want more. He got out his other fiddle, the one he had taken from Curry, and carefully let Quaninch explore it. "Nae too rough, littl'un," he cried when Quaninch waved the instrument too violently. "Gentle-like, now," and he guided the small hands to hold the bow and the fiddle.

By the next winter, Quaninch was able to hold the fiddle by himself. William tried to show him some technique, but at that age, the little boy only wanted to saw away at it. He resisted any attempt to show him proper form, but William felt that he should let the boy play with, it however he wanted, as long as he didn't damage the instrument. And play he did, scraping the bow over the strings for hours on end. William and Tsunnunk tried not to let the monotonous droning get under their skin though it often took will power to refrain from screaming, "Stop that noise!"

William had always left his carved fiddle at home and taken Curry's with him when he journeyed to the mountains in the summer. He didn't want to risk damaging the priceless instrument, as he lived and worked in the wild mountains where one might be caught in a downpour or take a fall on a steep trail. His stern instructions were that no one should touch the fiddle while he was gone, but the year that Quaninch turned five, William said, "Annie, I believe our little bairn is old enough to play that fiddle while I'm gone. Only take care that he treats it well."

"Are you sure, William? He's still so young."

"Ay, but he loves to play, and as you've noticed, he's even begun to try to make some notes instead of just sawing at it. He's a fiddler, of that, I'm sure. Let's give him a chance to play as much as he wants and see how well he takes to it."

Each time William returned to the village that summer – the year that Quaninch would turn nine, he was pleased at the progress his son showed on the fiddle. He decided that the time was right to show the boy a real fiddle tune. They sat in the teepee facing each other, William holding Curry's fiddle and Quaninch the king's head fiddle. "This is one I learned when I was a wee bairn ," he said. He played the melody for him and then helped the boy form his small hand around the neck of the fiddle. "They mostly call it 'Soldiers' Joy,' but in Scotland we also ken it as 'King's Head.' When I was just sma, I thought the song was named after this fiddle, maybe, but doubt that it's so."

Quaninch tried his best to follow his father's playing, and William lovingly corrected the many mistakes the boy made. By the time William had to return to the mountains, Quaninch was able to make the sounds on his instrument almost recognizable as the old fiddle tune.

When he returned for the season that fall, Quaninch could not restrain himself from showing his father how well he could play. "Da!" he shouted as William dismounted his horse at the teepee's door, "Listen to me! Listen!" William circled his arm around Tsunnunk and watched in pleased amazement as Quaninch played "Soldiers' Joy" without a single mistake.

"Ay, that's bonnie! I knew ye were a fiddler – just like yer old man. We'll have a great time this winter with these two fiddles." He turned to his wife and pulled her close to him. "Ay," he repeated, "we'll have a great time for sure this winter, my lovely, my Annie!"

Quaninch was a handsome boy, a little bigger than the other boys his age in the village. He ran and played with grace and strength, and he had learned much of the lore of his people. He had the dark, smooth hair of his mother and the inquisitive blue eyes of his father. As the weather turned colder, they spent more time in their teepee, Quaninch and his father began to play duets on their fiddles. William was patient with the boy and Quaninch was an eager pupil. "Let's do it again, Da!" was his cry day after day as he tried to master the fine points of fiddling.

William and Quaninch seemed inseparable that winter. Sometimes on cold, clear nights, William took his son outside to gaze at the glorious stars spread out over them. The high canyon walls blocked the horizon in every direction, but straight overhead they could see Orion the Hunter, the Seven Sisters in Taurus the Bull, and the Winter Triangle formed by Betelgeuse, Sirius, and Procyon. Tsunnunk joined them and told how the Nuwuvi called Sirius the Deer Star and the North Star was Quiami Wintook Pootsee and she told stories and legends she remembered from her own childhood.

And when Arcturus was seen rising over the canyon rim, and the people knew that another winter was passing, William was very reluctant to begin planning the summer's journey. "Qweets," he said to his father-in-law, "I'm worried about going to the mountains this summer."

"Why is that my son?"

"Ye ken that each year we hae had to go further into the mountains to find our quarry. Last summer was the hardest one yet. You remember how many days your traps sat empty. And in spite of the scarcity of animals, the number of trappers only increases. I wonder when we will arrive at the point where we will have to go so far and yet return empty-handed." He paused and then said, "And I will miss my wee boy – he's a canny lad, you know, and he's a great knack for the fiddle. In another year he could go with us, but I dinna think he's big enough yet."

Qweets put his hand on his friend's shoulder. "But what are our choices, William? If the pelts are scarcer, we only must look harder and farther. We need that money to buy goods for the winter."

"Ay, you're right there. Maybe the next summer, when Quaninch is old enough to join us, we could strike out farther west, find some undiscovered valleys in the Sierras where it will be like the old days with fat beavers aplenty. But still and all, I hate to leave Tsunnunk and the wee one."

The men set out in late May and William's foreboding was justified. There were more trappers roaming the mountain valleys than ever, and fewer pelts to be had. Fighting and stealing had become commonplace, though William and Qweets always kept a safe distance from the other groups. When William made his first return visit to the village in July, he had only one pack mule lightly loaded with fur.

There was a joyous reunion with his family, but they couldn't help noticing the scarcity of pelts. "It's lean pickings, Annie," he told his wife. "I can't make another return trip before the fall unless we find more animals in our traps."

He delighted in the inches Quaninch had added to his height and the increasing skill that the boy showed on the fiddle. They played many a duet and laughed away the few days William could stay. "But I must be on my way," he said to a downcast Tsunnunk and Quaninch. "You keep a-practicing that fiddle, my lad. By next summer, ye'll be big enough to go along with your Da to the mountains."

Seeing Tsunnunk's quizzical stare, he added with a broad smile, "In fact, I don't see why the whole family can't go next year. We'll be heading much further away than before with no visits back to Mukuntuweap. So maybe we can all just ride along together."

The farewell was tearful, as it always had been, but William promised to be home in October, hopefully with a better harvest. He waved goodbye as he rode off to join with Qweets and the others in the high country.

The remaining season was no better than the early days. The animals had either been hunted out of their homes or fled deeper into the mountains to escape the inexorable flood of trappers. "We might as well call it a season," William said to Qweets one frosty morning. "The days are getting shorter, and we haven't seen any likely trapping sites for over a week. I know we've got a poor showing, but we have enough to see us through the winter. Let's head for home and try to find a better plan for next year."

Qweets looked thoughtful and turned his face to take in the vast panorama of mountains, forest, and river. "It is so huge, William, the land that Thuwipu Unipugant, 'the One who made the earth' gave us. Yet with the coming of the white men, this land has shrunk. There are too many people here now, taking too much of what has been given to us. We will not return to these mountains and valleys, William. We will seek out new places that haven't been overrun. But you see the way of the world, my son... soon all places will be hunted out and filled up and then where will there be a place for the Numu?"

When they were about a day's journey from Mukuntuweap, William was unable to resist his anticipation. "I'm going to ride out ahead," he said to Qweets. "You bring up the men and what little we have to show for our summer's work, and I'll meet you in the village."

He rode ahead rapidly, anticipating the joyful reunion with his wife and son. He was looking forward to another quiet winter of playing music with Quaninch and holding his wife Annie in her warm embrace. They would have to make some major changes in their lives by the next summer. The mountains that he had loved so well and known so intimately were now played out. Too many trappers and too few wild animals. And the prices for beaver pelts had been declining the past few years, too. Fashions in Europe were changing, the agents from the East said. William needed to think hard about how he would support his family and how his kinsmen the Nuwuvis would survive. The main project for me this winter, he thought, is to come up with a new idea for our livelihood.

All thoughts of the future though came to a sickening halt when he topped the rise where he could catch the first glimpse of Mukuntuweap. The place had been devastated. Looted and ransacked with charred remains of pine teepees lining the empty lane that should have been filled with people working. There was no smoke drifting up from friendly fires, no noise of yapping dogs and playing children. His blood chilled as he hastened toward the scene of destruction. Now his mind was whirling with a thousand dreadful horrors. Tsunnunk and Quaninch, where were they? What had happened here?

He reached the site of his ruined home, still unable to comprehend the disaster that had so suddenly befallen him. There was no trace of his beloved wife and child, only ashes and some scattered robes and hides. Through his trauma and bewilderment, harsh reality forced its way into his mind. He suddenly realized this had happened some time ago. While he was in the mountains seeking pelts, had his family been attacked and… killed? Enslaved? What should he do? He must seek them out, find them if they were still alive, but…

William was suddenly overwhelmed with primal grief. He screamed "Nooo!" to the skies, fell to his knees and lifted handfuls of ash to his face. "Oh, my Annie! My little boy! Why did I leave you helpless here? No, no, no…" His voice slid into unintelligible weeping as tears streaked through the caked ash on his face.

He was still sitting in the ruined teepee when he heard the quiet approach of Jack Bobbee Qweets and the others. Qweets dismounted and stood next to William in shocked disbelief. Even though he was a proud Nuwuvi who had endured much heartache, he couldn't keep bitter tears from welling in his eyes. He placed a hand on his son-in-law's shoulder and waited until he could speak without crying. "It has been many days since this happened, William. If they are still living, they must be many miles away."

"Slavers!" William growled. "There are no bodies, no bones, here. This wasn't a horse-stealing raid or thieving murder. It was a slave raid and all the people here have been taken. We have to find them, Qweets. We can't leave Tsunnunk and Quaninch to the mercies of slavers!"

Qweets looked at William with weary sorrow. "Yes, but they have been gone many days. By now, they have probably been taken to Los Angeles and sold in the slave markets there. If we left right away, it would be four weeks before we could get there. And what would we find? Would anyone remember a woman and a boy sold in the market some months ago?" William shook his head in bewildered sadness. "William my son, I would risk anything to find my daughter and my grandson, but what can we do?"

William didn't answer for many minutes. Then he said, "We'll go downstream along the river, see if anyone is still in the other villages and if they can tell us anything about when this happened, or if they saw our people being taken away. Once we know something about what happened, and when, we can make a plan."

Qweets saw that his son-in-law needed to do something. That action was the only way he could continue living. He had no hope that they could succeed in finding their missing loved ones, but for William's sanity, there was no choice but to try.

They followed the river to the next village. It was much smaller than Mukuntuweap and had been raided. It also showed signs of having been recently burned. But there were people living there and the pine bark teepees had been rebuilt and village life seemed to be going on as usual.

They found Tocho, a relative of Qweets' they had sometimes hunted with, standing by his teepee at the edge of the village. He looked at them solemnly and said "Qweets... William... there are no words to say."

"What can you tell us, Tocho?" William blurted out as he dismounted. "When did it happen?"

"It was almost two months ago. We heard the shooting in the dark of morning and we ran into the canyon with only what we could take in our hands. The next day, we scouted and saw that they were gone. Our village was in ashes, but thankfully, no one o died or was taken to be enslaved. Then we walked upstream to Mukuntuweap, fear in our hearts. It was as bad as we feared, all burned, no one alive."

"Tsununk?" William cried out.

"Tsununk is dead," said Tocho softly. "But she took a raider with her, both bodies in the door of your teepee. She was a warrior even in her dying."

"And Quaninch?" he asked in agony.

"None of the children were to be seen. They had all gone with the slavers."

The three men stood in silence. Then Tocho continued, "There were many other dead also. We built a pyre and sent their ashes to the heavens. Now we wait in fear for the next band of raiders to appear."

Two months ago, William thought. The journey from here to the slave market at Los Angeles would take no more than six weeks. That meant that Quaninch had already been sold two weeks ago. And it would take William at least four weeks to get there if he rode day and night. Who would remember one small Indian boy out of so many that came through the slave pens? How could he ever track him down? And rescue him?

"William," said Qweets tenderly, placing a hand on his shoulder. "It is a hard fate to accept. But I must do so. I cannot go to Los Angeles to try to rescue Quaninch. I do not believe you should do so, either. We cannot find him, William. I will stay in my own people's country as long as we have a land to live in. And when that is gone, so also will be the Numu."

Bitter tears coursed down William's face, and he wept uncontrollably. He couldn't speak for a moment and then he said, "I don't know, Qweets. I must think about this. How can I leave my little bairn to face a life of slavery? How can I live with that?"

In the cold light of the next morning, William understood what he had to do. This part of his life was over, and he had to move on. Tsununk was dead and Quaninch was lost beyond all hope of finding. The mountains no longer held the golden promise they had when he first came west. Jack Bobbee Qweets would stay with his own people and William would go back to his.

CHAPTER FOUR

Quaninch's nightmare had begun in the early morning as he slept with his mother in their cozy teepee. Even though the summer days in the desert could be blazingly hot, the nights were usually cool, and on this night Quaninch and Tsunnunk were happily wrapped in warm robes, oblivious to the men approaching the sleeping village.

The first noise Quaninch heard was a gunshot, followed by shouts and more reports. As he shook his head to see if he was awake or not, his mother sat bolt upright and reached for him. "What is it, Mother? Has Da come home?"

"Shh. I don't think it's your father – or anything good. Keep quiet and don't move."

Tsunnunk crept to the door flap and cautiously peeked outside. At first, she could see nothing, but she heard startled and distressed cries from all over the village. There was a sound of running feet, shouted curses, and continuing gunfire. She instantly realized that their village was being raided – likely by horse thieves or slavers – and she hoped they were horse thieves.

Before she had a chance to tell Quaninch what was happening, a gruff voice shouted "Salga! Rapido!"

She put her finger over her lips and looked desperately at her young son, shaking her head. "Out of there before I burn it down!" the hoarse voice shouted. She quickly pulled aside the flap and saw a Mexican on a horse holding a gun in his right hand and a flaming brand in his left. As she stepped outside, she saw a terrifying leer on the man's face. He would certainly rape her should she submit and hope that Quaninch would be overlooked? Her question was answered by the eruption into flame of the next teepee. There was going to be no safety in hiding.

She stood before the horseman trembling. "Anyone else in there?" he growled, starting to toss the torch on to the structure.

"Yes!" she shouted. She turned to the open doorway. "Quaninch! Come out right now!"

The terrified boy wiped the sleep from his eyes and stepped outside into the pale early light. The man dismounted and stepped up to Quaninch, put his hands under his armpits and lifted the boy off the ground. His face was fat and greasy with a dirty beard. He regarded the boy impersonally, as if appraising a pelt. Then he nodded and put him back down. "Yes," he said to himself, "This is a good catch. A fine young boy for the slave markets and a beautiful squaw for myself."

He turned to Tsununk, grabbed the front of her dress, and threw her in the open door. "Don't move, you little turd," he snarled at Quaninch and stooped to enter the teepee. Quaninch stood paralyzed with horror. He looked around his village that had been so comfortable and safe and saw teepees ablaze, bodies lying on the ground, and strangers on horses rounding up the young boys and girls into groups. Turning back to his own home, he saw a confusion of dark shapes and heard the man laughing. Suddenly, the laughter turned to a surprised shout of pain as Tsunnunk smashed a clay pot over her attacker's head. He put his hand to his scalp and stared curiously at his bloody palm. "You Indian bitch!" he screamed, but his movement was cut short by the sound of a gun going off. His body jerked backwards, and he lay half outside the teepee door, a gaping hole just above his mouth where his nose had been.

His mother stepped over the body with a smoking pistol in her hand. "Quaninch," she said in a broken voice. "They will kill me for what I have done to this beast of a man. He is dead, but I will be too, and very soon. I will not let them have me. I'm going to take my own life, my son. I'm so sorry, but there is no other way for me." Quaninch tried to speak, but he was shaking too hard to form a word. "You must try to survive, my son. They will take you away, but you are too valuable for them to kill. My heart breaks beyond words for you. I love you so much and I had such dreams for you and me and your father,but that is all over now. You must do as I say. Don't resist them, just follow along with the others. My prayer is that your father may find you and rescue you someday. But now, my Quaninch, my son, my love… you must go join the other children and try to… try to survive, my heart, my own!" She pushed him toward the group of children in the center of the village. He saw another mounted man riding toward them and suddenly heard another loud report behind him. When he turned, his mother was lying crumpled on the ground.

The man on horseback reined up in front of the teepee. He first looked at the small heap that was Tsunnunk's body and then toward the entrance where his compatriot lay sprawled in a pool of blood. "You were never a very smart son of a bitch, Luis," he sighed, shaking his head. He dismounted and pried the pistol from the woman's hand and dropped it in his pocket. Then he stepped over Luis's body and quickly glanced around the room. From long experience, his eye was quick to pick out anything of value, but there was not much here other than a few furs, nothing more. "Hello," he said aloud. "And what are you?" He lifted the fiddle with the carved king's head on its scroll. He turned it over in his hands and sighted along the fingerboard. "A fine piece of work," he muttered. "Well, you might be worth something, anyway." He returned to his horse with his small haul of loot, threw a burning torch in the doorway, and rode back to the rest of the troop.

The Mexican slaver gangs that operated along the Old Spanish Trail were businessmen. The items they dealt in were young Indian boys and girls. There was no value in the old ones. They couldn't make the trip to Los Angeles, and they wouldn't fetch any price in the markets anyway, so they were killed immediately. The slavers liked to attack when most of the men were out of the village, but if a few men happened to be there, they were also killed outright. The young women might be worth taking on the long overland trip, but they might also be designated as companions for the raiders. The real money was in the youth, and if they were not necessarily well-treated, they at least had to be looked after so that they would fetch top dollar when they got to market.

So Quaninch and the other children of the village were not beaten or shot. They were collected a short distance from the village and tied in a train – about twenty boys and girls. The children looked around to see their mothers and grandparents dead on the ground, their homes aflame, their possessions destroyed or stolen. The sudden and incomprehensible blow had left them all in a state of total bewilderment, shock, and grief.

The raiders finished their work in the village and set out at a slow pace toward the southwest, along the river that many people were now calling the Virgin. The small villages they passed through were deserted, fires still smoking and food in pots. Word of the raid had spread quickly, and the residents had grabbed what they could and fled to the highlands. The children walked in stunned silence, fearful of bringing the wrath of their captors down on them. They walked all that day, stopping often for short breaks. The men gave their captives water and food during the short rest breaks. Then they were off again. When they stopped for the night, they threw robes at their prisoners, who huddled miserably against the desert chill. They cried and whimpered throughout the dark hours, sleeping fitfully in the midst of their unbearable sorrow and fear.

The first stage of their hopeless journey took almost two weeks. Day after day of plodding along the trail had numbed the captives. After each endless night of cold and tears, they were fed and tied in a line to begin their trek again. To keep himself sane, Quaninch tried to focus his mind on every detail of his surroundings. He learned to distinguish the men from one another. There were fifteen riders who herded the motley collection of Indian children, stolen horses, and pack mules laden with plunder. They were a disreputable lot, mostly slovenly and grizzled. None of the men were kind. Most didn't seem any more aware of the children than they did of their horses. At least a couple of them seemed to have a trace of humanity.

The man called Fernando often rode next to the young captives. He was the first to call for breaks when he saw the children stumble or noticed their lips becoming parched from thirst. Quaninch also saw that Fernando had a piece of loot in his pack that filled him with hope... and despair. The carved king's head on the scroll of his father's fiddle could be seen poking out of a loose wrapping of cloth. He mourned for the lost times when he and his father played their fiddles while his mother happily hummed along. But the sight of that instrument also reminded him that he had a father, and he would surely be looking for him when he returned from the mountains.

The valley that Rafael Rivera had named Las Vegas had changed since William Kennedy visited it in 1830. Those seven years had seen a small permanent settlement grow up there, a watering hole and resting spot for caravans moving along the Old Spanish Trail. The small party of slavers didn't stick out from the others gathered there. Some of the others also had Indian captives and pelts, tobacco, foodstuffs, and trade goods. Amid the bartering, jostling, swearing, fighting, drinking, and whoring, groups disbanded and re-formed. Some would go on to the mission at Los Angeles, others would return to Santa Fe.

The group that had raided Quaninch's village was one that split up. There was no need for fifteen armed riders to escort a group of captive Indian children to the slave market. Four men were chosen to make the trip, while the others would return to Santa Fe to await the next season's pillage. Quaninch felt some relief to see that Fernando was among those going on to Los Angeles. At least he would remain close to his father's fiddle for a while.

The trail to Los Angeles was well-travelled. Many packs of traders passed them coming and going as they moved inexorably southwest. The four guards who tended the children from Mukuntuweap were reasonably considerate of their captives' well-being and more so as they approached their destination, the slave market at Los Angeles. They wanted the children to fetch the highest price at the auction, so they increased their food and water and made rest stops more frequently.

At one stop on a cool autumn afternoon, Quaninch was sitting on the ground near Fernando's horse. He could see the king's head of his father's fiddle poking out of the saddlebag. Glancing furtively around, he quietly got to his feet and reached out to touch it. Suddenly his heart chilled with fear as he heard Fernando shout from a short distance, "Hey! What are you doing there?" He quickly walked back to where the captives were resting, a scowl on his face. "What are you reaching for, little thief?"

He pulled his hand back to give the boy a blow, but Quaninch blurted out, "I'm sorry, senor! I only wanted to touch my Da's fiddle."

Fernando gazed at the headstock and back to the boy. "Your padre's fiddle, eh? Yes, I remember I found it in the teepee where you lived." His glance travelled again to the fiddle in the pack. Then he grabbed Quaninch by the wrist and pulled him close. "Well, little thief, it's my fiddle now. It should bring a good price in Los Angeles, and I don't want anything to happen to it before we get there!"

Quaninch was cowering, fearful of the blow that was surely going to fall on him. "What do you want of this thing?" Fernando asked.

"I just wanted to touch it, to remember my father," he cried, tears forming in his deep blue eyes.

"Is your father Nuwuvi?" he asked, noticing the boy's eyes and light complexion.

Quaninch struggled to catch a breath and said through his tears, "No. He is a white man, a Scot."

"A half-breed, eh? Well, all the better. You should be in demand at the market." A thought struck him. "You don't play this yourself, do you?"

Quaninch nodded hopefully. Perhaps he would escape a beating after all.

"You're pretty young to be able to play a fiddle. Are you lying to me?"

"No," Quaninch yelped. "I don't say that I'm good, but my Da is a great fiddler and he said I had the gift, too."

Fernando unloosed the cord tying the saddlebag and drew the fiddle out. Quaninch was grief-stricken to see the beautiful instrument he and his father had played together so many times. Yet it was something from home, from his former life, and that gave him some strange comfort.

Fernando handed the fiddle to Quaninch. "Careful, now don't harm it. Play me a tune if you can."

Quaninch held the fiddle reverently in his hands. He lifted it and plucked the strings; they were badly out of tune. He turned the pegs and soon brought it up to pitch. Then he looked around, puzzled.

"What's the matter?" Fernando barked.

"Where's the bow?" Quaninch asked, peering at the saddlebag.

"Bow? Well, I never thought of that. Can't you play without one?"

Quaninch plucked out a melody with his fingers, but it sounded thin and weak. "I see," said Fernando. "It's plain that you do know something about playing this thing. Give it here."

Quaninch watched broken-heartedly as Fernando returned the fiddle to the pack. "We're ready to move out," he said. "Everyone up!" he shouted to the rest of the children, and they resumed their journey along the parched desert trail. A struggle was going on in Quaninch's heart. He felt hope, and joy, that his beloved fiddle was so close, and despair that he would never again be able to play it.

That evening, after they had stopped for the night, their guards gave them food and water. Their rations were even bigger than before on the trail; they must be getting close to their final destination, where their appearance and health would determine their value.

As they settled into their blankets for the night, Fernando walked over to the group huddled near the fire. His eyes searched the children until he found Quaninch. "You there!" he pointed. "Come with me."

Fear quickly drove sleepiness from Quaninch as he hurriedly rose and approached Fernando. The night air was chilly, and the boy kept his blanket pulled tightly across his shoulders. Fernando turned and walked back toward the place where the horses were tethered for the night. Quaninch followed wordlessly, fear and curiosity mixing in his mind.

Fernando approached his own horse and pulled the fiddle from the saddlebags. The sight of its carved headstock gleaming in the firelight bewildered the young boy. What was he going to do with the fiddle that he loved so much?

He handed the instrument to Quaninch and turned again to the pack draped over his horse and pulled something else out, keeping it behind his back.

Quaninch looked lovingly at the fiddle and then questioningly at the slaver. "Did you want me to play again? Without a bow?" he asked tremulously.

Fernando didn't allow a smile to reveal his feelings as he slowly pulled from behind his back, a bow. "I want to see if you really can play this thing," he said softly. "I borrowed this from a friend who is travelling to Santa Fe with his own fiddle. I must return it to him tonight, but this will give you a chance to show me what you can do." He handed the bow to Quaninch and said, "Play!"

It had been nearly a month since Quaninch had played this fiddle, though the terror, sorrow, and despair he had lived through made it seem like an entire lifetime. He checked the tuning, tightened the bow, and placed it under his chin. Then he closed his eyes and began to play.

Fernando was no music critic, and Quaninch was not an expert fiddler, yet as the boy played the Nuwuvi melodies and Scottish tunes that his father had taught him, he could tell that this young Indian had a remarkable gift for this instrument. As for Quaninch, the thrill of playing this precious fiddle turned back time to before the start of this nightmare, back to the wonderful life he had in the little village of Mukuntuweap with his brave, beautiful mother, Tsunenk, and the strong and loving father, William. The grief and tears of his present life melted away and he lived only in the melodies of the past.

Fernando let the boy play as long as he wanted, and when he finally stopped, having played every tune he knew, he stood holding the fiddle for a moment and then proffered it to the older man. Fernando gently took the fiddle and the bow from Quaninch and with a trace of a smile, said, "Well, done, boy. You seem to have been born to play this instrument. Perhaps you will have a chance to do it again. Now go back to sleep." With that, Quaninch returned to his fellow captives and settled down with his blanket pulled up to his chin and allowed his memories to lull him to sleep.

As he walked back across the camp to return the bow, Fernando mulled the significance of this Indian boy's talent. A boy with this ability shouldn't be sold at the market to become a field worker or domestic servant; no, he could fetch a much bigger price from a man Fernando knew well, Father Xavier, the rector of the mission at San Fernando Rey de España. He was a priest who loved music almost as much as he loved his God.

Since the Revolution, fifteen years earlier, had established Mexican independence from Spain, the territory of California had seen great turmoil. Slavery had been outlawed by the Mexican government, but that prohibition had been aimed at the American settlers, who were bringing their African slaves into the territory of Tejas. California was far away from the center of national authority, and the relatively mild institution of Indian slavery was untouched there.

The mission system which had ruled New Spain's vast wilderness empire was also suffering under the revolutionary government at Mexico City. The dust had not yet settled from the secularization of the missions, in 1834, just six years before Quaninch's arrival there. Father Xavier faced an uncertain future, as did all the mission priests, but he continued to say Masses every day and to maintain a church for the local population. He also had several Indian slaves, or, as he called them, servants. These had been chosen by Father Xavier from among the Indian children who regularly appeared in the slave market of Los Angeles. He took only the ones who seemed bright and malleable – those who could be trained to read and write, to master the intricacies of serving at Mass, and, most importantly, those who displayed musical talents.

Over the years, Father Xavier had established contact with a few of the slavers. The more humane ones, who kept watch for latent abilities among their victims, would be taken directly to Xavier, bypassing the bustle of the slave market. If the candidates met the standards of Father Xavier, there would be a quiet transaction, and the new servant would enter the service of San Fernando Rey de España.

After listening to the young Indian captive play this fiddle, Fernando knew that not only could he sell the boy at a good price to Father Xavier, but he could also get a handsome return for the unique fiddle with a king's head carved in the headstock.

During the remaining two days of their journey to Los Angeles, on the trail blazed by Jedediah Smith and Antonio, old friends William Kennedy, Fernando did not approach the boy again, or even look in his direction. As far as Quaninch could tell, Fernando had satisfied his curiosity and that was an end of it.

On the morning of their arrival, however, Fernando again approached the group of Indian children and gestured to Quaninch to come with him. The captives, who had become inured to their harsh life on the trail, were filled with anxiety now that this phase of their journey had ended. What would come next in this endless nightmare?

Quaninch hesitantly followed the slaver away from the others to Fernando's mount. There, the older man placed Quaninch on the horse's neck and then heaved himself into the saddle. They rode wordlessly a short distance to a large, open courtyard of a mission. The brilliant morning sun illuminated the white bell tower against the blue sky, and Quaninch could see a scattering of people walking through the busy courtyard, some of them in white robes tied with thick rope, others in their native garments. They were all engaged in a variety of tasks. Quaninch couldn't really make much sense of what all the activity was about. In any case, no one paid any attention to the grizzled Mexican with a very young Indian boy riding in front of him as they approached the mission.

Fernando paused as an Indian dressed in a white robe carrying a stack of books walked by. "Por favor," he barked as the man hurried by. "Where can I find Padre Xavier?"

The young Indian quickly took in the image before him, a grizzled man in trail-stained clothes and a little Indian boy riding in front of him. He immediately understood the situation; this was another servant being brought to Father Xavier by a slaver. "Father Xavier is at prayer in the chapel saying the Terce. He should be done very shortly. Shall I tell him he has a visitor?"

Fernando allowed himself a slight smile. The good padre certainly civilized his Indian slaves. "Yes, por favor. We will wait on the veranda." He dismounted and let his horse drink from the trough while he and Quaninch moved to a shady spot.

They stood in an awkward silence for about ten minutes before Father Xavier appeared. He was a short man in a brown robe and sandals, tonsured head, and shaved cheeks. He sported a mustache and well-trimmed goatee. "Fernando!" he said with a wide smile. "The Lord be with you. It is good to see you after so long an absence."

"And also, with you." He gestured at Quaninch. "I have brought this boy to you because I think he may have a rare gift." He turned to his horse and drew out the fiddle. "And I also have this instrument which comes from this boy's home. He can play it despite his youth."

Xavier first looked at the fiddle. He hefted it and examined the carved headstock, then sighted along the neck and peered into the body. "A tolerable instrument," he remarked casually. Then he turned his attention to the nervous boy standing in front of him. "And you, little one, you needn't be afraid. No harm will befall you now that you are in God's keeping. You play this instrument?"

"Yes, Padre," Quaninch stammered. He didn't know much about the Church or its servants, but he followed Fernando's lead in addressing the priest with respect.

Father Xavier looked back to Fernando and asked, "Is there a bow?"

"No, Padre, but I borrowed one on the trail so that I could see whether the boy could really play. I don't know music, of course, but it seemed to me he has some skill."

"Come inside with me, child," Xavier said to Quaninch. "Wait for us here, Fernando. This won't take long." Together they walked into the cool interior of the church and then into a room off to the right of the altar. Quaninch saw that there were many instruments hanging on the walls. Fiddles of different sizes, tambourines, flutes, and others that he didn't recognize. Father Xavier reached up to the wall and pulled down a violin bow. He handed the fiddle to Quaninch and then gave him the bow. "Will you play a little for me?" he asked. "Don't be nervous. There is nothing to fear now."

Quaninch, again, thrilled to the feel of his beloved fiddle in his hands, quickly tuned it and then tested the bow. He tightened it a bit and asked," Is there any rosin? It feels a bit slick."

Xavier laughed gently and said, "So you really are a musician. We always want our instruments to be just right, don't we?"

"Do you play also, Padre?" he asked.

"Oh, I'd say I play a bit. But let's hear you now."

Quaninch began playing his limited repertoire of his people's music and then moved on to the Scottish melodies that his father had taught him. He glanced a few times at Father Xavier's face to see if he liked what he was hearing, but he caught no clue there. The padre's face was inscrutable, but Quaninch sensed a bit of distaste in the priest's attitude. He played his best, but perhaps he didn't rise to the standard that Father Xavier expected.

When he finished, he dropped the fiddle to his side and waited for the friar's reaction. Xavier didn't speak for a moment, apparently assessing the abilities of this youngster. Finally, he spoke. "Yes, you play very well for such a young boy and one who has not had any proper training, I see."

"Thank you, Padre. But I have had some lessons from my father, who is a great fiddler," he said proudly.

"I see," Xavier said softly. "Your father, apparently a rustic fiddler who played only the melodies of the untutored, the songs of Scotland and, as it seems, some of the barbarous music that your own people sing. But this is not real music, my son. I can teach you to play music of real worth, music to accompany the Mass and music of Spain that can uplift the spirit. But you would have to work very hard; you would have to do your exercises and study your assigned pieces until you perfect them. Of course, you must also be schooled in the true religion so that your soul may be saved. And there are many other tasks that we set for those like you, who are coming to our community from the lands of savage wilderness. If you think you can apply yourself to these tasks and be meek and willing in your efforts, I would be glad to talk to my friend Fernando to arrange for you to remain with us. If you do not feel that you can give us the very best that you are capable of, Fernando can take you back to your compatriots to share their destiny."

Quaninch didn't like hearing his people's music called barbarous or his father deemed a rustic fiddler. But even at his young age, he realized that his choice was simple: stay here and at least be able to play the fiddle or leap into the unknown, to be sold at a market and put to work in the vineyards and fields.

"Please, Padre, let me stay here. I promise to work hard and learn all that you teach."

"That pleases me very much, my son... what is your name, child?"

"Quaninch," he replied.

Xavier frowned and thought for a moment. "Quaninch... you will also need a Christian name. I will call you Jaime, James, after Our Lord's brother."

Quaninch let the name drift through his mind. "Thank you, Padre. It has a fine sound."

Father Xavier took the fiddle from Quaninch and led him by the hand down the long aisle of the church and out into the late morning sunshine. Fernando was sitting in the shade near the horse trough. He hastily stood when the priest approached.

"Well, Fernando, I won't say the lad doesn't have potential. But he's rough, he's really going to need a good deal of effort, and I can't say if even then he'll amount to anything. But I can always use him as a gardener if nothing else. As to the fiddle," he held the instrument up to eye level, "it's a bit garish, don't you think? However, we can always use practice instruments for our beginning students. Come with me inside and we'll finalize the details. You stay here, Jaime," he said to Quaninch, and they disappeared into the padre's room.

"Jaime?" thought Fernando as he followed Xavier inside. "I wouldn't have taken him for a Jaime." He had never thought to ask the boy his name.

CHAPTER FIVE

Quaninch's new life began immediately. He was given new clothes – white robes that tied with a sash and thoroughly cleaned up. He was assigned to a room with another young Indian boy, Diego, a Cahuilla Indian whose real name was Nakai, and who was studying the cello under Father Xavier's tutelage. Quaninch was assigned his chores – the most menial ones since he was the most recent arrival.

He was disappointed that he didn't begin to study the violin right away. First, he had to learn the routine of the mission. The prayers of the hours, the simple but ample meals, the daily domestic tasks, and the intense catechism lessons. Quaninch's religious life had been complicated. His father had been a Presbyterian, though not devout, and his mother, like the rest of her people, had absorbed some of the Catholicism that had been spread by Spanish priests throughout the colonial era. They still remembered their tribal religion, though, and revered Thuwipu Unipugant as the creator of the world.

But in Father Xavier's classroom there was no room for any religion but the "one, true faith." The recitation of questions and answers from the catechism was punctuated by painful blows to the hands from Xavier's rod for a wrong answer, or even for a pause before answering. Quaninch was a quick study and he soon learned to parrot the required sentences immediately. Xavier was pleased that he had read the boy well. He was bright and eager, and surely would make a valuable addition to the mission and to the orchestra, the great passion of Father Xavier's life.

So as the weeks passed, Quaninch was kept too busy to mourn for the life he had lost with his mother, father, grandfather, and his people of the Mukuntuweap village by the beautiful canyon walls. At night, after the lights were extinguished, he let his mind wander and often cried for his family, but his body was tired from the strenuous schedule and soon he drifted to sleep.

One spring morning, as Quaninch scrubbed the slate floor of the entrance to the church, his friend Diego ran breathlessly across the courtyard.

"Jaime," he panted, "Padre wants you to come immediately to the music room."

A bright spark of hope flared in Quaninch's mind. Could this be his chance to return to playing his beloved violin? "But I'm not finished with the cleaning," he said.

"Don't worry, I'll finish for you. Get going. He said right away!"

Quaninch stood and brushed off his robe. "Should I go clean up first, do you think?"

Diego pushed him away with a quick grin. "You look beautiful! But Father will not be happy if he waits for you any longer – go!"

Quaninch took off at a quick pace, his mind whirling with possibilities. How long it seemed since he had cradled his father's fiddle low against his chest and brought forth the stirring music of his people, both the Nuwuvi with whom he had grown up and the Scots, whom he had never even met. He knew his playing would be rusty, but he hoped he could impress Father Xavier with his talent. Maybe he would be able to play music instead of the backbreaking chores he had been assigned.

When he arrived at the music room, the Padre was waiting outside. "How long could it take to walk here from the church, Jaime?" he scowled. "I sent Diego to fetch you some time ago. Are you dawdling on this fine spring day?"

"No, Padre, I came as soon as Diego told me. I didn't even take time to change from my dirty work clothes."

Xavier nodded and said, "Well, be that as it may, you're here now. Do you know why I sent for you?"

Quaninch looked at the priest hopefully, not sure how to respond. "Well, Padre, I don't know, but I hope it is to begin my music studies – though, of course, I am ready to do your will, whatever it may be."

Father Xavier smiled benevolently and nodded. "Yes, that is exactly why you have been summoned. You have done well, Jaime, in your catechism and your work here. Never forget that work is a form of worship, highly pleasing to our Lord, and I have decided that the time has arrived for you to take up your studies. Come in, my boy, and we will begin."

They stepped into the music room, which seemed dark and cool after the brilliant morning sun of the plaza. Xavier walked to the wall where the instruments hung. Quaninch could see his father's fiddle with its carved headstock hanging there, but the Padre didn't reach for it, rather, he pulled down one of the other plain violins and held it up to his eye, sighting along the neck and turning it in his hands. "Yes," he murmured, "this one should do to begin with."

Quaninch was disappointed that he hadn't been given his own fiddle, but he had learned through hard experience not to ask too many questions of the priest. He took the violin in his hands and waited for the instruction to begin to play.

"First, examine the instrument," Xavier commanded.

Quaninch copied the Padre's movements and sighted along the neck and turned the fiddle in his hands. "It seems like a sound instrument, Father," the boy answered.

"Yes, I think it will be a good fit for you." Neither one made any reference to the king's head instrument hanging on the wall.

Quaninch wisely waited for instructions before he began to play. Father Xavier smiled enigmatically and said, "All right. Prepare to play."

Quaninch pulled the fiddle to his chest and clutched the bow in his hand like a breadknife the way his father had taught him. He was stunned by a sharp blow to his buttocks from Father Xavier's rod.

"Surely you know that is not the proper way to hold a violin, Jaime," he said affably.

Fighting back a tear, Quaninch said, "I'm sorry, Padre, but that is the way my father taught me."

"You must forget all that he showed you, my boy. I realize that you have love for your father, but he was not a true musician, merely a homespun fiddler. We will begin from tabula rasa, a blank slate. First, place the violin higher, under your chin, like this." Xavier pulled another fiddle from the wall and demonstrated. Quaninch imitated him and tucked the tailpiece under his jaw. It felt very awkward.

"Now, keep it just like that while we look at the bow. You must hold it in this fashion," and he showed the boy how to squeeze his hand around the handle with his thumb inserted in the frog of the bow and his fingers curled over the top. "Now place the bow on the strings and draw it downward."

This posture was so unfamiliar to Quaninch that he was unable to create the smooth, pleasing tone he wanted. Xavier was not pleased with the sound and gave him a sharp rap on his right knuckles. "Again," he sharply commanded.

Quaninch tried again and again, and soon he did manage to improve the results of his efforts. He practiced on an open string, pulling, and pushing the bow in up and down strokes. His right hand began to cramp, and his left arm grew tired from the burden of holding the instrument in this unnatural way. He wondered why the Padre insisted on this strange, awkward position, when the style his father played was so comfortable and easy. Still, the frequent blows and raps kept him focused on the style that Xavier insisted on.

After about a half hour of this practice, Quaninch's limbs felt on fire from the cramped muscles. He was greatly relieved when he heard the order to put down the violin. "Now we will learn our first scale," Xavier intoned. He lifted his fiddle to his chin and demonstrated a simple scale. "Now you try," he urged.

Quaninch was a very quick learner, but this was an unfamiliar pattern to him. He was more used to using open strings as a drone and playing a melody over the top. He tried the scale and was rewarded by a rap on the hand. "Again," the priest barked, and again Quaninch was unable to match the scale Father had played. For another half hour, he struggled to imitate the scale, improving each time, but still being urged by the Padre's method of smacks on fingers and knuckles.

By the end of the lesson, Quaninch was more exhausted, physically, and emotionally, than if he had continued his scrubbing chores. He wondered, not for the last time, if he had erred in choosing to stay with the Padre. This wasn't playing music as he had known it. It was mechanical, dull, and lifeless.

Father Xavier was surprisingly kind as he took the violin from Quaninch's aching hands. "That was not too bad, Jaime. You have many bad habits that we must root out, and you have a long journey to learn even the basics of the instrument, but I believe you have the natural ability to do it, if you have the discipline and motivation. Now return to your work. We will meet again tomorrow after prayers for our next session."

Quaninch hurried back to the church to relieve Diego of his scrubbing. As he worked with the warm, sudsy water and the stiff scrub brush, he was overwhelmed by longing for his mother and father, and a world now vanished, his tears mixed with the wash water in the slate floor.

The next morning after the terce, the mid-morning prayers, Quaninch promptly went to the music room. "Good morning, Jaime," Xavier said. "Are we ready to resume our studies?"

"Yes, Padre," the boy meekly answered. Xavier handed him the violin and they resumed where they had left off, playing a major scale over and over. The lesson had stuck with Quaninch, because he was able to hold the instrument in the manner prescribed by the Padre and he played the scale quite acceptably.

"Very good, Jaime," he said, smiling broadly. "Now for our next scale." Quaninch's heart sank a bit as Xavier demonstrated another scale, but he was able to learn this one much more quickly than the first, with only a few light blows from his teacher. The unnatural positioning of his arms began to feel a little less strange, though the repetitive scales were no more enjoyable to play.

In this way, Quaninch's life continued through the spring and on into the early summer. Scales, practice exercises, and blows for errors, prayers, and chores. He was not allowed to play anything like a recognizable melody or song, and he was sternly forbidden to play anything that he had learned from his father or from the Nuwuvi. But his skills did improve, and at a faster rate than Xavier had thought possible. Not only did the boy have talent, as the priest had surmised the first time, he heard him play, but he seemed to be a prodigy.

Quaninch still hungered to play the music he loved though on one hot summer day, during the siesta, he left his bed and stole quietly into the music room. Xavier's rooms were at the other end of the plaza, so he didn't think he would be heard. He didn't dare to take down his father's fiddle, but instead, reached for the one he had been using in his lessons. He first held it in the way his father had taught him, but he was surprised to realize that it no longer felt comfortable. He tucked it under his chin in the way Father Xavier had showed him and very quietly, he began to play one of the first melodies his father had taught him, "Soldier's Joy." His heart welled with happiness at the remembered fingerings and the memories of his family that came rushing back. He then played one of the Nuwuvi melodies that he had worked out on the fiddle when his father was away in the mountains. The sad drone overwhelmed him with nostalgia, and he broke down and wept. When he recovered himself, he quickly replaced the violin on the wall and surreptitiously crept back to his room where his friends were dozing. Diego, lying with his face to the wall, had noticed Quaninch's coming and going, but he pretended to be asleep and said nothing.

Quaninch didn't dare to repeat his escapade for some time, because he knew Father's wrath would be violent if he were caught. However, as the days slipped by in their predictable pattern, he occasionally went back to the music room and let his fingers trace the familiar and beloved memories. The fourth time he did this, Diego heard him leave their room. Waiting just a few moments, he quickly got up and looked out into the bright plaza to see Quaninch just disappearing into the practice room. He scanned the courtyard to be sure no one was about and then he followed his friend.

When Diego reached the room, he glanced around furtively and quietly slipped through the door. Quaninch was in the corner softly playing a fiddle, his eyes closed and a smile on his face. Diego stood silently for a second and then cleared his throat. Quaninch started and turned a frightened face to him. Then with relief, he said "Oh, it's you, Diego. You scared me. If Padre ever caught me doing this, I'd get a whipping sure."

"What is that music you're playing, Jaime? It doesn't sound like anything we've been practicing."

"That was a tune my father and I used to play together. I could show it to you if you wanted to try it on the cello."

Diego nervously turned to the open door and peered out at the blazing plaza. He turned back to his friend. "But what's the point, Jaime? Why take the chance of angering the Padre? Let's just stick to our lessons and leave this other music alone."

"But Diego, this is the music I really love. There's no fun in playing pointless scales and exercises when I could be learning how to play the music of my people, that of my father and of my mother."

Diego frowned. "When you've been with the Padre a while, he'll give you other pieces to play. I'm working on a solo for cello written by Elizaga. It's really quite beautiful, though I have to work very hard at it."

Quaninch thought for a moment. "Well, maybe it will get better after a while. But even so, I never want to forget the music of my childhood – my people." He hung up the fiddle and said, "We'd better be getting back, Diego. I'll play my music another time." The boys quickly made their way back to their room without being seen.

Diego's advice proved true. A week later, the Padre listened to Quaninch play his scales and exercises and said, "You are making good progress, Jaime. I think you are now ready to begin working on a real piece of music." He rummaged around on his desk and pulled forth several sheets of hand-written music. "This is a sonata by Antonio Soler, a Spanish composer of the last century. It was written for organ, but I have arranged it for the violin. Let's have a look at it, shall we?"

Quaninch pondered the notes scrawled across the staffs of the manuscript, symbols which would have had no meaning to him two months earlier. But now he understood what they represented. He put his violin to his chin and began to slowly feel his way through the piece. Xavier hummed along, stopping Quaninch often to correct some error or explain some unfamiliar construction.

As Quaninch reached the bottom of the first page, the priest said, "Let's stop there for today, Jaime. What do you think of it?"

The boy pondered the question for just a moment before replying, "It will be a challenge, Padre, but I think I will like it very much." He didn't voice his thought that at least it's better than those endless scales you want me to play!

The summer passed and autumn came, though the weather in Los Angeles didn't change as much as it did in the Canyonlands of his home. It had been a year since he was taken away from his village, since his mother had died in the door of their pine bark teepee, and more than a year since he had seen his father. He missed his old life, but Quaninch was mature enough to realize he would never regain it. He had to go on with the life God had given him, for he now believed that God was in charge of his life, that there was a plan behind the suffering and loss he had endured. His catechism with Father Xavier had penetrated his spirit to that extent. But he never wanted to forget; that was why he hungered for the music of his childhood.

He had continued his clandestine visits to the music room to play the Scots and Nuwuvi melodies that transported him to a happier time. Diego did not return with him on these visits, and though he warned his friend repeatedly that Father Xavier would catch him someday, Quaninch could not keep away from the music room with its wall of instruments.

It was when the days were becoming shorter that his secret was uncovered. His eyes were closed as usual while he played a Nuwuvi chant that he had sounded out on the violin when he was shocked to hear an angry shout.

"Jaime! What are you doing?" Father Xavier had been in the town and as he returned, he heard the strains of music coming from the rehearsal hall. Quaninch stared in horror at the red-faced priest advancing toward him.

"Father..." he began, but Xavier reached out quickly and swept the instrument from the boy's hands. He stared at it in anger and then raised it tremulously above his head as if to crash it down on Quaninch. At the last minute he restrained himself and let the violin sag to his side. "Jaime, I am so disappointed in you. I hear such potential in your playing, and I believed you had realized the value of real music. And now I see that you have never lost your love for this primitive, savage... I won't even call it music! It's far, far beneath your abilities, and it's an insult to me and all I've done for you," he said in sorrow as much as anger.

"Father..." Quaninch repeated. "Please, don't be angry with me. I do love the music you are teaching me, and I do appreciate all you have done." The boy fell to his knees and looked up at the priest, eyes full of tears. "And I'm sorry... but I must explain that these songs from my people have great meaning for me and..."

"Your people!" Xavier spit out. "Your Scottish vagabond father and your ignorant savage mother! You should be grateful that you were rescued from them or else you'd be sitting today in your mud hut, never knowing the true joy of music, never knowing the true God." He lashed out with his left hand and struck Quaninch hard across the cheek. The boy reached up to protect himself, but Xavier delivered a stinging backhand blow that knocked him to the floor.

The Padre carefully hung up the violin and turned to the weeping boy prostrate on the floor. "It is not enough to punish you, Jaime. I must, for your own sake, drive this demon out of you. I cannot allow you to turn your talents, given you by God, to be used in such low and unworthy pursuits. Stand up!"

Quaninch struggled to his feet, his face streaked with tears and glowing red from the blows he had received. Xavier regarded him with stern, unforgiving eyes. "I must give this matter much thought. But for now, you are barred entrance to this room. You will not touch a violin again until I am certain that you have left your savage ways and ideas behind you. Return to your room until vespers and then come to my chamber. I will tell you then what I have decided must be done."

When Quaninch walked into his room, Diego saw at once that what he had warned his friend about had come to pass. "Jaime! What has happened? Did Padre catch you in the music room?"

Quaninch collapsed on his bed and between tearful gasps, told Diego what had happened. "I'm to go to his quarters after vespers," he choked. "What do you suppose he will do to me, Diego?"

Diego shook his head. "I don't know, Jaime. I wish you had listened to me. I was afraid that this would…"

"Stop!" Quaninch shouted. "Don't tell me 'I told you so.' I know that you were right – what difference does it make now?" He buried his head in his pillow as Diego left to attend to his afternoon chores.

It was a long day for Quaninch, alone in his room and fearful of what Father Xavier had in mind for his punishment. If a whipping, then he knew he could stand it, unpleasant though it might be. But what if he decided to bar him from playing music? Or sent him away from the mission to be a domestic servant or field hand on the nearby farms? As much as he disliked the repetitive scales and exercises that the Padre had made him play, at least he was playing music, and he was just beginning to learn some real musical pieces. Finally, when the vespers bell rang, he went to the chapel with the other boys and prayed fervently that he would not be cast out.

After the prayers, while the other boys filed out to return to their rooms, Quaninch walked nervously to Father Xavier's quarters. He knocked quietly and waited to hear the Padre's voice. "Enter."

Xavier was seated at his small desk. He looked up at Quaninch with inscrutable eyes and softly said, "Come over here, my son." Quaninch moved directly in front of the older man and stood stiffly. The priest waited a long moment before beginning.

"Jaime, I have told you many times that you show much promise. I tell you now that you are the most talented boy I have ever taught in this mission, and there have been many talented boys here over the years. And yet your talent is of no avail to you, or me, or our music here, if you cannot reform yourself and lose these savage impulses. I have tried to show you that the crude melodies you learned from your father and the demon-inspired chants that your savage forebears howled in the wilderness are of no value. How can you hear the works of our great Mexican composers, men like Elizaga and Soler, and still wish to desecrate the violin with such trash?"

Xavier became angrier as he spoke, and he rose to his feet. "I have decided to save you from yourself, Jaime. It is a mighty task that I set for myself, to overcome the barbarous demons that you stubbornly hold on to. But I will do it! "

Father Xavier's punishment wasn't medieval; it was not torturous or disfiguring. Rather, it was lenient, wise, and effective. There were the ten swats on the bare buttocks, but many boys had endured that for far less serious breaches of good conduct. After a good deal of liniment and two days lying on his stomach, Quaninch's sore behind was healed.

Xavier's method was the intuitive one of fear and reward. He would dangle the boy over the abyss and then offer him salvation in return for his whole-hearted acceptance of these conditions: that no trace of his father or mother's people remain in his music or his life. To this end, he went to see his friend Don Juan Alvarado, who owned the large rancho that had formerly been the property of the mission. It had been taken away by the Secularization Act in 1833, leaving only the immediate mission grounds as church property. In the ten years since, Xavier and Juan had become friends, their love for music forming a bond between them.

"Padre!" Juan exclaimed as he approached the priest in the sunny courtyard of the main house. They embraced warmly and Juan ushered him into the cool veranda and beckoned to a seat. "Bring wine for our guest," he said to the young servant who stood at the ready. Xavier noted the resemblance of this slave boy to the Indian boys he kept at the mission and smiled.

"Now, my friend, what is the happy occasion for this long-overdue visit?"

"You are right to chide me, Don Juan. I have allowed my duties at the mission to keep me from my dearest and oldest friends. But to come right to the point, I am here to ask a favor."

Don Juan, assuming that the padre had come seeking funds, suppressed any inkling of a wince on his face. "Anything, Father," he answered broadly. "You know that all I have is yours for the asking." Both men knew that there was a double meaning in these words, since, in fact, the rancho had been taken from the Church and given to Don Juan by the Mexican government.

Xavier smiled and gestured with his palms outward. "No, my generous friend, I am not seeking any contributions... at least not at this moment. Rather, my request must be prefaced with a short tale."

"Please continue," said Don Juan. "Sharing this time with you is the only pressing business for me today."

"About a year ago, I acquired a young Nuwuvi slave I named Jaime. This boy seems to have a remarkable gift for the violin." The ranchero's face warmed at the mention of the violin: he was a great aficionado of the instrument. "However," the padre continued, "he had learned a corrupted form of playing from his father, an itinerant Scotch trader. Also, he was deeply attached to the primitive music and culture of his mother's people. Over the past year, I have struggled to rid the boy of these defects, to impart the true faith to him, and to correct the baneful influence of his upbringing. I thought I was making good progress, and indeed, the boy shows wonderful quickness of wit and agility. We had advanced as far as to begin work on an organ piece by Antonio Soler, which I have transcribed for the violin."

Don Juan smiled contentedly as he remarked, "A very great composer. I am sure your work is worthy of him."

"Thank you, Don," Xavier replied abashedly. "You do me too great a kindness. But to continue, this Jaime was making the most remarkable progress until just a few days ago, when I found him in our practice room playing some barbarous, savage melody he had learned from the Nuwuvi. Questioning him revealed that he had been surreptitiously playing this... I hate to call it 'music'... as well as the crude melodies he had inherited from his vagabond father. I punished him, of course, but I feel that he is worthy of a much greater effort, an attempt to truly rid him of his demonic past and create a genuine artist to play music to the glory of God."

Don Juan crossed himself piously and said, "A most admirable undertaking, Father. But how can I be of help to you?"

The priest took a sip of wine and continued. "I want to frighten this boy into forever abandoning his savage history. This is my plan: I would like to have you take him for a few months – say until Ash Wednesday. I will tell him that he has been sold and may never return to my service or to the study of the violin. Then, if you would simply put him to work as the lowliest of your servants and let the reality of life as a slave sink into his very soul, I believe he would be ready to embrace life at the mission with a desperate intensity and would truly and finally turn his back on his backward and savage ways."

The Don sipped his wine and thoughtfully considered the padre's proposal. "My old friend," he began, "it seems that far from asking a boon of me, you are offering me a generous gift. Of course, I will help you. In addition to doing a good deed in urging this boy towards salvation, I will be enjoying the fruits of an extra laborer on the ranchero. It seems that we all will benefit from your remarkable plan."

And so, it was agreed. The very next morning, Father Xavier appeared at the door of Quaninch's room accompanied by a burly stranger. "Jaime," he began harshly, "you have forfeited any claim you had on my generosity. I offered you the gift of religion and civilization and you betrayed my trust. I wash my hands of you! You are now the property of Don Juan Alvarado. May the Lord have mercy on you!"

Before the stunned boy could respond, Xavier turned on his heel and the rough-looking man took hold of his arm. Quaninch cried out to the padre's receding back, "Please, Father! No, don't let them take me away. I will be good – I promise." But his words fell lifelessly to the paving stones as he was pulled across the courtyard and out of the mission.

His life as a slave on an Old California rancho was as bad as he had feared. From dawn to dusk, he labored in the vineyard, in the stables, in the vegetable garden, in the blacksmith's shop – and everywhere he was assigned the lowest, most menial, most difficult, least interesting tasks. He desperately rued the foolish willfulness that had driven him to defy the Padre's commands. Every day blurred through sweaty, aching hours that crept slowly toward the short, blessed time of rest in the night, and the nights blurred with the bitter tears of loss.

The food was meager, and poor compared to the large, wholesome portions at the mission. Sunday was the only day of rest, and most of it was spent in church, where he stood with the other servants from Don Juan's estate and had to endure the sight of his old friends serving at the altar. And at the Midnight Mass on Christmas Eve, Quaninch shed hot, forlorn tears as he listened to his friend Diego playing villancicos, Spanish Christmas carols, on his beautiful cello. He despaired of ever playing the violin again. He could see no future for himself but the endless drudgery of a slave's life on a California rancho.

The New Year arrived, and his life remained unchanged. The Christmas Season ended and the few weeks of Ordinary Time in the church calendar passed; winter in California did not keep the slaves indoors. Their work continued in field and stable without hiatus.

The first day of Lent, Ash Wednesday, arrived, though Quaninch had no reason to mark the fact. Except for the Mass and the ashes marked on his forehead, it was just another day of hard labor, and the coming penitential season promised to be even more dismal. That night, when he stumbled into his adobe hutch that he shared with three others, he was stunned to the point of breathlessness to see Father Xavier standing by his bunk. The Padre had arrived at the rancho to collect his property after the three-month term of service, but Quaninch had no idea that his earthly Hell had been only temporary. He fell to his knees at Xavier's feet and clasped him about the knees, wetting the priest's coarse robe with his tears.

Father Xavier waited for Quaninch to regain his composure and then he urged him to his feet. "Jaime," he softly said. "How have you been, my son?"

"Oh, Father," Quaninch gasped, "This is a terrible place. Please don't leave me here! I promise I'll never ignore your words again!"

Xavier held the boy at arm's length and regarded him quizzically. "So, you think you would be able to leave behind the memory of your father and mother? All of it? The music and language and beliefs?"

"Oh, yes, Father," Quaninch gasped urgently. "I know I could – I would! I will! Please just let me come back to the mission and I swear that I will never disappoint you again!"

Just as the old priest had planned, the fear of a lifetime as an agricultural slave had broken this boy's spirit. Now to rebuild that spirit with the reward of re-admittance to the comfortable life of a mission boy, and the chance to return to music and the violin.

The Padre held Quaninch's shoulders and stared directly into the boy's wide, anxious eyes. "I will give you another chance, Jaime." Quaninch's face relaxed with joy and relief. "But only one!" the priest thundered. "Another such lapse in your behavior and you will be a slave on this Rancho for the rest of your life!"

Quaninch's return to the mission was a joyous time for him. He was given back his old quarters and his former roommate Diego was there to greet him. They embraced and Quaninch sobbed joyfully, "Oh Diego – you were so right to warn me against defying the Padre. How I have suffered, and how good it is to see you and be back in the mission!"

"I never gave up hope, Jaime. I didn't believe that Father Xavier would abandon you forever. He knows you have the gift for music, and he just wanted to teach you a lesson."

"Oh, I have learned that lesson. Never allow me to speak again of the past, of my... my father... my mother." He could see and hear them in his heart, his good, loving mother and grandfather and all the happiness of his youth in the little Nuwuvi village at the mouth of the beautiful canyon. And his brave, loving father who laughed as he played the stirring, happy tunes from Scotland in the long winter nights. Could he really drive them from his mind and never again hear in his heart the songs of his people?

CHAPTER SIX

The next few years were a golden time for Quaninch. His relief at being returned to the mission after the harsh months as a rancho slave was so great that he seemed to truly leave his past behind. He no longer thought of playing the forbidden music of his father and mother and was thrilled to experience the classical music that Father Xavier revealed to him.

As Xavier had suspected, the boy was not only talented, but a genuine prodigy. He soon surpassed the efforts of his fellow musicians in the mission orchestra and became the soloist in every piece they practiced, even soaring beyond the talents of Father Xavier himself. At the Midnight Mass on Christmas Eve, 1842, Quaninch's violin and Diego's cello filled the church with the soaring sound of strings as they played the beloved villancicos and accompanied the choir's singing.

Quaninch felt the tears of joy course down his face as he remembered the dark despair of the previous Christmas when he listened hopelessly to his friend's cello. He was so grateful to God and to the Padre for his earthly salvation. All he wanted from now on was to be a loyal servant to Father Xavier and the Church and to play the violin.

The time drifted away in the routine of work, study, practice, prayer, and performance. He passed his thirteenth and fourteenth birthdays, growing in body, mind, and artistic sensibilities. Xavier had given him the best violin at the mission to play, though the old

King's Head fiddle still hung forlornly and almost unremembered on the wall of the practice room.

As he grew into manhood in the isolated life of the mission, the world outside had been in ferment. Old California was in its twilight years as a new California awaited its violent birth. Ever since Mexican independence in 1821, the modern world had tried to seep into the timelessness of California, but it was such a remote province that Mexico City exerted little direct influence on it. That is why slavery, while outlawed in Mexico since before independence, continued in California, fed by the marauding bands of slavers like those who had taken Quaninch and killed his mother.

While Quaninch practiced his violin in the sunny courtyard of the mission, outsiders were moving into California. The main port and provincial capital at Monterey was becoming a cosmopolitan outpost, with ships from all over the world docking in its bay. American merchants, contemptuously called "Bostons" by the Californios, walked the marketplaces of San Diego, Los Angeles, and Yerba Buena, and American settlers had moved into northern California in large numbers, congregating around the lands of John Sutter.

Far away from California, in Washington D. C., politicians had been casting acquisitive eyes on the Mexican territory for some time. Washington and Mexico City had been at loggerheads over the breakaway province of Texas, and political storms swirled over the question of admitting the huge Lone Star Republic into the United States. While the phrase "Manifest Destiny" wasn't coined until 1845 by editor John O'Sullivan, the reality was that Americans were expanding relentlessly into Texas, New Mexico, Utah, and California. And war was looming over the horizon.

These rivers of fate were destined to engulf Quaninch before very long, but to him, the earthshaking concern of that time was Father Xavier's health. The Padre was not a very old man, though to the young boys in his service, he seemed venerable indeed. He turned sixty in 1843, a respectable age in that place and time, but hardly a remarkable example of longevity. He was active and hard-working, always bristling with energy as he supervised the activities of the mission, visited the sick, said daily Mass, and directed the mission orchestra.

In the summer of 1845, though, Xavier began to experience some disturbing symptoms. He noticed that a short walk would leave him out of breath. His face lost some of its ruddy glow and he simply didn't have the energy anymore to fulfill all his duties. He requested an associate priest to help him and in September of that year, Father Julio arrived to ease the Padre of some of his burdens. Julio was from Mexico City, of an old and proud Castilian family. His assignment to the mission at Los Angeles had been an unwelcome one. He tried using his family connections to dissuade the archbishop from sending him to the godforsaken reaches of California, so far from the centers of civilization, but his overweening assumption of superiority had alienated many in the Church and his reassignment far away was welcomed by his fellow priests.

He was a man of average stature with a medium build, though his fleshy face and jowls belonged to an older man, and he prided himself on the lightness of his skin and his European features. He made it clear to all that the mestizos were much inferior to him, with his Spanish lineage so apparent in his appearance and deportment, and, of course, that the Indians were so far beneath his status that they were hardly to be considered human at all. When his efforts to avoid his fate turned out to be in vain, he resigned himself to the purgatory to which he had been condemned and reluctantly set out for the remote mission which was to be his new home. He was comforted by the thought that his stay there might be a short one and that he would soon return to the comforts and enjoyments of Mexico City.

As an assistant to Father Xavier, he was hardly energetic and enthusiastic, but he did take over the duties of performing the Mass and loosely supervised the business affairs, such as they were, of the mission.

Quaninch assumed an ever-larger role in the operations of the orchestra, selecting music, rehearsing the group, and giving individual lessons. In spite of the lessening of Xavier's responsibilities, though, his strength continued to decline and by November, he was confined to his bed. Quaninch stayed by his side as much as possible, often playing for him to pass the weary hours. In the last week of Ordinary Time, just before the season of Advent, Father Xavier called Quaninch to his bedside. He was gaunt and pale and struggled to make his words audible.

"Jaime," he rasped, "I want you to know that you have given me great joy in my last years."

"No, Padre, these aren't your last years," Quaninch began to interrupt, but the priest continued.

"Do not try to buoy me up, Jaime. I know it is my time and I know I am going to be in the presence of Jesus, and I will hear the heavenly music very soon now. But I want to tell you while I still have breath that you have been the brightest glow of my life. Not only because I have been allowed to help uncover your rare, God-given talent, but because I have been able to save you from a barbarous, heathen life and lead you to your rightful place as a child of God. You come from savage peoples, the Nuwuvi and the Scotch heathens without true religion or civilization. But look at you now, Jaime." Xavier struggled to lift himself into a sitting position. "You are nearly a man, and a fine man. Your future is a mystery to all but God himself, but I feel that you will retain your faith in Him and in the talent, he has given you." He grasped Quaninch's arm feebly. "Only resist at all costs the siren voices that call you back to the godless and uncultured life of your forbears. Keep me always in your heart and in your prayers, and I will watch over you from heaven." He slumped back onto the bed. "Go now, my son. Come to me in the morning."

In the morning, Quaninch was told that the Padre had died during the night. The funeral Mass was long and beautiful, and the mission orchestra read their music through eyes blurred by abundant tears. Quaninch, who had memorized his part, played a solo with his eyes closed, his heart leaping from the violin and filling the church with the love he had for this dead priest.

Father Julio had been tending to the duties of rector of the mission for several months while Xavier was ill, but now that he was the sole head of the parish, he determined to make some major changes in the operation. First, it must be said, Julio was no musician. He did not play, nor did he enjoy listening. He thought of music as a great distraction from the practical matters of life as well as from the spiritual needs of the mission and the parishioners. Furthermore, the orchestra was comprised of Indian boys who he viewed as barely civilized savages. It galled him to see them receiving the praises of the community for the music they created. He would rid himself of that irritation as soon as the opportunity presented itself.

Quaninch was the natural choice to take over the music of the mission; in fact, he had been the de facto director for some time as Xavier's strength had declined. He wanted the music for the upcoming Christmas Season to be glorious, not only as accompaniment to the birth of the Lord, but in memoriam to their departed leader, now in Heaven. He rehearsed the musicians every moment that could be spared from their other tasks. He carefully chose pieces that would do honor to Xavier's influence on the orchestra, and the result was truly stunning. The Christmas Masses were ablaze with candles and awash in the haunting sounds of the lush strings. Quaninch stunned the congregation with a solo rendition of "Ave Maria" during the preparation of the gifts. This piece, written twenty years before by the German composer Franz Schubert, was new to the ears of the Californios and its compelling melody held every worshiper transfixed. Father Julio, saying the Eucharistic Prayers over the sacraments, was not pleased that this young Indian boy had diverted the minds of the people from the Mass and instead drew them into a piece of showmanship – an entertainment! He determined that changes would be forthcoming, and soon.

The New Year arrived, the Christmas Season came to an end with the Baptism of the Lord, and the brief Ordinary Time led on toward the season of Lent. Julio patiently waited until Ash Wednesday had arrived to reveal his plans to Quaninch. Lenten Masses did not feature instrumental music other than the minimum required to accompany the choir, so Quaninch had given his musicians some time off to rest from the rigorous rehearsals and performances of the past six weeks. Father Julio judged that this would be the time to make some major changes in the life of the mission.

Quanninch was summoned to Julio's office one bright February morning. He had asked the orchestra to meet after the sext, the midday prayer at noon, to make plans for the Easter Season, when they would again pick up their instruments and play joyfully to the glory of God. He had no inkling of the storm that was about to break over his pleasant and settled life.

He knocked at the rectory door and respectfully entered when bidden to come in.

"Jaime," said the priest as he fixed Quaninch with his watery pale eyes. "I have, after much prayerful consideration, decided that our mission orchestra has become a distraction from the urgent needs of this community." Quaninch was unable to conceal the surprise and disbelief that showed so clearly on his face. Julio continued without pause. "I know that there is no need for me to explain or justify this decision to you, or to anyone. I am the rector of this mission, and my authority is absolute in these matters. Still, since this activity has apparently meant so much to you…"

"And to Father Xavier, too," Quaninch blurted out.

Julio frowned and continued, "Father Xavier is no longer in charge of this mission. Of course, he was a good man, God rest his soul, but all men have their foibles. Perhaps my late predecessor was led by his own love of music to some excesses. Be that as it may! But I have no such fixation. I realize the true purpose of this mission is to bring lost souls to Christ." He waited briefly to see if Quaninch had any reply.

"Of course, what you say is true, Father. But I believe we have brought many to the true religion through this orchestra. I myself am an example of one whose faith began in the study of the violin."

Julio allowed a slight smile to come to his lips. "And we are joyful for your conversion and the faith of your fellow… natives. But you are a small group and represent California's past. Outside these mission gates, the world is ablaze with violence, war, and conquest. If we mean to take our Holy Church and our sacred Spanish heritage into the future, we cannot afford such distractions. My decision is final, Jaime. You will inform your fellow players of it. When Lent ends, we will rely upon our church organ to support what singing is necessary to our liturgies. That is all."

"But Padre," Quaninch began.

"That is all, I say!" Julio bellowed and rose suddenly from his seat, his face flushed and angry. "There is no debate – you will do as I say without questioning me! Now go!"

Quaninch stood trembling for a moment, then started to say, "Is there no way to appeal to you to reconsider, Padre?"

Julio briskly stepped around his desk and slapped Quaninch full in the face. "Father Xavier had a great blind spot regarding you savages! He thought you could be civilized and turned into white men. I have no such delusions! You are Indians and slaves and that is all you will ever be. I will not tolerate disrespect and dissension from you or your benighted brethren. Go now, disband your troupe of clumsy bow scratchers and devote yourself to your duty and that duty will be determined by me and me alone!"

Quaninch mumbled "Yes, Father" through his tears and made his way blindly out of the room. The brilliant sun of the courtyard stung his weeping eyes. He didn't know what to do or where to go. His pleasant and regular life of the past three years had been suddenly and inexplicably shattered, gone beyond recapture. What the future could hold for him was hidden from his mind. Only black despair welled up inside him and accompanied him as he slowly made his way to his quarters.

Thankfully, Diego wasn't there when Quaninch entered the cool, dark room. He didn't know how he was going to tell his friend that his days of making soaring music on his beloved cello were over. He fell on the bed and wept for his loss. And for the first time in years, the memory of his even greater loss returned to his conscious mind. Perhaps it had lingered there, out of view, all along, but the horrifying memories of his mother's murder, his capture and enslavement, the grueling march to Los Angeles and the separation from his father all flooded into his grieving mind and mingled with the new despair and hopelessness that he felt.

Eventually his tears dried, and he sat up. He had many tasks now, foremost of which was to tell the boys that the orchestra was dissolved, that their studies were at an end. For the first time, it occurred to him that Father Julio was not only ending the musical training of the boys, but that he was turning away from Father Xavier's purpose to educate and uplift the boys. Xavier's belief that the Indians were barbarous, and savage was an evil delusion, of course. Quaninch had always been aware of that, even when he felt deep love for the man. But in his own way he had been a kind man. He was acting according to the command of his faith, no matter how misguided that faith might be, and his purpose was ultimately for the good of those he taught, at least in his own understanding of it.

Julio was an altogether different kind of man. Quaninch understood that this priest felt no love for the youngsters in his care, no belief in their salvation, whether in this world or the next. They were going to become what they always had been in truth – slaves. Xavier's treatment of them had created a sense of community among them, a feeling that they were students and apprentices rather than domestic slaves. But now that thin veneer was torn off forever.

Quaninch stood and walked to the bureau where the ewer stood full of fresh water. He rinsed the streaks of tears from his face and regarded his reflection in the mirror. The face that stared back at him was no longer a vulnerable boy at the mercy of the winds of the world. There was the face of a man in the mirror. He was now 15 years old, strong, and slender, with black hair cut in short bangs. He could see in the chiseled face before him, the traces of both the dark and artistic expression of the Nuwavi and the stern, angular face of the Scots. His eyes also displayed his joint heritage, not the deep brown of his mother, but the pale blue eyes of his father.

He contemplated his image in silence for some time, trying to make sense of the confidence and strength that was growing within. The years of submission to Xavier and the life of the mission had served a purpose. He had mastered the violin and grown to the stature of a man during this peaceful interlude. But he saw that he must no longer accept the dictates of anyone now. He must be his own man and chart his own course no matter the cost.

He turned from the mirror and sat on the edge of the bed, his mind a flurry of conflicting thoughts and ideas. There was no plan yet, but there was a purpose. He would free himself from Julio and the bondage of the mission life. When and how were the great questions, but there was no doubt that this, he would do.

The door cracked open to allow a brilliant flood of light to engulf the cot where Quaninch sat. "Jaime," said Diego in surprise. "Why are you sitting alone here in the dark? The boys are gathered in the rehearsal hall to begin our plans for Easter. We're waiting for you."

Quaninch looked at him with a serious, somewhat detached expression. "Yes, it must have slipped my mind. Let's go." The two young men walked in silence across the courtyard and found the seven other boys who made up the little orchestra seated in the rehearsal room, instruments still hanging on the wall. The season of Lent was just beginning, and they knew they would not play in the church during that penitential time. They would, however, be able to devote all their energies to the Liturgies of Easter, that joyous feast that awaited forty days in the future.

There would be no easy way to do this, Quaninch realized. He bade them sit and began to speak softly. "I'm afraid I bring some very bad news, friends." The relaxed and eager faces clouded with uncertainty. He decided to come to the point immediately. "Father

Julio has just told me that he is discontinuing our music program, disbanding the orchestra and ending all lessons and studies."

There was no response for a few seconds; then the stunned silence was broken by a flurry of distressed questions to which Quaninch had no satisfactory answers. "No, there is no chance of his changing his mind; no, you will not be able to keep your instrument and play on your own; no, I do not know what other changes Father Julio has in mind; yes, I too am shocked and heart-broken, but there is no appeal. We must each make our own choices and seek our own fates."

During the stunned murmur, Diego spoke up bitterly. "What choices do you mean, Jaime? What of our fates? We are slaves who have no choice and whose fates are in the hands of our owners. In the hands of Father Julio!" He nearly spat the name.

Quaninch looked deeply into his friend's eyes but had nothing to say – yet. The boys scattered to their quarters and their tasks, each pondering the portent of this unwelcome development. When Quaninch and Diego were left alone in the forlorn rehearsal hall, he turned to his friend and said, "Be patient, Diego. I must muse deeply on this. I must find some way to deal with this catastrophe. And I will want you to be with me, whatever comes."

Diego looked at his friend sadly and said, "There is no way, Jaime. There is nothing to be done, nothing to ponder. We have lived in a fool's paradise and now we are thrust into the cold light of day." He turned and walked out without looking back.

While Quaninch struggled to find some way out of his quandary, events far beyond his experience were moving inexorably toward him. In April of that year, a clash occurred in Texas that resulted in the United States declaring war on Mexico, though this news would not reach Los Angeles until the following August. In addition, American interests had been working assiduously for years to separate California from Mexico and bring it into the United States. The Americanos were strongest in the north, along the Sacramento Valley and in the port towns of Yerba Buena and Monterey, but many agents of the United States government, official and unofficial, had been active in Southern California from San Diego to Los Angeles.

The towns and missions of Old California were small. Los Angeles held about 1500 souls, and so were the military units that were forming to take part in the looming struggle. Nevertheless, there were many plots and negotiations afoot in the rich but isolated territory. Mexico City was much too far away to exert real control, and many of the Californios had been so alienated by the central government's neglect and authoritarian pronouncements that they hoped for annexation to the United States or even to Great Britain.

Of these currents of history circulating around him, Quaninch had no knowledge, and he would not have understood them if he knew. His life had been remote and isolated, a childhood in the remote Nuwuvi village and coming of age in the confines of the mission. He had rarely ventured into the village of Los Angeles, and on the few occasions when he did, he was bewildered by the bustle and confusion of the town. There were so many different languages and skin colors, everyone in a hurry to buy and sell, to make a profit, to gain advantage. He always felt a cool relief when he entered the mission grounds and shut the cacophonous world out of his mind.

Now, in the black rage he felt toward Father Julio, he was beginning to form a plan to leave the mission and enter into the life of that unknown and incomprehensible world. He would bide his time, no point in moving rashly before he could form a plan. He needed to learn about the world outside of his world, the streets and markets of Los Angeles and the hinterlands beyond. He remembered well the hot, dry desert through which the Old Spanish Trail blazed from the Colorado River to Los Angeles. He didn't think that way would offer any chance to an inexperienced traveler on the run from slave catchers.

He also knew that there was an ocean which accommodated men in ships and led to places so mysterious that they might have been settings for fairy tales. That would remain an option, but he must learn much more about ships and sailors and the ports to which they sailed before attempting an escape in that direction. Should he run away alone, or should he see if Diego would join him? There were many things to consider, and Quaninch had learned patience under the tutelage of the good Padre. He would bide his time, keep his eyes and ears open, and think, think long and carefully before he acted. He was too young and inexperienced to realize that events might overtake his most careful deliberations and hurl him headlong into his   future.

CHAPTER SEVEN

That Easter Season of 1846 was joyless for Quaninch and his friends. There was no music to match the beauty and wonder of the holiest of days in the Church year. Only the wheezy organ to accompany the singing, and there was not much of that.

The time that had formerly been spent in rehearsal and practice was now devoted to longer hours of work in the fields and vineyards surrounding the mission, and Father Julio expanded the practice of renting his slaves out to local rancheros. Most of the boys were fatalistic about the change in their lives. They came from a variety of tribes throughout the Southwest, and they all had suffered the trauma of being stolen from their villages and families and brought to this new life at the mission. Some, like Quaninch, had even seen their parents killed before their eyes. This new turn of events, while unwelcome, was just one more example of the mysterious workings of fate, or of God – that simply must be accepted and endured.

Even Diego had slumped into a state of apathy and depression. Quaninch did not see the bright spark in his friend's eyes that had sustained him in troubled times, nor hear the laughter that had always helped to lift his own spirits. Nothing he said could get a rise out of his old friend. Diego simply turned away whenever Quaninch tried to talk about an escape plan. "Jaime," he would sigh, "Please stop dreaming these impossible things. All you will accomplish is to receive a terrible beating and be sold to a back-country rancho where you will be treated as an escapee, a dangerous slave that must be controlled and isolated. Here, at least, you face the devil you know. Out there is the devil you do not know, and that is worse."

Nothing would deter Quaninch from his planning, however. If he couldn't entice his friend to join him, he would act alone. Throughout the spring and early summer of that year, while war and revolution were stirring in the north at Sonoma and Yerba Buena, Quaninch used the errands he was assigned to gather information. Knowledge that he hoped he could use to escape. With his newly opened eyes and ears, he listened to strangers' conversations, noted the arrivals and departures of traders with their long mule trains loaded with goods, and began to look at the few ships that anchored far out in San Pedro Bay.

Los Angeles did not have an attractive harbor, unlike San Diego, Yerba Buena, and Monterey, the main port for the province. It was shallow, with a muddy bottom, so that the relatively few ships that called there had to anchor in the nearby harbor of San Pedro. Still, there was a lively enough trade that there were always a handful of ships for Quaninch to study.

He also was able to eavesdrop on the talk of the seamen. They spoke many languages, most of which he did not understand, but he knew enough English to learn some of the ways of the sailors. It appeared that their greatest interests were in liquor and women, since those were what the men from the ships talked about incessantly, and they always headed directly to the taverns and burdels when they debarked from their vessels. Quaninch knew nothing of drinking or sex, though as he approached his sixteenth birthday, he noticed unfamiliar feelings prompted by the senoritas with painted faces and low-cut gowns who loitered in certain streets and disappeared with sailors on their arms into darkened doorways.

There was some talk of other matters where the sailors congregated. Quaninch first heard the names of Commodore Stockton and Captain Fremont, Americans who were busily engaged in removing Northern California from Mexican sovereignty and adding it to the United States. He had no inkling that the course of his own life would be swayed by these men and the forces they led.

In spite of his newly acquired curiosity about the world outside the mission, he was unable to come up with an escape plan. He certainly couldn't sail away on one of the ships since he knew nothing of sailors' arts and would surely be identified as an escaped slave. Likewise, the land caravans offered little hope. Any Indian faces in those groups belonged to captives, though the slave trade had dwindled to almost nothing in recent years. Perhaps Diego was right – it was pointless to resist fate. But whenever this thought entered Quaninch's mind, he quickly rejected it. Sensible or not, practical, or foolish, possible, or impossible, he was determined to escape his lot in life as a mission slave. He would seek his freedom whatever the cost.

His planning was overtaken by events as so often happens. As the hot, dry month of August arrived in the dusty village of Los Angeles, two things happened. One private and one public, that would propel him into his unknown future. The first of these occurred when Quaninch, who was working with some other boys unloading a shipment of holy wine from a pack mule, saw Father Julio approach the long-shuttered rehearsal hall with another man at his side. He recognized this man, Gabriel Ortez, as the owner of the violin shop in the village. Before Father Xavier's death, they had often taken damaged instruments there for repair, and Father Xavier had sometimes bought supplies and music from him.

Why the padre would be taking Gabriel into the music room was a puzzle, until it flashed suddenly in his mind that Julio was going to sell off the instruments. He was a greedy man, and the violins and one cello surely would fetch him a substantial amount. The two men emerged from the room into the blazing courtyard and Gabriel departed with a handshake, while Father Julio returned to his quarters with an unmistakably pleased look on his face.

Quaninch had long since given up any hope that the little orchestra would ever play again, and if Julio sold off the instruments it would really make no difference. There was one fiddle in that room though, that he was determined would not be sold, the one with the ornate carving of a Scots king on the headstock. That was his father's, and it was his by right of inheritance. He knew he had to act immediately if he were to save the precious heirloom. Gabriel was probably planning to come back the next day to take his purchases back to his shop. Whatever he would do must be done that night Quaninch realized.

As he sat in the church during the night prayers, he recited the ancient words with one part of his mind. The rest of his thought was bent on his dilemma of how to rescue the king's head fiddle. The prayer ended and the boys returned to their rooms. Diego fell asleep quickly as the boys usually did after their long days of hard work. But Quaninch had no trouble staying awake. His mind was whirring, trying to devise some plan. But no plan came to him. Still, he would not allow the fiddle to be stolen, yes stolen, because it was his, not Father Xavier's, not Father Julio's, not the Church's.

He rose and carefully felt in his nightstand for the key to the music room which Xavier had entrusted to him. Julio had not thought of asking him to return it, and he silently crept out of the room. The courtyard was jet black in the warm night as he made his way to the once-beloved rehearsal hall. He kept to the darkest shadows until he reached the door and quickly inserted the key. He turned it slowly and gently pushed the door open without a creak.

His eyes had adjusted to the darkness of the courtyard, but the music room was completely black. He couldn't see anything on the wall or on the floor. He had not visited this room since the previous February when Julio had disbanded the orchestra, but he remembered where the fiddle hung on the wall, untouched since the day so long ago when Father Xavier took it from him. Even before the Padre had caught him playing forbidden music, he never dared to reach for this instrument. But he had gazed on it reverently every time he entered this room, and he knew its location even in the ink of darkness.

He cautiously shuffled over to the wall to avoid stepping on anything that might have been left out on the floor. With his hand tentatively stretched in front of his face, he touched a violin. Two rows up and on the left – there it was. He gently pulled it from its peg and brought it down, cradling it like a newborn baby. He could not see it, even though he held it only inches from his eyes, but there was no mistaking it by its feel. He didn't even need to trace the carved headstock. This was an instrument he would never forget no matter how long it had been since he held it.

He quickly slipped out of the music room with the fiddle held under his nightshirt, but he had no inkling of where he could hide it. His simple cell had no recesses in which he could conceal anything. He couldn't risk leaving it where someone might accidentally discover it. He decided to simply keep it in his bed until he could think of a better place. There was a chance that it wouldn't even be missed, since Julio had never taken any notice of the musical instruments and perhaps it hadn't caught Gabriel's attention, either. Diego was sound asleep and didn't waken when Quaninch slipped into the room and crawled back into bed, placing the fiddle under the covers near his feet.

The next morning, he let Diego leave the room just ahead of him on his way to lauds, the early Morning Prayer, and arranged his bedclothes to accommodate the violin between the bed and the wall. He looked back as he left, satisfied that it was hidden from a casual observer, though it would be found by the most cursory search of the room. He would have to think very hard today to find a safer hiding place.

The fiddle remained in its perilous hiding place for that day and the following night. On the day after that, Gabriel arrived with two helpers to remove the instruments from the mission and take them to the luthier's shop. They busily wrapped the violins and carefully placed them in the hand-drawn cart they had brought. Whenever their tasks took them within sight of the courtyard, Quaninch and Diego stole glances at the men working. Diego's eyes welled up when he saw his beloved cello wrapped in muslin and placed in the wagon.

The men took about an hour to remove all the instruments and safely stow them in the cart for their short journey to the shop. Quaninch saw Gabriel enter Father Julio's office and leave a short time later. The three men then slowly pulled their wagon out of the courtyard and headed into town. He allowed himself a little inward sigh of relief. It seemed that his father's fiddle had not been missed.

As he left after Vespers, however, Father Julio motioned to him to stay. After the others had left the church, the priest confronted him with an icy tone of voice.

"Jaime, I know you are aware that I have sold the musical instruments, since we have no more need of them here."

"Yes, Padre, I saw Gabriel removing them today."

"But Gabriel was disturbed that one of them was missing. He seems to think it is of some value, a unique piece, he said with a strange carving on it. Do you know this instrument?"

"Of course, Padre," Quaninch answered. "That fiddle was originally given to me by my father."

Julio looked intently into Quaninch's eyes. "And do you know the whereabouts of this unusual item, Jaime?"

"No, Father," he answered immediately. "I haven't seen it since you halted the music program last February."

"Jaime," the priest continued, "It is to your credit that you are a terrible liar." I ask you again if you know where this fiddle is?"

"Padre," Quaninch protested, "I don't know anything about..."

He was cut short by a violent blow to the face. Julio said nothing. Quaninch fought back tears and said, "No, Father, don't hit me. I don't know..." Another slap harder than the first staggered Quaninch.

Julio brought his florid face closer to the crying boy. "No more lies, Jaime," he scowled. "Tell me where you have put the fiddle!" He unleashed another blow to the boy's face and Quaninch fell to the floor. The priest unleashed a hard kick to his stomach and the boy retched and curled up in pain.

"You are a savage and a thief," Julio shouted. "Xavier's naiveté was never so apparent as it is now, when you stand revealed as an ungrateful cur who bites his master's hand!"

He brought his foot back to deliver another blow, but his foot caught in his long brown robe, causing the priest to lose his balance and fall heavily backward. The boy huddled on the floor, quaking with dread at what the priest would do next when he arose. But he didn't rise. Quaninch pushed himself to all fours and saw Father Julio lying still with his eyes closed and a trickle of spittle draining from the corner of his mouth.

Without waiting to see what Julio's condition was, Quaninch leaped to his feet and rushed from the room. There was no one out in the courtyard. Dusk had begun to fall, and all the boys were in their cells. He breathlessly burst into his room and surprised Diego, who was reading on his bed.

"Jaime!" he blurted out. "What is the matter?"

"Oh, Diego, I'm in the worst trouble! Father Julio was beating me, and he fell down and isn't moving. I didn't touch him! But what will that matter? I'll be blamed for attacking him or murder if he's dead. Do you know what the fate is of slaves who assault their owners?"

"But why was he beating you?" Diego asked, bewildered.

Quaninch went to his bed and pulled out the fiddle. "I took this from the music room before Gabriel could load it up. It's mine, you know! I couldn't let them take it away where I would never see it again."

Diego rose from the bed and faced his friend. "Jaime, I don't know what to say. The only choice for you is to run. You could be killed for what you have done, whether the padre lives or dies. You must leave, and right away!"

"But where can I go? I don't know anyone in this town who could take me in."

"I don't know, Jaime," Diego sadly whispered. "But it is certain you can't remain here. Go, now! This minute! Father Julio may have come to and might be headed here as we speak!"

Quaninch could not deny the truth of what Diego was saying. He had almost no belongings, so it was a matter of minutes for him to grab a change of clothes, pick up the fiddle in its wrapping, and start for the door.

He turned for a second and looked at his friend. "Diego, you have been my brother, I hate to leave you, but I hope we may meet again someday in a happier time. Adios."

"Adios, my friend. May God protect you."

Quaninch turned without another word and stepped out into the fading twilight. He quickly made his way to the entrance to the mission and slipped off into the evening.

He stepped directly into that other event that was to change his life that day. Commodore Robert Stockton had arrived in Los Angeles with an army of 350 men and declared that the city was now part of the United States of America.

CHAPTER EIGHT

Quaninch was stunned as he quietly crept into the town. He had expected a typical sleepy evening, with a few drunken sailors fighting over a girl in an otherwise quiet village. Instead, he found the place ablaze with torches, fireworks exploding, and exuberant crowds cheering and walking with linked arms down the center of the streets.

Everywhere people were carrying the flag he had seen on some of the ships in the harbor, the red, white, and blue American flag. He noticed three different versions – most of them were the twenty-six-star flag, but there were a few twenty-seven starred ones, reflecting the addition of Florida to the Union the previous year. Here and there, small detachments of Commodore Stockton's men displayed the most up-to-date version. The twenty-eight-star flag that included the newest state – Texas.

He was bewildered by the unexpected chaos in the town, but he quickly realized that it could all work to his advantage. The commotion would overwhelm any hue and cry over his disappearance. He decided to blend in with the revelers and simply await some opportunity to make good his escape.

The cheering crowds were not altogether sure of what they were celebrating. The only thing that they knew was that the disorder and confusion of the past few years was at an end and a new order had arrived. Mexico City had long treated California as a troublesome stepchild and appointed a string of ineffectual governors, including Juan Alvorado, the ranchero who had taken Quaninch as a slave at

Father Xavier's request. The neglected province had thus become a tangled nest of corruption and chaos. While the United States was an unknown quantity in Los Angles, it represented change and the future. That was something the Californios were ready to celebrate.

Quaninch joined the procession of revelers and added his voice to those shouting, "¡Viva los estados unidos!" and, "¡Hurra por Stockton!" He was relieved to see that the impromptu parade was heading away from the mission and toward the area of bars and burdels where the celebration was centered, fueled by an abundance of mescal and wine. The procession gradually broke up as marchers drifted off to find a seat at taberna or to disappear into a dark room with a pretty puta.

Above the cries and shouts and the explosions of fireworks, Quaninch could faintly hear music being played in some of the taverns and even on a few street corners. He quickly realized that he could possibly make a few pennies by playing his own violin in the street. While he hadn't touched the fiddle since February, he was sure he could make sounds at least as pleasing as some of the wheezy accordions and clumsily strummed guitars that he heard.

He glanced around in the darkness, illuminated only by the burning torches, and found a cracked piece of pottery. This he placed on the ground by his feet. He then unwrapped the king's head fiddle and gently wiped it clean. It had been so long since he had played this wonderful old instrument, his father's fiddle, handed down to William by his own father, and who knew how far back in time his ancestors had owned and played it? The excitement in the streets, the euphoria of being free, the boundless happiness he felt of once again holding his rightful inheritance, all combined to overwhelm Quaninch with a joy that vanquished the fear and uncertainty of the past few hours.

The fiddle was very badly out of tune, as could be expected after its years of inactivity. He guessed at what might be close to pitch and tuned the four strings. Then he tightened and rosined the bow. He did not attract any attention by this. The crowds were still large and noisy, and a young man preparing to play a fiddle wasn't exciting enough to gain their attention.

Quaninch took a breath and began to play the first tune he had learned on his own, back in the far-off days of his childhood in Mukuntuweap at the mouth of the beautiful canyon, "Soldiers' Joy."

His fingers were stiff, but the mechanics of playing came to him subconsciously. When he finished that one, he tried a few other Scots songs that he had learned from his father. He didn't attract great notice, but a few coins began to tumble into the cracked bowl at his feet. He didn't attempt any of the Nuwuvi melodies he had learned on the violin. They were too somber and mysterious for this audience. He tried to keep it light and fast, but he soon ran out of songs he remembered. So, he just started over with "Soldiers' Joy" and repeated his repertoire. The crowd moved by so swiftly that no one noticed the repeats.

Long after midnight, the crowd finally thinned to nothing, leaving the streets to a few idlers, drunks, and Quaninch. He had garnered enough coins to pay for a place to sleep, but he didn't know where to look, and he thought the hour was too late to try to find a room. He wrapped up the fiddle, shook the coins out of the bowl into his pocket, and walked away from the village into the countryside where he found a sheltered spot to lie down.

The next day he walked through the entire town keeping his eyes and ears open. He wanted to know if Father Julio was searching for him. He wanted to find out where he might be able to rent a room with his meager funds. Most importantly, he wanted to come up with a plan for his survival. He knew he couldn't stay in Los Angeles indefinitely. He had as yet, no idea where he could go.

Quaninch was almost sixteen, tall and well-built, and he easily passed for two years older than he was. He had become a handsome young man with the dark hair and olive skin of his mother and the fair eyes and angular face of his father. He fit in easily among the diverse peoples of Los Angeles – Mexicans, Indians, Americanos, Chinese, European, Africans, and many mulattoes and mestizos. He passed the day walking around, occasionally spending one of his coins on a bunch of grapes or some tortillas to assuage his hunger. He didn't see any signs that he was being hunted, no familiar faces from the mission mingling with the crowds that still filled the streets in response to the American invasion.

When dusk fell, hoping to duplicate his modest success of the previous night, Quaninch looked for a good spot to play some music and hopefully increase his small collection of coins. He placed the battered bowl at his feet, pulled out his fiddle, and began to play. As had been the case the night before, he managed to garner a few coins as he tried a variety of tunes to catch the interest of the crowds. He felt stronger on the instrument now after playing all those hours yesterday.

Quaninch noticed a young man who seemed to be watching him very carefully. After finishing a group of songs, he nodded to the stranger. "Hola," he said quietly.

"Hola," came the response. "You play very well."

Quaninch regarded him quizzically. "Do you also play?"

The young man chuckled and replied, "I don't play the fiddle, and I'm not nearly the musician that you are, but I do play a bit on my banjo."

"Banjo? What's that? I don't think I've ever heard the word."

The stranger laughed heartily. "They're very popular in the East," he said. "They come from the slaves originally, but lots of white folks have taken up the instrument. It's kind of hard to describe. Maybe I could go get mine and show you."

Quaninch thought for a second and replied," Yes, I'd love to see it, but I think I should continue to play for a while here. I'm getting a few tips, and I certainly need the money. Perhaps you could come back in a little while when the crowds have thinned out."

"Yes, I'd like that. Maybe we could even play a few tunes together. Banjo and fiddle make a very good combination." He stepped up to Quaninch and proffered his hand. "My name is Jack," he said. "Jack Ferguson. I'm on the brigantine *Abigail*. We're in port for a week and I have some time on my hands to see what this land of California is all about, especially since it seems that it's going to be part of my country now."

Quaninch took his hand and said, "My name is Jaime. Glad to meet you. I'm very interested in seeing your... what do you call it?"

Jack replied, "It's a banjo. Once you see and hear it I think you'll remember. I have a room at Bella's Saloon on North Main Street. Do you know it?"

"I'll find it," Quaninch replied. "I might play pretty late if the crowd sticks around."

"That's no problem," Jack smiled. "Bella's is not what you would call a quiet place. They go on there late into the night, and I don't think a little fiddle and banjo will bother anyone. See you soon."

When Quaninch arrived at Bella's later that night, he was pleased to have a pocket full of coins to show for his night's work. Bella's was a lively place, a favorite of sailors ashore and therefore, a place of great drunkenness and revelry. He enquired at the bar about Jack Ferguson and was told to go around back. There he found a ramshackle stairway leading to a balcony with several doors opening onto it.

As he gingerly ascended the creaking stairs, he heard a door open, and Jack's voice call out. "Jaime! You made it. Come on in."

Jack's room was small and dingy, but his seaman's training showed in the neat way his gear was stowed. He held a strange object in his hands — something that looked like a tambourine with a long neck attached. There were four tuning pegs on the headstock, just like a fiddle, but halfway down the neck was another tuner stuck on as a seeming afterthought. Jack offered it to Quaninch saying, "Here. What do you think? See if you can make any music on it."

"Is there a bow?" he asked?

"No," Jack laughed, "You pluck it with your finger or rather your nails. I'll show you."

He took the banjo back and cradled it in his arms. The first notes had a shocking, brassy, percussive quality quite unlike anything Quaninch had heard before. Jack only played a few chords, demonstrating the technique he used of striking the strings with his fingernails using a downward motion and plucking the forlorn fifth string with his thumb. It was more rhythmic than melodic, Quaninch realized.

"You try it," Jack said, again offering the banjo to Quaninch. He took it awkwardly and touched it gently, as if afraid it would fall apart in his hands.

"You needn't be so careful, Jaime. That banjo has survived a trip around the Horn. I doubt you will harm it by playing a few notes."

Quaninch strummed on the strings as he had seen his new friend do. The bangy tone made him wince a little. He tentatively pushed a string down along the neck, but it was so different from his own musical experiences that he quickly handed it back. "Why don't you play a tune?" he asked Jack. "I'll get out my fiddle and maybe I can follow you on something."

As Quaninch tuned his fiddle and rosined his bow, Jack began to strum a melody on his banjo. "This one is called "Ol' Zip Coon," he said. "It's a favorite at the minstrel shows and it couldn't be any easier."

Quaninch listened once through the melody and then joined in. At first, he simply sawed away at the chords, but he soon got the hang of the melody and took a turn at it. Suddenly the music took on a new life. The banjo provided a solid rhythm underneath the fiddle's melody line. This delighted both of them so much that when they had exhausted the simple melody, Quaninch asked, "Do you have another? This is really fun!"

"Well, this one is a bit harder. I can't play the melody all the way through, so I'll sing it. Maybe you can catch on that way." He began strumming and said over the music, "It's called "Turkey in the Straw."

This melody was considerably more complex than the first song, but it posed no obstacle to Quaninch, who had learned and memorized very long and intricate classical pieces as well as Scot's melodies he learned by ear from his father. They continued to play through the night until they had run through all the songs that Jack knew. It was harder to do the songs Quaninch played. Jack wasn't really a very accomplished musician, and his instrument was largely limited to one key, that of the open-tuned strings.

Jack had been right when he said that they wouldn't bother anyone at Bella's. No one seemed to hear anything, and in fact, in between their songs, they could hear the uproar from the saloon continuing deep into the early morning.

As they took a breather after their long session, Jack asked, "Where do you stay Jaime?"

Quaninch was suddenly reminded of his precarious status. How much could he confide to this total stranger? But Jack wasn't from the area, and he would be leaving shortly. Perhaps he might risk letting his new friend in on his situation. Maybe Jack could even help him.

"I haven't had a chance to find lodging just yet," he began.

"But where did you sleep last night?" Jack asked.

Quaninch looked sheepish and said, "I found a little gulley outside town. It wasn't too bad. I've slept in worse places."

"Well, let's have no more of that! You'll sleep here tonight. Maybe we could play some more music tomorrow and even turn a bit of a profit from it."

The next day proved very profitable for the two young musicians. The addition of the banjo was something new to the Californios.

They loved the rhythmic percussive sound that supported the fiddle's melody. There was handclapping and dancing on the corner where they played, and many coins were dropped into the little bowl.

Quaninch saw a face in the crowd that alarmed him, though. Gabriel Ortez, the owner of the violin shop, peered through the throng and stared at the unique headstock on Quaninch's fiddle. He instantly turned and was lost from view, but Quaninch didn't doubt that he had recognized the fiddle and was headed to the mission to tell Father Julio.

"That was quite a night," Jack bubbled as they returned to his lodgings with a bowl full of coins. He saw the grim expression on his friend's face and asked, "Well, what's the matter with you? Didn't you have fun? And look at this money!" He filled his cupped hands with coins and let them trickle through his fingers into the bowl with a merry clink.

Quaninch looked soberly at his new friend. "Jack, I have to tell you something about myself. I'm on the run." Jack really wasn't too surprised. He had wondered why this young man would be wandering the streets of Los Angeles with only a fiddle and a change of clothes. He thought that eventually Quaninch would tell him his story when he wanted to, so he didn't pry.

"I'm a runaway slave," Quaninch announced. This did take Jack by surprise. He had guessed a runaway from home or maybe some trouble with the law.

"A slave?" Jack said with gaping mouth. "Why, you're not black. I thought you were maybe Mexican or part Indian. It didn't matter to me, so I didn't ask. But a slave! How is that possible?"

"In California, slaves are Indians. My mother was Nuwuvi, that's a tribe far away from here in the desert, and my father was… is… Scots. It was from him that I learned to fiddle. I was taken from my home and my mother was killed when I was very young. I've been at the mission here ever since, and I ran away with this fiddle just a few nights ago. It was my father's, but now it's mine."

He paused while Jack took in his words. "Tonight, in the crowd I saw a man who knows where this fiddle came from, and he has reported it to the priest at the mission already, I'm sure. I don't think we'll be able to play the streets anymore. They'll be looking for me now."

Jack regarded his friend silently. Then he said, "Well then, here's an idea. You lie low in this room for a few days. We've got enough money here to buy ourselves plenty of food and we can while away the time practicing."

"But, Jack, I just told you…"

"You haven't heard all that I have to say, Jaime," Jack replied. "My ship *Abigail* will be weighing anchor on Tuesday. I'll talk to the captain and ask if he could use another hand on board."

"But I know nothing of ships or the sea," Quaninch protested.

"Oh, I can teach you what you need to know to be a common seaman. It's your fiddle that will sell the captain. He loves music on deck in the evening, but he's pretty tired of my poor efforts on this banjo. He'll want you along sure. And anyway, we're just sailing up the coast to Yerba Buena to take on some cargo. We'll be back here in six weeks before we head out across the Pacific. If you don't like the sailor's life, you can come ashore. I doubt the search will still be hot by then."

Quaninch didn't have to ponder this offer long. He knew he couldn't stay in Los Angeles, and he had no place in mind to escape to. This would be a few weeks of safety at any rate. "All right, Jack. That's a good plan. When can you see if your captain will have me on board?"

"That's fine, Jaime. I know we'll have a great time on the old *Abigail*. I'll look up the skipper tomorrow afternoon. No use bothering him early in the morning – not when he's ashore and off duty. Meantime, let's have a good night's rest and see what the day will bring us."

Jack found his skipper, Benjamin Truxhall of Massachusetts, sitting at a streetside café in the hot sun. It was past noon, and many shops were closing for the siesta, but Captain Truxhall had a hangover to attend to, and he was drinking copious amounts of coffee.

Jack stood at loose attention and spoke up. "Captain, sir. Good day to you, sir. I trust you are in good health?"

Truxhall peered blearily at the young sailor. "Is that you Ferguson? Am I accursed? This terrible headache, and now I'm pestered by my banjo-playing so-called 'seaman.' What burdens do you have to lay at my feet now?"

"Begging your pardon, Captain, I have no burdens for you today. I bring good news."

The captain pushed his coffee away and opened his eyes a bit further against the bright glare. "So? Are you jumping ship, perhaps? Maybe found a little wife here who will convert you to a Mexican landlubber?"

Jack laughed quietly. "No, sir, nothing like that. I've met a man who plays the fiddle like an angel does the harp. He and I have joined forces and are making some very pleasing music. I know you have disparaged the banjo on occasion, but if you could only hear how well it blends in with a good fiddle. We could have fine music for dancing in the evenings all the way to Yerba Buena and back."

Captain Truxhall lowered his face and massaged his temples with both hands. "Is he an able seaman?"

Jack's face betrayed his answer. "Well, no, sir. Actually, he's never been at sea." The captain's face lifted, and his eyes opened in disbelief. "But before you go off, sir, I'm sure I can teach him what he needs to know for this short voyage. And really, we mostly want him for the music, you see."

"Jack, you are many things, not all of them good. But I believe you know your music, and if this fellow is willing to come on as an apprentice, no wages for him beyond his keep, I don't have any objection. Tell him though, and I tell you, that if this causes any trouble, I'll put you both ashore without a second thought."

"Thank you Cap'n," Jack said as he backed away hurriedly, "They'll be no trouble. I can promise you that."

Truxhall barked at Jack's back as he turned to leave. "Hold up! What kind of a man is he? What's his name?"

Jack caught himself and turned back to the captain. "He's about my age, I would say. Tall, well-muscled, quick-witted. His name's Jaime. He's part Indian and part Scots. Do you want me to bring him to you?"

"No, that's fine. I'll see him when we sail Tuesday. Mind that you're at the ship with your friend at four bells sharp!"

"Aye, skipper, and thank you," Jack shouted over his shoulder as he headed back to tell Quaninch the news.

Quaninch chafed at the three days of isolation in the little room, but he had no desire to risk being taken back to the mission and sent to a life of harsh slavery on a rancho. Besides, the hours didn't drag since he and Jack honed their repertoire with constant playing.

Jack also used the time to teach Quaninch a few essentials of the life of a seaman like knot-tying, nautical terminology, and shipboard routine. By six o'clock Tuesday morning he knew that the time was four bells of the morning watch. Jack waved at Captain Truxhall who stood on the quarter deck observing the activities as the men and cargo came aboard. Truxhall's eye caught the young man with Jack and sized him up as an able-bodied fellow with plenty of muscle for the work to be done. And he saw the fiddle the young man carried. He was looking forward to hearing some music other than Jack's rather monotonous banjo playing.

The world of the sea was a revelation to Quaninch. He quickly learned his way around the small craft, and he showed himself to be a valuable hand on deck. As Jack had predicted, the fiddle was welcomed by all the men and officers when they gathered on deck in the evening for a ration of grog and dancing. Captain Truxhall was a lenient skipper by the standards of the day, and he had learned that a happy crew is a hard-working crew.

Quaninch was blessed with a good stomach, and he was immune to the tortures of mareo, which often kept landsmen to their hammocks and the ship's rail with interminable nausea. He liked the life on the sea, the fresh breezes, the beautiful views of ocean and coast, the hard work, and the pleasures of music in the evening.

Their voyage northward to Yerba Buena, the sleepy village at the entrance to the San Francisco Bay, was pleasant, uneventful, and brief. The air of Yerba Buena was cool and bracing, a nice contrast to the hot and dusty streets of Los Angeles. They were put to work unloading hides and tallow from the ranchos of Southern California, and taking on salmon, lumber, and British manufactures for re-sale. The town was abuzz about the summer's events of the Bear Flag Revolt and the annexation of all Northern California to the United States. Here, as on the streets of Los Angeles, Quaninch saw the American flag flying everywhere, mostly the newest twenty-eight-star flag distributed by the American forces under Fremont.

A week of hard work was made pleasant by the company of a good friend, the fresh air of Yerba Buena, and the nightly music that drew crowds of locals as well as his shipmates. Soon, its business completed, the *Abigail* weighed anchor and turned south on its return voyage to Los Angeles. There they would take on more trade goods before commencing their long voyage across the Pacific to the Sandwich Islands and on to China.

Quaninch pondered his future in the nights as he lay awake in his hammock or stood the watch in the small hours of the morning. He did enjoy the life of a sailor, but he wasn't sure he wanted to embark on such a long journey. While he had no one tying him to California, it had been the only home he'd known since his childhood, a childhood now almost lost in the mists of memory. When the ship rounded the point and entered San Pedro Harbor, he had nearly decided to stay with the *Abigail* and see the world.

To his great surprise, the village of Los Angeles was in turmoil. After Stockton had been given a hero's welcome and the Californios had enthusiastically welcomed their new American status, the Commodore had left the town in the care of one Captain Gillespie, who had foolishly declared martial law in the area, closed the saloons and enforced a curfew. Gillespie's men insulted the women and ordered the men about with curses. The unrest which arose in response had built up until on September 23, the night before the *Abigail* arrived, gunshots were exchanged between about twenty Californios and U. S. soldiers, and the village of Los Angeles erupted.

Captain Truxhall was informed of the situation as soon as the pilot came aboard at the port of San Pedro. "I don't recommend you staying on here any longer than necessary, Cap'n," the pilot said. "The crowd has just chased the American army out of town, and they are ready to keep going until all Americanos are kicked out of California. They've got that idiot Gillespie surrounded on a little hill with no water. He won't be able to hold out there for long. Then you'll have all Southern California in the hands of Jose Maria Flores and his Californios. You'd better load your goods and be away as soon as you can."

Truxhall didn't have to mull over the pilot's advice for long. He had no desire to be engulfed by a civil war and have his ship quarantined or looted. He assembled his crew on deck and said, "Men, a situation has arisen that changes our plans. There is revolution in the streets of Los Angeles, and it looks the worse for the American side. We don't want to get caught up in any of that mess, so we're going to take on cargo and depart right away." The men looked dejected, and a few let slip a groan.

"Enough of that!" the captain shouted. "I know you've been looking forward to a bit of liberty, and some of you have your 'wives' to visit, but the town is in a roil and it's too dangerous for American sailors to visit. Now to your tasks and look sharp!"

Quaninch considered his choices as he helped Jack prepare the hoist to haul aboard the ox hides and tallow to top off their cargo. He had very nearly decided to stay with the ship before they arrived in port, but this news of revolt and turmoil fascinated him. He wanted to see just how this would affect life in the quiet village where he had lived for six years. He wanted to be in the thick of things and perhaps find the pathway to his future that had eluded him for so long.

"Jack," he said quietly, "I think I'm going to stay here and see how everything works out."

"No, Jaime, don't! We've been having fun, haven't we? Come with us and see the beautiful South Sea Islands with their friendly women, the Far East, China, India. It's a mighty big world out there and we can see it together."

Quaninch looked sadly at his friend. "Yes, I had almost determined to stay on the *Abigail*, but I just don't want to leave when everything is turning upside down. I want to be in on it, please understand, Jack, I would feel like I was missing something that comes along once in a lifetime. The sea will always be here, and my path may take me there someday. But for now, I want to be a part of whatever is going on here in Los Angeles."

They finished their work in silence and then Quaninch went to see the captain. "We're sad to see you go, Jaime, "said Truxhall. "You've been a good seaman, and we have loved your music, and now we're condemned to hear that banjo all by itself all the way to China. But I have no desire to keep you against your will, boy. Best of luck to you and may our paths cross again."

"I hope they do, sir. And thank you for everything."

"Jack!" the captain shouted, "Get this lad to shore right away and get back to the ship. We're shoving off with the tide."

Jack morosely rowed the skiff to the wharf as the two sat silently. When they reached the dock, Jaime stuck out his hand. "I doubt that this is farewell forever, Jack," he said huskily. "I hope to reunite our fiddle and banjo again. We have a lot of music left to play."

Jack shook Quaninch's hand with great emotion. "That is my hope, too, my friend. Goodbye, and may God be with you."

"Adios, mi amigo," Quaninch choked out. He quickly hopped out of the boat and stood on the pier watching his friend row back to the waiting ship. Then he settled his sea bag under his arm and began to walk toward the town.

The crowds were very like the ones he had seen before he left on the *Abigail*, but these carried no American flags; instead, the crowds waved the green, white, and red flag of Mexico. They were angrier than the celebratory mob had been in August when American troops were welcomed as liberators. These Californios were still in the middle of the armed insurrection. They had twenty-nine American marines surrounded on Fort Hill and their leaders issued a fiery proclamation calling for all men from ages fifteen to sixty to come to the aid of their country and drive the invaders from their soil. It demanded "freedom from the chains of slavery" and an end to "barbarous servitude." These phrases thrilled Quaninch. And end to slavery? Yes, that was what he longed for, though he had never before seen how it could be accomplished. But here was the pathway to freedom, to join with his brothers and chase the oppressors out of their homeland.

Quaninch had no hatred for Americans. His father was an American in a way, and that made Quaninch part American. He had been very well-treated on the American ship *Abigail*, and he had made a close friend of the American, Jack Ferguson. And he had no great love for Mexicans. It was a band of Mexican slavers who had killed his mother and kidnapped him, and Mexican priests who had kept him in slavery and tried to eradicate his identity as a Nuwuvi and a Scot. Still, the excitement was contagious, and he was swept up in the hysteria, as well as being inspired by calls to freedom and breaking of chains.

He milled with the crowds, trying to find out how one joined in this righteous crusade. There seemed to be a great deal of drinking and swearing, of ferocious threats and martial posturing, but there was no clear direction to the mob, no leaders to harness the inarticulate rage. Across the dusty street, amid a jostling throng, he caught a glimpse that both delighted and frightened him. "Diego!" he called out above the furor. "Diego! Over here!"

Hearing his name being called out over the noise of the street, Diego turned and was elated to see his friend's face in the mob. The two ran together as rapidly as the chaotic jumble would allow.

"Jaime!" Diego called joyfully. "Jaime! I never thought I would see you again."

The two young men embraced: their happy reunion unnoted by the clamorous crush of excited Californios. "Where have you been, Jaime?" Diego asked breathlessly and then continued before his friend could reply. "Such changes have occurred – I tried to find you right away, but you had vanished from the earth without a trace. I found some people who remembered a young Indian playing the fiddle, but no one knew what had befallen you."

"I've been at sea," Quaninch tried to explain, but Diego went right on.

"Father Julio is gone – back to Mexico City the day after the Americans arrived. He wasn't badly hurt by his fall, and he feared that the Americans would arrest him and confiscate his property, so he loaded up all that he could pack on a few mules and headed south. The mission is empty! We are all free! You, too."

Quaninch smiled happily at his friend. He suddenly realized that he had felt free ever since his departure from the mission, but he was thankful for the freedom now enjoyed by Diego and all the other boys he had grown up with. "But what now, Diego? What will you do with your freedom?"

"Oh, I'm going to join Flores and his men and chase the Yankees out of California. Then we will have our own country, free from the United States and Mexico, too! Come with me, we'll join up together and be heroes!"

"Heroes?" Quaninch laughed.

"Yes, why not? The Yankees are on the run! Why shouldn't we join with the victors and share in the glory?"

"Have the Americanos ever done anything to you, Diego?"

His young friend looked thoughtful for a moment and then replied, "No, not to me personally. But when the Yankee Gillespie took charge, he and his men were very insulting to the women, and they tried to keep people off the streets. They didn't like the Mexicans and cursed us with English oaths. I didn't think we could live with those kinds of roughnecks in charge, and I was very happy yesterday when the crowd rose up and showed the Americanos that we are a people not to be trifled with!"

Quaninch didn't think very deeply about it. The mood of the crowd was contagious, and Diego's enthusiasm swept him along in spite of any misgivings he might have entertained. "All right!" he shouted. "Let's be heroes! Where do we go to sign up?"

Diego happily grasped his friend's arm and then paused with a puzzled look on his face. "I'm not really sure where to go, Jaime. General Flores is in charge of the town now. Let's try to find out where he is and see if we can join up with him."

Jose Maria Flores was a captain in the Mexican Army when the Americans invaded. His commandant, General Jose Castro, had sent him to the American Commodore Stockton to negotiate a peaceful transition of power, but Stockton refused to recognize Castro's authority. Castro, Governor Pico, and other leaders then abandoned Los Angeles for Sonora, presumably hoping to return with a victorious Mexican army to liberate California from the occupiers.

Flores and the other lower-ranking officers were left to fend for themselves. They remained inconspicuous while the Californios welcomed their American conquerors and celebrated their delivery from the grasping, bony hand of far-away Mexico City. Then, when Captain Gillespie's rule turned harsh and tyrannical, Flores and his friends assumed command over the rioting crowd and led them to a string of victories, which though quite small, had the effect of ridding all of Southern California, from San Luis Obispo to San Diego, of the American forces.

The boys roamed the boisterous streets, asking strangers where they could go to join the army. They followed several false leads until they accidentally stumbled on a large crowd gathered in front of a military-style tent set up in the city square.

There didn't seem to be any sort of organized line, but they joined the milling throng and eventually pushed to the front, where they saw several uniformed men sitting at long tables with large books open before them. Quaninch stood before one of them and waited for the man to look up at him. The soldier kept his eyes focused on the paperwork in front of him and did not so much as glance up until Quaninch loudly cleared his throat.

The man regarded Quaninch briefly and then asked, "You? Are you here to sign up for military service?"

"Yes, I am," Quaninch answered proudly. "The proclamation called for all men to join in the fight to free our country, and so here we are."

"The important word that you are missing in the proclamation is 'men,'" he said condescendingly. "How old are you boys?"

"Sixteen," Quaninch blurted out.

"And I'm seventeen," Diego thrust in.

The soldier looked skeptically at the two eager faces. "Well, there are many things to be done in this struggle. You may not be old enough to fight, but I'm sure we will find a useful employment for you. Sign your names here."

He turned the book toward them, and the boys signed their Spanish names in the clear, flowing hand that they had learned so painfully at the side of Father Xavier. The soldier took the book back and then wrote out two small chits and handed them to the boys. "Find Captain Pico and see what use he can make of you." He dismissed them by returning his gaze to the open book in front of him.

They located Pico's headquarters but were told that the captain was on an inspection and would be back shortly. They should wait for his return. They found a shady spot to sit and finally had a few minutes to share their experiences since they had parted six weeks ago. Diego was especially interested in Quaninch's description of Jack's banjo and how well the fiddle and banjo fit together.

"And you, Diego," Quaninch asked, "Are you still playing the cello?"

He regretted the question as soon as it fell from his lips. He had almost forgotten that the cello, along with all the other instruments except his own kings-head fiddle, had been sold to the violin maker. "No," Diego said, sadly shaking his head. "I haven't touched a cello since last winter."

The two sat in silence for a moment and then Diego brightly added, "I do have an instrument, though – a guitar!"

"A guitar?" Quaninch replied. "Can you play it?"

Diego laughed. "Well, it's nothing like a cello, really. There are six strings, and you pluck it with your fingers rather than bow it, and it has frets on the fingerboard... but it is just a stringed instrument, after all, and I should be able to play anything with strings. I want to show you how well I've learned it, Jaime, and maybe it will fit in with the fiddle as well as the banjo did."

"Where is it, Diego?"

"It's in my room at the mission. I'm still staying there, even though it's closed. Actually, it's a very pleasant place now that there are no priests around."

Quaninch glanced around the milling crowd. "Can you go get it? I think we may be here quite a while before anyone notices us, and it would help the time pass to play some music."

"I don't know, Jaime... I don't want to miss out on joining the army. What if they call my name and I'm gone to the mission to get a guitar?"

"Hurry, and you'll be back long before they call our names. And if they do, I'll stall them until you return. Go quickly, now!"

Diego wasn't sure about it, but he accepted his friend's reasoning and said, "I'll run the whole way, just don't let me get passed over while I'm gone." He flew down the dusty alley and was gone from sight.

Quaninch didn't really have a chance to feel bored before Diego returned with a somewhat weather-beaten guitar in hand. "I came across it right after Father Julio left the mission. In all the turmoil in the town, someone didn't want to be bothered with an old guitar, so they just left it in a heap of rubbish behind a storefront. It was in pretty bad shape..."

Quaninch smiled broadly as he interrupted, "You mean it looked worse than it does now?"

Diego looked only slightly hurt. "Well, I did do a lot of work to make it playable. And by now, I've grown rather fond of the old thing, so please, none of your insults."

With that, Quaninch pulled his fiddle from his sea bag and the two boys tuned up. "What do you know on that thing?" he asked.

"Oh, just play some of your tunes, the simpler ones, please, and I'll see if I can follow."

Quaninch fell back on his oldest standby and began to play "Soldier's Joy." Diego strummed a few chords tentatively and then joined in with the rhythm. The result was so pleasing that the boys broke into joyful laughter. And there, in the disorder and noise, in the dust and heat, in the middle of an impending war, the two old friends lost themselves in their private world of music.

A small crowd of would-be soldiers gathered around them as they played, but their performance was abruptly cut short by the arrival of Andres Pico, acting comandante de escuadrón. He was a brother of Pio Pico, former governor of the province who had fled when Stockton arrived in Los Angeles in August. Andres was now third in command to General Jose Maria Flores.

The group of men surrounding Diego and Quaninch quickly queued in front of the open tent where Pico, his blue uniform covered with dust, settled himself. One by one, the men presented their handwritten chits to the comandante, who briefly looked them over, glanced at the man standing before him, and then handed the paper to an aide, nodding to the recruit to move to the next line. When Quaninch and Diego reached the front of the line, Pico took their chits and then broke into a broad smile as he regarded the two young volunteers.

"Signing up to play music for our dances?" he asked.

The two boys had forgotten that they still held their instruments in their hands.

"Oh no, sir," Diego protested. "We were just playing while we waited your turn. We want to help to expel the invader from our sacred land!"

Pico's smile erupted into a deep laugh. "Would that all our good Californios had your enthusiasm, my friend." He glanced at the paper the boy had handed him. "Diego," he repeated. "Seventeen? Perhaps you exaggerated your age a bit?"

"No sir," Diego replied. "I was born near the time when the days are the longest. I just turned seventeen this past June."

"Well," Pico muttered, "perhaps. And Jaime?" he asked, turning his gaze to Quaninch, "You are sixteen?"

Quaninch looked a bit sheepish and responded, "I will be sixteen in just a couple months, sir. And the proclamation called for all men from fifteen to sixty."

"So, it did. I assume the two of you are friends?"

"Oh yes, sir," the boys simultaneously blurted out.

"And you play music. Do you play well?"

"Can we show you?" Quaninch boldly asked.

"Please do," the smiling officer nodded.

Diego looked nervously to Quaninch, who said, "Let's do 'Soldiers' Joy. ' That one's simple and it sounded good."

The boys began to play, and all the bustle of the dusty plaza came to a halt. Comandante Pico clapped along and all the others standing nearby forgot their earnest business of war-making and for a moment were transported by the simple joy of these two young men and their music.

When they finished their piece, there was general applause and laughter and then all returned to their tasks. "Very fine, boys," Pico said, still smiling contentedly. "I think we can use you at headquarters. There will be plenty of errands to run, messes to be cleaned up, messages delivered... and music to be played in the evenings. Report to the quartermaster for your uniforms."

They began to thank him, but he waved them away with a preemptory gesture and they moved along, searching for the quartermaster in the midst of a bustling sea of people.

CHAPTER NINE

The days of early autumn, 1846, were exciting times in old California. On September 29th, Flores accepted Captain Gillespie's surrender at Fort Hill. He generously allowed the tiny American garrison to keep their small arms and to depart safely for the merchant ship *Vandalia* in San Pedro Harbor. In the days that followed, the Americans evacuated their forces from Santa Barbara and San Diego as well, leaving all of Southern California in the insurgents' hands.

Quaninch and Diego were kept very busy in their new positions as orderlies to Comandante Pico. They proudly wore their new uniforms, blue trousers, and blouse with white belts across the chest, and Pico and his officers grew reliant on having the young men close at hand. "Jaime! Diego!" frequently rang out in the headquarters and the boys would be quivering at attention before the echoes faded.

And there was music. The evenings were times of relaxation for the officers and men, and their ladies, and the sweet music of Diego's guitar and Quaninch's violin filled the plaza night after night. It was a war from the pages of a romance novel. Long on pageantry and exhilaration and short on bloodshed and perspiration.

General Flores was one of the few who realized that the American retreat would only be a temporary one. They still had forces in the north, and there were rumors that an American army was winding its way westward from Santa Fe. The general tried to instill his foreboding into his commanders and troops, to make them take their training seriously, but most of the Californios were sure that the war was over. They had defeated the cowardly Yankees and now all that remained was for the politicians in Washington and Mexico City to make peace and leave California to its own dreams. It was a time to celebrate, not to worry.

The most effective weapons in the Californios' arsenal were their mounted lancers. This cavalry, led by Andres Pico, boasted riders bred to the saddle from birth, each one dressed in a bright serape and carrying a seven-foot-long, needle-sharp, ash wood lance, its tip hardened in fire. Their tactic was to fire one round from their muskets and then charge with the lance. They also had a scattering of cannon of various ages, materials, and bores, which could be employed along with the lancers if the opportunity arrived. The first test of these forces came suddenly.

Just before Gillespie surrendered, he had sent young Juan Flaco – "Skinny John Brown" with a message for Commodore Stockton detailing the plight of his command. Against formidable obstacles, Juan Flaco managed to ride over four hundred miles in fifty-two hours to deliver his message to Stockton at Yerba Buena. Now being called San Francisco by the Americans, Stockton's response was swift, ordering the *Savannah,* a fifty-four-gun warship skippered by Captain William Mervine, to send reinforcements to Gillespie.

The vessel reached San Pedro Harbor on October 6, where they found Gillespie's men awaiting them aboard the *Vandalia.* With a total of over 360 sailors and marines, Mervine immediately started out for Los Angeles, certain that the Californios would flee in terror at the sight of the approaching Americans.

Flores, who, unlike Mervine, was very familiar with the lay of the land, ordered his forces to set up an ambush for the approaching invaders. Pico's lancers were to establish a battle line on either side of the narrow road that led from the port to the town while an old brass four-pounder was to be placed athwart the Americans' route.

Pico's headquarters was a hive of activity as the Comandante shouted his orders to his officers. Quaninch and Diego stood in the midst of the chaos, seemingly forgotten. As Pico dismissed one commander and was turning to another, Diego stepped toward him and asked, "Pardon me, Comandante, but isn't there something Jaime and I can do? We want to fight the Americans also."

Pico looked tolerantly at his two orderlies. "Diego, Jaime… no, my good soldiers. You are untrained in the arts of war. There will be cannons, muskets, swords, and lances. A battle is a dreadful thing. I'm afraid that most of my troops don't really know what lies ahead for them, despite the training we have given them. It is no place for the untrained, no matter how fiercely their manhood is flaming. You boys wait here at headquarters. I will be sending messages from the front, and I need to have reliable men such as you to receive and act on them. You have earned my trust, now show me your obedience."

With that, Pico turned to the crowd of officers that had gathered around him, pulling them close to him one by one to give them their orders. Diego turned away despondently. "Don't worry, Diego," Quaninch said. "He is right. We aren't fighters. I'm sure we would only be a burden and a danger to our men if we were in the battle. The Comandante says we are needed at headquarters, and I believe he is right. We have our part to do."

"Yes, I know," said Diego sourly. "But this may be the only battle of this war. We could be missing out on the only chance we'll ever have to be heroes."

"I hope you're right, Diego. I hope this will end the war as bloodlessly as possible. I have no desire to kill Americans or to be killed by them, either! Come, let's see the men off and get ready to receive the messages from the front."

The messages that came to headquarters contained the best kind of news. The Americans had been completely repulsed by Flores' ambush. They had fled back to their ship and abruptly departed for Monterrey, leaving four of their number buried on Isla de los Muertos – the Isle of Death. The Californios had no casualties, not even any wounded. The Battle of Dominguez Rancho was a victory that only strengthened the people's confidence that the war in California was over.

Throughout the remainder of the year, Old California inhaled the final breath of its long life. Flores, Pico, and the other leaders tried to keep their troops in camp, to improve their training and discipline, to upgrade their weapons and strategies. But it was hopeless. Almost everyone knew that the mounted Californios with their bright colors and wicked lances had scared the Americanos away. They wouldn't be back. The victorious soldiers relished their status as conquerors and defenders. Fiestas blossomed every night with dancing and colored lanterns and endless fountains of tequila and wine. And music of course. Diego and Quaninch were constantly in demand, and their countless performances forced them to expand their repertoire and skills.

Only a few soldiers and leaders were disturbed by the accounts they heard of Fremont raising troops in the north and beginning to move overland toward Monterrey. Or the word that General Stephen Kearny had conquered New Mexico and guided by wilderness legends Kit Carson and William Kennedy, was on his way west, armed with a Presidential proclamation naming him as governor of the newly-won territory.

Flores had a large area to try to defend, much of it close to the sea, where Yankee ships dominated the coast. His forces kept shrinking as soldiers returned to their ranchos and homes, confident that their work was done and their country safe. His supply of munitions was meager and his supply of money to pay his troops nonexistent. But his people danced on to fading melodies, secure in their past and confident of their future.

And the good fortune of the Californios continued for one more battle. On December 6th, in a freezing rain, Pico's lancers held off the combined forces of Kearny and Gillespie at San Pasqual. Three American officers and nineteen men were killed, all but two by the lance. All the leaders, including Kearny, were grievously wounded. If any had doubted the power of the Californios' armed might, let this be proof.

The American troops, exhausted, wounded, and lacking food and water took refuge on a small rise they called Mule Hill, because they were forced to use some of their mules for food. Andres Pico's lancers surrounded them, and for three days they were besieged, though Pico, with gallantry from a bygone era, gave them some sugar and tea and arranged for a swap of prisoners. The fate of the Americans was decided when a relief force from San Diego arrived and allowed Kearny's battered men to retreat from Mule Hill and rejoin their compatriots.

After the battle, Diego and Quaninch watched as 11 wounded Californio lancers were brought back into Los Angeles, cheered on their way to the military hospital tent. Most of them had fairly minor wounds and were able to wave cheerfully to their neighbors, but the sight of blood-stained uniforms and bandaged injuries brought home to the boys the harsh reality of combat.

That evening, the victory was announced in the plaza and the people celebrated with renewed joy, in spite of the cold rain that continued to drench the area. To those in the ebullient crowd, this seemed to be the ultimate confirmation that the war was ended, and they had secured their freedom. Only the leaders knew that enemy forces were moving toward Los Angeles from south and north, coming closer each day with overwhelming numbers and strength. The days of easy triumph over the Yankees were over.

As Christmas approached, Quaninch began to wonder how the Holy Mass could be celebrated without a priest. Amid war and chaos, none had been named to succeed Father Julio. When he idly mentioned this to his friend, Diego snapped, "I don't care! I'm not going to be here anyway."

"What does that mean? Where are you going to be if not here?"

"At the front," Diego asserted defiantly.

"We've been over that before," Quaninch sighed. "You know we don't have the training or skills to help in the war, and it looks like our soldiers don't need any help from us, anyway."

"But this is different," Diego said hotly. "You know I'm Cahuilla. My people, they don't live that far from here out in the desert. Anyway, I was talking to one of the wounded men, and he told me they weren't hurt in the fight against the Americans." Diego pulled Quaninch closer and whispered harshly, "But they were hurt in an ambush by the Luiseno! My people's oldest enemies, and now they are attacking Comandante Pico's men! I must join in the fight. My people's honor is at stake!"

Quaninch was surprised at the intensity of his friend's feelings. He had often reminisced about his own people, the Nuwuvi, but rarely had he heard Diego talking about his family or how he came to be a slave at the mission.

"Still," Quaninch went on after giving Diego a chance to cool off. "There is the problem of exactly how you can be of assistance, since you can't ride a horse or wield a lance, and you can't shoot a gun either. What does that leave… swordplay?"

Diego didn't return his friend's smile. "I've been taking target practice, Jaime. I can shoot a musket as well as most of these infantrymen. I mean it this time. I'm going to join the others at the front."

Quaninch looked somberly at Diego's face. "Well then, I guess I'll have to go too," he said.

"You?" Diego snorted. "Now there is a case of someone who would truly be a hindrance to the cause. Don't even say it in fun. I'm going and you must stay here and do the work of both of us. You'll be run ragged, I'm sure."

"We'll have to see what the Comandante says," Quaninch replied. "Probably neither of us will be going anywhere."

But as December wore on, Quaninch's prophecy proved false. Comandante Andres Pico joined General Flores at his headquarters north of Los Angeles in San Fernando, and he took his orderlies along. He quickly dismissed Diego's plea to join the infantry. "Diego, wars are won by infinite efforts put forward by many different people. Some are front-line fighters; some are generalissimos who plan the battle from afar. Some are cooks, some mule drivers, some blacksmiths… and some are orderlies and messengers. And that is also an important effort to make in the victory. Do your duty and remain at your post."

General Flores was now in an untenable position. He had five hundred men in his command, but they were unpaid, ill-equipped, and resentful at having to remain on duty in the bleak December weather. With this tenuous force he had to prepare to meet the brigade of frontiersmen that Fremont had collected in Northern California, which was beginning to advance from their base at Santa Barbara. He also was aware that Stockton had assembled a force of over six hundred from his ships and survivors of Kearny's men in San Diego, and that this force was also on the move.

Christmas was a slightly noticed event. Quaninch and Diego played villancicos on Christmas Eve, but the days were filled with troop movements, scouts' reports, requisitions, appeals for more men… and there were never enough men.

Flores expected that he would meet Fremont's force first, and then, if victorious, would turn to the south and face the larger army under Stockton and Kearny. His plans changed however, when his scouts brought word that the southern force was moving much more rapidly. He would have to reverse the order of his battle plans and meet Stockton first. He moved his army south to a bluff overlooking the San Gabriel River and completed his arrangements. Pico's lancers were placed along the fifty-foot-high bluff, while sharpshooters and other cavalry faced the direction from which the Americans would have to come. It was a good plan and the terrain offered good hope for surprise. Stockton's scouts discovered the Californios' dispositions though and crossed the river at a lower ford.

As always, Quaninch and Diego were in constant demand for errands and messages. Roaming the lines of soldiers along the bluff on their rounds, they felt the confidence of the men. The positions selected by their general were superb, and the prospects were good for yet another rout of the invading army. As they visited the lines of sharpshooters, who were busily occupied with cleaning their weapons, arranging their ammunition, and sighting in on landmarks in the valley below, Diego whispered to Quaninch, "When the battle starts, I'm coming down here. This will be my chance to strike a blow against the Americans, the friends of my enemies the Luiseno."

Quaninch shook his head. He had often heard his friend making plans to get into the fighting, but so far, he had obeyed Pico's orders to remain at his post as an orderly. This time though, Quaninch knew that Diego meant to act on his plans. This would certainly be the last battle in this war. After they drove this American army off the field in disarray, the Americans would surely realize that they couldn't defeat the proud Californios and they would open negotiations. If Diego were to be able to strike a blow for the honor of his people, the Cahuilla, it would have to be now or never.

"Diego," Quaninch began, but Diego cut him short.

"Please, Jaime, I know what you have to say; I'm not trained, my efforts are needed elsewhere, Commandante Pico has ordered me away from the fighting. But this is my last chance to do something brave and honorable. I don't want to tell my children that in the great war for California's freedom, I was a messenger boy!"

"As you will, my friend," Quaninch sighed. "I suppose that in the confusion of battle, no one will notice that you're missing. I'll do my best to cover for you. Only be careful, amigo... remember the blood that poured from the wounded men. The Americans fire real bullets, and just because we've beaten them in every battle so far, that's no guarantee that you couldn't get shot."

"I will put my fate in the hands of Dios," Diego said firmly. Quaninch could only smile at his friend's bravado.

On the morning of January 8, 1847 – the twenty-second anniversary of Andrew Jackson's epic victory at the Battle of New Orleans, the Americans struggled through the quicksand bed of the San Gabriel and, despite the advantageous position of the Californios, managed to train their cannon on the defenders' positions.

When the firing began, Diego turned to Quaninch and said, "This is it! If they discover I've gone to fight, so be it. When the battle is over and we are victorious, no one will hold it against me."

"Diego, can't I say something to convince you to stay here with me?"

Diego turned to his friend with what he thought was a wise and heroic expression, though it seemed comical on his smooth young face. "I'm sorry, Jaime. I must do my duty. Cover for me." He retrieved his old musket from his tent and slipped off into the confusion of men, mules, and horses heading for the bluff.

Quaninch watched Diego disappear, saying a silent prayer for him. Then he returned to his duties. There wasn't much to do now that the battle had begun. Pico was with his lancers and the other officers had their assignments and were on the front line. After a few minutes of idle frustration, Quaninch began to drift off in the direction that his friend had gone a short time before.

He neared the edge of the bluff and could see the battle developing below him. Pico's lancers made a brave charge, but the Yankee cannon cut their horses down under them. The charge broke up in disarray and the proud lancers struggled to get back to their positions, some now without their mounts.

The line of sharpshooters wasn't having much luck, either. He could hear curses from men whose inferior powder didn't fire or fizzled out in the firing pan. He could also hear the bullets from the Americans whistling over his head. He ducked low and crept closer to the firing line, hoping to catch sight of Diego. In the smoke and confusion, it was hard to make out exactly what was going on, but the line of infantry was gradually thinning out as men ran away or were wounded. He finally caught a glimpse of Diego lying prone at the lip of the bluff, carefully aiming his musket and firing. Quaninch spotted an abandoned musket nearby, picked it up, and took it toward the firing line, crouching low to avoid the whizzing bullets overhead. He moved next to Diego and shouted over the din, "Here's another musket. I can load for you while you're firing."

Diego quickly glanced at Quaninch and then intently returned his gaze to the battle below him. "You shouldn't be here, Jaime," he grunted. "Get back to safety."

Quaninch didn't answer, but only passed the loaded weapon to Diego and took his empty one to reload. They continued wordlessly to shoot and load, but the men around them were disappearing one by one. The Americans' cannons were shooting canister now – each blast sending hundreds of sharp, hot metal fragments through the air like a massive shotgun blast. Each explosion left a smoking wake of destruction marked by wounded men and animals.

"I think we'd better get out of here," Quaninch said. "The rest of the men are retreating. We don't want to be out here all alone."

Diego turned away from his musket and saw that Quaninch was right. "Yes, I see. We'll make our stand further back. Let's go."

As he rose to a kneeling position, they were sent flying by a terrific burst to their left. A round of canister had blasted through their lines about three feet from where the boys were crouching. Quaninch struggled to open his eyes, but they were crusted shut with sand. The battlefield had suddenly become completely silent and when he managed to wipe one eye enough to open it, he saw Diego, covered in blood, lying several feet away. He opened his mouth to shout "Diego!" but no noise came out. He had been rendered completely deaf by the thunder of the canister shot.

He saw, rather than heard, that the Yankee cannons were still at their work, blowing swathes of destruction through the sparse desert vegetation. He could not see any other Californios standing. They were alone.

He never knew he could crawl so close to the ground, but he moved in Diego's direction trying to stay as low as a snake. He reached his friend, fearful that he would find him dead. He heard a low groan however, so he knew that Diego was still alive, at least for the present. He began to drag him away from the edge of the bluff and from the merciless blasts of the American artillery.

Once they were far enough back from the lip, Quaninch looked around and tried to come up with a plan to rescue Diego and himself. He was not going to be able to carry or drag him to safety. He saw several horses and mules nearby, some of them running in mindless panic, while others were inexplicably calm, pausing to nibble at some dry grass. He rose halfway to his feet and stumbled toward a horse that didn't seem to be aware of the battle at all. "Easy, boy. Easy, now," he whispered as he reached for the bridle and led the creature slowly back to where Diego lay.

He urgently shook Diego, trying to wake him enough to mount the horse. His friend moaned and cracked open a blood-clotted eye. His lips moved, but Quaninch could hear nothing.

"Later," Quaninch blurted out. He couldn't hear what Diego was saying, and his own voice sounded like it was coming from somewhere far away. "Where are you hurt? Can you get on this horse?"

"I don't know, Jaime," he whimpered. "I hurt all over." He looked down at his chest. "And I'm bleeding!" He glanced in fear at his friend kneeling by his side. "And you're bleeding too, Jaime! What are we going to do?"

While he couldn't hear the words his friend was mouthing, he could gather the meaning from the fear and pain on Diego's face. "Nothing for it but to get out of here!" he shouted, and he tried to lift his wounded partner to his feet. Diego struggled and managed to rise, leaning heavily on the horse. Quaninch could see many wounds and much blood. He assisted Diego onto the horse and then began to pull himself up. He felt searing pains in his shoulder and hip, but he managed to settle himself behind his friend. He looked toward the Californios' encampment but could see no one there. They had all fled. The battle must surely be lost. To his right was the steep slope leading down to the river, now alive with American troops clambering up the bluff.

He could see no way of escape except directly in front of them, upstream from the battlefield, to the southwest. He kicked their mount gently and started off at a walk, holding tightly to the seriously wounded Diego, who had lost consciousness again. He had no plan, but only a hope, that they would find a rancho or Indian village where they could find help and safety.

Immediately to their right, two Americans summated the bluff. They were clad in the buckskin jackets of the wilderness scouts and trappers.

The men raised their guns, but one reached over and pushed the other man's rifle down. The second man looked at his friend, puzzled and a little angry. "Why'd you do that?"

"I dinna ken why… they're just lads, anyway. They'll nae be a threat to us. Leave'm be."

"They're big enough to shoot at us," the second man snarled, starting to lift his rifle again.

"Nae, I say!" the first man shouted, again pushing the weapon toward the ground.

The second man looked incredulously at the first. "Why in blazes are you so het up?"

The first man looked at the other with deep sadness. "I dunno… I had a bairn once who would be just about that age if he yet lives. My son… Quaninch."

CHAPTER TEN

When William Kennedy rode away from the ashes of the Nuwuvi town of Mukuntuweap in that terrible fall of 1840, he had no idea of what to do or where to go. His family, his beautiful Annie and his talented Quaninch were gone. Her ashes were scattered in the desert and Quaninch was gone forever, too. Perhaps still alive but sold away by a slaver gang.

Along with the grief of his loss, he also had to recognize that the work he had done for the past eighteen years was at an end. He had been a fur trader and wilderness guide ever since he left St. Louis back in 1822 with Jedediah Smith as a member of Ashley's Hundred. But the fur trade was gone. Changing fashions had reduced demand for pelts, and unbelievably the seemingly infinite numbers of beaver, mink, fox, and otter had dwindled to the point of scarcity.

What does a man do, when at age forty, his life is upended? William had no answer to that question. He only knew that there was no future for him in the mountains. Where then? By default, he turned his horse east and began the long, and at that time of year, dangerous journey to the great metropolis of the West, St. Louis.

He rode alone, finding solace in the empty wilderness and stark landscapes of the Great Plains in late autumn. His fiddle remained in his pack. Even catching a glimpse of it brought back the unbearable pain of losing his family. It brought to mind the warm times huddled in the pine bark teepee, safe from the howling winter gales, showing his son, Quaninch how to hold the fiddle and bow while Tsununk looked on, her face aglow with love for her husband and child.

Even though William knew many Indian villages along the route where he could seek shelter from the rapidly deteriorating weather, he chose to remain alone on the trail. He wasn't sure of his ability to control his sorrow, and he didn't want to make a spectacle of himself in front of old friends. The days and nights blurred as he journeyed eastward, riding alone by day, sleeping alone in sheltered spots, huddled close to his horse for warmth.

He headed northeast toward South Pass, then straight east through the endless grasslands. Even an experienced mountain man had to be wary of the blizzards that swept the unbroken spaces with blinding winds and many feet of snow. Twice on his journey he had to hunker down for days to wait out a storm, but the cold and danger seemed like a dream to him. For William, survival was instinctive, not something he had to focus on. He knew the ways of the wilderness so well that, even in his dark despair, he could withstand the many dangers and hardships of winter travel in a land where no one, not even the Indians dared to venture far.

As the year neared its end, William began to enter a tamer country. The road became wider and worn. There were occasional sod houses and dilapidated wooden cabins along the way; and, of course, he began to encounter people, the first he had seen in over two months on the trail.

The grief which had ridden with him across the desolate prairies had not gone away. It would never completely disappear, but it no longer debilitated him, so that when he finally had to interact with people, he was able to put up a façade of a strong man from the wilds. A mountain man.

Finally, just after the new year of 1841 began, he arrived in St. Louis. He was physically exhausted, his face darkened by months of braving freezing winds and his body emaciated from little food and grueling travel. It had been five years since he had last visited the "Gateway to the West," but he found Mrs. Jenner's boarding house was still open for business and the widow Jenner was still hale and healthy.

She opened her door to his knock and stared warily at the stranger before her. "Olivia!" he said with a smile that looked grim on the weathered face. "Dinna ye recognize me?"

She peered closer and ventured a guess. "William?" she cautiously asked.

"I suppose I have changed a wee bit since last I was here," he grinned. "But ye haven't aged a minute."

"Well, the face looks pretty beat up, but the old line of balderdash is still the same. Come in, old friend, and catch me up on what's happened to you, and why you show up in the middle of winter looking like a dried-up bit of jerky."

She looked him up and down as he entered the foyer of the boarding house where he had stayed many a winter in the days when he annually returned east after trading in the mountains. "First order of business will be a bath," she said, wrinkling her nose. "And maybe we can do something about those rags you're wearing, too."

"Sorry, Liv," he sheepishly replied. "I've been a long time on the trail, and in this season, there's no bathing to be had out on the plains."

"Get out of those filthy things while I boil some bath water. Once you've scraped off a layer or two of grime, you can tell me why a man with any sense at all would be travelling in the wilds in the dead of winter."

The bath did feel luxurious, and as he soaked, some of the miles and hardships began to fall away. Every fifteen minutes, Olivia would bring in the big steaming kettle and pour scalding water into the tub. He didn't feel embarrassed to have her walking in while he sat naked in the tub; they were old friends between whom modesty wasn't a factor.

Olivia Jenner was a widow in her early sixties, about twenty years older than William. He had first met her when he arrived in St. Louis almost twenty years before as a young man with a fiddle who was trying to leave trouble behind him. He lodged with her until departing with Ashley's Hundred in the spring of 1823, and he had returned each autumn for a few years. Then, one winter, he didn't come back to St. Louis. Olivia looked for him to arrive, but when he didn't, she didn't give the matter much thought. There were many reasons why a man might not return from the West, some bad and others not so awful.

There had been no romance between the two. She had been widowed a short time before William first arrived, and the age difference was substantial. The main reason she remembered

William among the countless boarders who had passed through her establishment was his fiddle playing. Over the years since he had last stayed at her place, her thoughts were often turned to him when she heard a snatch of a fiddle tune. "That's good," she would think, "but not so good as William."

Once the long, sensuous bath was done, he sat in the kitchen while she rustled up some food for him, and he told her his tale. His voice broke when he described the loss of his wife and child, and she put her hands on his shoulders and said, "You don't need to be so brave, William. Let out your tears if you need to." And he did.

By the time he finished telling his saga, he was drifting in and out of sleep, and she pushed him into a bedroom where he slept all that afternoon and night.

As he walked through the city the next day, his thoughts flew back to the St. Louis that he had first seen in 1822. Then, it had been a thriving town of about 5,000, still largely French, home base of the expeditions that were tentatively probing the distant Rocky Mountains. Now it was a real city, over 16,000 in the town itself, and other thousands in the outlying area. No longer would he meet up there with old friends from the mountains to plan the next year's expedition. What was there for a wilderness scout to do in this alien metropolis?

The modern St. Louis had at least one thing in common with the old one: an abundance of taverns, and William arrived in one on his first day in town. He ended up stumbling into Mrs. Jenner's boarding house well after midnight. This established his pattern for the next few months. Olivia knew the kind of grief and despair he was dealing with, but after several weeks of his nightly bouts of drunkenness, she began to be concerned.

"William, I know it's none of my business," she began one morning as she poured coffee for her bleary-eyed boarder.

"Aye, that's the truth," William interrupted.

She put down the coffee pot and put her hands on her hips. "How can you know that before I can even say my piece?"

"There is only one thing ye would say, Olivia: I'm drinking too much, and I need to get on with my life and find a job."

"Well, you can't deny it, then."

"I dinna deny anythin' Liv. Nor admit anything, neither. It's my own devil to face, and none can help me!"

She picked up the coffee and bustled at the stove. Neither spoke for an awkward, long moment. Then William broke the silence. "I'm sorry Olivia," he said. "I dinna mean to make ye worry. I know you're right in what ye say. And I've been thinkin' the same thing, in fact. It's time I got meself a job and got on with things. And besides, I'm plumb out of money!"

Olivia turned back to him with a smile. "Well, that's better. I don't like to hear you talk so mean. And if you're serious about looking for work, you might want to read some of the handbills that are posted around the town."

William's bloodshot eyes opened a little wider. "What d'ye mean? Someone looking for workers?"

"You better go see yourself what it's all about, but there's a party forming up to take wagons to Oregon this summer. They need some scouts and hostlers. It sounds like it might be just your kind of work."

He mulled over her news as he finished his coffee and tried to shake the cobwebs out of his mind. It had been a long time since he had given any thought to anything but the need to escape his feelings of pain and despair. He knew it was time to leave all that behind and start over. The days of the mountain men might be past, but there was still a huge, wild country to cross, and the old trappers and traders were the ones who knew the lay of the land. It just might be that there was a future for him, and not one of drowning his troubles in the taverns of St. Louis.

That day, when he walked the streets, he wasn't looking for a drink; he was searching for one of the posters that Olivia had mentioned. There weren't any on the streets of the business district, but as he drifted toward the stockyards, he found a piece of paper nailed up to a wall of a stable. "Men Wanted! Emigrants to California and Oregon Departing May 15 from Westport. Looking for a few men who know the country and can work with horses, mules, and oxen. Apply Tho. Fitzpatrick, Planter's Hotel, Fourth & Pine."

Tom Fitzpatrick! Old "Broken Hand." Many were the miles he'd travelled with Tom Fitzpatrick and Jedidiah Smith, across the plains to the Rocky Mountains, through South Pass and in the desert lands of the West. Tom would surely give an old trail-partner a job. He made straightaway for the newly opened Planter's Hotel to find his old friend and see what he could arrange.

The hotel had opened just a few weeks earlier, replacing the original Planter's Hotel which had burned to the ground. It was the most luxurious, up-to-date lodging in the city. "Looks like Tom has some money behind him to take rooms like this," William thought as he entered the plush lobby, redolent of new wood and fresh varnish.

He asked at the desk for Tom Fitzpatrick, and the clerk, barely looking up from his newspaper, nodded toward the hallway leading off toward the right. Down a short corridor, he saw a few men milling around and talking quietly. Behind a table sat a large man talking to an applicant standing before him and occasionally writing something on the paper in front of him. William peered closely at the seated man. He was clean-shaven, with salt-and-pepper hair cut short and a pair of rimless spectacles perched on his nose.

The last time William had seen Tom Fitzpatrick was in 1827 – fourteen years ago. His last memory of him was a mountain man with full dark beard, long hair, and buckskin clothes waving farewell as they parted ways at the end of the trapping season. William had decided not to make the trip back east. He would spend that winter in the village of his friend Jack Bobby Qweets. He hadn't heard anything about Tom since then.

Was this clean, respectable-looking clerk the same ferocious mountain man with whom William had crisscrossed the American wilderness? He watched closely while the applicant was handed a slip of paper and turned toward the door. Tom looked up and glanced around the room to see if there were any other job seekers. William moved toward the table and Tom began to quietly assess this new fellow. He moved like an outdoorsman, and his deeply lined face clearly showed the effects of a life in the sun. As William reached the table, Tom was struck by the knowing grin on the man's face. Something in that face was so familiar.

"Billy? No, it can't be you, you old snake! What in blazes happened to you, to turn you into an old coot?"

William laughed and Tom rose to shake his hand. "I was just wondering what hae happened to ye to turn ye into a bank teller," William replied, his face breaking into a huge, happy grin. Tom walked around the table and grabbed his old friend in a fierce bear hug.

"My, my," he wondered aloud. "This is a good day for the Bidwell-Bartleson party, you old mountain goat!"

"The Birdwell – what?" William asked through his laughter.

Tom, still holding William by his shoulders shook his head. "And ain't that just like an ignorant old Scotch fool? Don't even know what job he's after! Sit down here and I'll give you the lowdown."

The two men sat on either side of the table. Tom looked at William, still shaking his head in wonder. "This'll be good times, Billy. Just like the old days, but a little bit plusher. We won't have to sleep in the open with a rock for a pillow and a pine bough for cover on this trip."

"From the looks of ye, I'd say it's been many a year since ye've slept in aught but a couthie warm bed or missed many fine meals."

"Be that as it may," he said, "I can see that you've weathered some rough winds of late." He glanced over William's shoulders to see some new applicants entering the room. "Let's get to business now and we'll meet afterward to catch up.

"Here's the whole prospect: You know, don't you, that a few settlers have followed the trails we blazed back in the twenties to Oregon. A small group made the trek two years ago, and last year three wagons made it from Fort Hall to Fort Walla Walla. So, the thing can be done, not just by mountain men who live in the wild, but by wagon loads of people, women, and children, too.

"John Bartleson and John Bidwell are organizing a party to take the trail west to California, if they can make it. I'm the wagon master, and I'm putting together my crew. And now that you're here, I know who my head scout will be."

William, trying to keep his excitement hidden, coolly asked, "How many in the party?"

Tom glanced down at the papers before him. "Twenty-six wagons as of right now, and I believe there'll be about sixty souls with us."

William pursed his lips. "That's a big lot of fowk," he said. "And lasses and bairns, too?"

"Yes, we'll have our hands full, and not a one of them knows anything about the West. But I don't doubt their courage if they're willing to take on this adventure."

"Courage, aye, but it may be that they dinna ken what they're in for."

Tom again glanced at the growing crowd of applicants milling around the room. "That's so, Billy. But Bartleson and Bidwell are offering good money for us to get them there. You know it's been hard times for us old scouts to find a job; this is a chance to get back in the mountains with a decent pay at the end of the road. I've got to get on to these other folks. What do you say, Bill? Are you with me to go back on the trail?"

"I don't even hae to think about it, Tom. I've been here aw winter, sure that there was no work for a man like me. I've tried to drink ma sorrows away, but that was nae good. It's a new chance at life for me, Tom, and I thank ye for it."

William signed the papers and the two old friends parted. When William reached the boarding house, Olivia could see immediately that he had gotten the job. "Oh, William," she said as he walked in the door, "it's so good to see that bounce in your step and the spark in your eyes. It's been gone a long time. I was afraid it wouldn't come back."

"Aye, it feels good to hae something to look forward to." He stared into her kind eyes. "And I must gie the thanks to ye for it. And for aw ye hae done for me. I dinna think it's too far to say ye've saved my life, Olivia."

That evening William returned to the Planter's Hotel, and Tom and he talked late into the night, reminiscing and planning. Tom was dismayed by William's story of loss and despair, but they were both mountain men, not accustomed to self-pity and tears. When they parted, Tom said, "We're gathering the party at Westport, departing around the fifteenth of May. I'll stay here in the city to finish recruiting and attend to supplies. You can go to Westport as soon as you like and help assemble the wagon train. I'll join you there soon."

William had been very careful to limit his drinking, so he was still reasonably sober as he stood to take his leave. "Tom, I want ye to know..."

"None of that!" Tom shouted. "I'm hiring you because you're the best guide there is. Not for old times' sake or because you've had a rough go lately. You get on out to Westport and get busy. I'll expect everything to be in good order for the journey when I arrive there. Now, go!"

In his room at the boarding house, Olivia helped William pack up his meager belongings. When his eye fell on the fiddle, the very one that he had taken from old Curry's room almost twenty years ago, he experienced anew the sharp pang of loss. But then he gingerly picked the instrument up and blew the dust off the dark finish of the old wood. He plucked the strings with his thumb, twisted the tuning keys, and hefted the fiddle to his left shoulder, high on his chest.

Olivia's eyes welled with moisture as William began to draw the bow across the strings, tentatively at first, and then with his old confidence and strength rapidly returning, the fiddle sang with its full-throated voice that had been silent for so long. He played a few quick tunes and then looked sheepishly at Olivia. "I reckon I didna forget how to play this old thing. It sounds aw richt, don't it, Liv?"

"It sounds fine, William. I wish you had felt like playing it all this time you've been here, but I'm just so pleased that you're bound for the West again, playing your fiddle again... why, it's a rebirth, William, a new life!"

He looked into her eyes, revealing the depth of the sorrow that would never leave him, and said, "Ay, Liv. That's what it is, I ken. And who do I thank for it? Only you, lass. Ye've put up with more than I could ever hae expected, with ne'er a glower and always a smile, and I will always be beholden to you for it."

The next morning, he loaded up his horse, took his leave of Mrs. Jenner, and headed for the village of Westport, Missouri, a journey of about 250 miles. William expected to make the trip in ten days, which would allow him two weeks to prepare for their departure. It was an uneventful ride, with only a few rainy days marring the delightful late April weather. He stayed at inns and settlers' homes occasionally, but usually he slept out under the stars. Whether in company or alone, he never let an evening pass without playing a few tunes on his fiddle. He had been away from it too long, and it was his delight to play it again.

Westport wasn't much of a town. It had only been settled for about ten years, but it had the unique advantage of sitting on the Kansas River at the western edge of the state. Just across the river was the beginning of the Great American Desert, the vast grassland that served as the highway for migrants seeking new lives in Oregon and California. From the top of the bluff overlooking the settlement, William could see the large gathering of covered wagons, tents, livestock, and open wagons, piles of equipment and belongings, and people. Streams of people who resembled nothing so much as an ant whose hill have been stirred by a child's stick.

He found his way to John Bidwell's tent, where the co-captain of the venture was immersed in paperwork, checking the list of stores, and dealing with complaints from emigrants. He introduced himself to the harried leader and handed him the letter from Fitzpatrick. Bidwell looked it over quickly and then looked directly into William's eyes. "Welcome to our group," he said cheerfully, extending his right hand. With his left, he waved the paper at William. "Tom indicates you're an old trail hand from the days of the mountain men. Good! We need scouts who know the territory."

"Aye, I've been over these lands many a time since '22." He couldn't resist a little bragging. "When I was with Ashley's Hundred."

Bidwell nodded with genuine respect. "Bartleson is out trying to convince folks to lighten up their wagons. You have no idea what some of them think they'll need in California! He should be back soon. See Willie over there, he'll show you where to bunk."

William got acquainted with the rest of the hands and some of the emigrants. He tried his very best to make the travelers understand some of the conditions they would be encountering along the way. He saw brass bedsteads, boxes of treasured books, even a treadle organ loaded into creaky wagons. He had to convince their owners that they wouldn't be useful on the trail, that they would be too heavy for their animals to pull over the mountains and long uphill slopes of the Great Plains. "It's possible we may have to leave our wagons behind at some point, especially if you want to cross the Sierras into California." His words failed to achieve their intended effect; many of the wagons were seriously overloaded when they crossed the Missouri River on the first leg of their long journey.

Tom Fitzpatrick arrived on the 13th, just two days before their scheduled departure. He sported a two-week growth of grizzled beard and a buckskin jacket. No trace of the rimless spectacles he wore in St. Louis. "You look a wee bit more like yourself, Tom," William yelled at him as he rode into the camp.

"And sure enough, I feel more like myself! Nothing like the fresh air out on the prairie, have to get the city air out of my lungs."

"With all these mules, oxen, and horses, the 'fresh' air mebbe a little too strong for ye!"

"So, it may," he laughed, taking a big sniff of air, "but still and all, give me the open air!"

The night before they departed, Tom called a meeting of the entire party. The twenty-five wagons had been lined up in five rows, ready to form a long line of travel when they pulled out in the morning. There were sixty-nine people, men, women, and children gathering in a large circle around the fire when Tom called for quiet.

He walked back and forth for a moment before he raised his voice to address them: "Friends, I think you all know me. If not, I am Tom Fitzpatrick, 'Broken Hand' as I'm known in some circles." He held up the crippled left hand that he owed to a firearms accident years before. "You also know your leaders John Bartleson, our newly elected captain and John Bidwell, whose relentless efforts brought this enterprise into being.

"In matters that touch on discipline and rules of the wagon train, Bartleson is your captain. His word goes. But when it comes to decisions about route, speed, dealing with the Indians, and all other issues concerning the successful completion of this journey, you had better rely on me. I've lived and traveled in these lands for many a year, and the fact that I'm here talking to you means that I've outwitted wild animals, fearsome storms, droughts, floods, thieving Indians, hunger, thirst, heat, and freezing cold. I've survived these many years because I listened to those who knew better and took their advice. I hope that all of you will be as wise as I have been.

"We leave at dawn tomorrow. The trumpet will sound at four, so you have time to take care of the animals and have your breakfast. We have a great adventure before us, my friends. Get a good night's sleep and off we go in the morning!"

When William reached the bunkhouse, he pulled out his fiddle and softly played some slow, sad songs of Scotland. Haunting melodies filled with the foggy glens of his mother country so far away.

The first morning on the trail was an adventure. The weather was fine, and although the task of crossing the river was grueling labor, the excitement of finally being underway infected every member of the company. The second day was also fresh and thrilling. The third day began to seem more routine. By the tenth day, the routine had become an endless rut. The landscape didn't seem to change at all, day after day, mile after mile. Endless grass and more grass; gentle slopes to labor up followed by gentle slopes to coast down, and rivers with cottonwood groves along the banks to be forded or floated over.

Almost everyone walked. The wagons were loaded with foodstuffs, gear, and family possessions, so there was no room for passengers. Only the sick, the very old, and the very young rode in the back of the wagons, and that was a jolting, bouncing horror.

William had light duty for the first weeks out. There was little scouting to be done on the featureless prairie. He rode out ahead of the train every day, searching for game to supplement their supplies, watching for bands of Kansa or Pawnee that might want to steal a horse or mule, and scouting for rivers and other obstacles. On his return, he rode with Tom at the head of the column, sharing what he had learned on his reconnaissance. They often noticed some landmark that reminded one of them of a story, and that led to another, and another, and the day passed quickly.

In the evenings, the wagons circled, more for the convenience than for safety. They ate their meals, visited with neighbors, tended their livestock, and often, if the weather allowed, there would be music and dancing under the stars. William was in great demand for his fiddle tunes, and Ella Mueller, the lady who had insisted on taking her treadle organ along, would roll up the canvas cover and play popular tunes of the day, with William often joining in. "On Top of Old Smoky" and "The Blue Juniata" were among the favorites of the emigrants. Many a rugged farmer would turn his face to conceal tears as William played the bittersweet melody of "Home, Sweet Home," filling the small circle of light and emanating through the infinite sea of grass.

Ella's organ also was put to use on Sunday mornings. Alton Seivers, a lay minister of the Baptist Church, held services. In deference to the many different religions represented in the group including Methodist, Catholic, Baptist, Congregationalist, and some, like Thomas Fitzpatrick and William Kennedy, who disinclined to follow any organized church, these observances consisted of singing hymns, saying prayers of thanksgiving, and reading a few scripture passages. A Methodist clergyman, the Reverend Joseph Williams joined the train at the end of May, near Alcove Springs. He also conducted Sunday services, as well as two weddings and a funeral over the course of the journey. But then the train would re-form and continue its journey. They could afford no days of rest on the trail if they hoped to reach their goal before the winter set in, which could be as early as November in the higher elevations.

The Reverend Williams was going west to convert the Indians. When he met Thomas Fitzpatrick for the first time, he shared his mission to "bring the light of truth to the savages."

"I don't know that we've got anything to teach them," Thomas gruffly replied.

Shocked, Williams sputtered for a moment and then said, "But surely, sir, we have the revelation of the Bible and the love of Christ to share with our misbegotten brothers. You know of the Great Commission: 'Go therefore and make disciples of all nations.' My mission is to make disciples of the miserable heathen who unknowingly yearn for God's love."

Fitzpatrick stared at the clergyman with a stony face. "I've lived in the cities and towns of the 'civilized' folk, and I've lived with the Arapahoe, the Lakota, the Cheyenne, and the Shoshone. I don't know that we've got anything to teach them, I say again, and they could teach us a great deal, if only we had ears to hear." He turned and walked away from the gaping man of the cloth.

"An ungodly man," he breathed to himself. "I hope his blasphemy doesn't bring disaster upon our heads."

William got to know many of the travelers. Most were farmers who were seeking new, fertile, affordable land in the West. They were a sturdy group, stoic in the face of hardship and willing to heed the advice of the seasoned guides who rode at their head. He especially admired the eighteen-year-old Nancy Kelsey, who walked beside her husband every day with her infant daughter on her hip, even though she could have ridden. In general, William was pleased and surprised by the harmonious relationships among the group. There had certainly been a lot more fights and hard feelings in the bands of trappers he travelled with twenty years previously. These were serious folk who had a fixed goal and were willing to do what needed to be done to accomplish it.

Gradually, almost imperceptibly, the grass became shorter and the rivers farther apart. The landmarks that the mountain men had used to find their bearings on the endless sea of grass disappeared. Courthouse Rock, Jail Rock, Chimney Rock, appeared on the horizon, grew in size as they approached, and then retreated behind them as they continued on their westward course.

When they caught sight of Scotts Bluff, they knew they were getting close to Fort Laramie, and that the prairie part of the journey was nearing its end. As Thomas and William stood contemplating the massive bluff, Thomas said, "I'll always wonder what exactly happened to old Hiram."

"Ay, it's a great puzzle. They found his bones on yon bluff, but many's the tale that that's told to explain wit happened to him."

"You remember him, Billy? A big feller, always at hand with a joke and a drink. Was he abandoned by his mates when he got sick? Was he wounded by the Blackfeet?"

"Old Hiram Scott – one of the first of Ashley's company to go. Wit's the wonder is that maist of us are still kickin'."

Thomas loosed a hearty laugh. "Yes, and still on the move, always on the move. Will we ever settle down, Bill?"

William turned and looked toward the west. "We may have nae choice, Tom. This country is filling up fast, and a day may be comin' when there are naw places to roam free."

The two mountain men stood lost in their private thoughts for a short time. Then the lead wagon of the party caught up with them and they turned once again to their business.

Another four day's hard travel found the wagon train at Fort Laramie. Thomas Fitzpatrick had been one of the early owners of the fort, established during the heyday of the fur trade. It changed hands several times and was owned by the American Fur Company when the emigrants arrived there at the end of July. They took several days to replenish their larders, repair equipment, and give some needed rest to animals and humans alike.

The refreshed group started off again through a landscape much different than the endless plains. They were in the open range now, with sagebrush and fescue grass replacing the tall prairie grasses. It was big sky country, with distant mountain peaks visible above the reds and ocher of the land.

All along the route, the travelers had discussed their ultimate destination. The easiest and safest route was along the Snake River to the Oregon Country. A handful of emigrants had taken that route in 1839 and 1840, and there were no unsurpassable obstacles that way. For John Bidwell, however, the entire point of the journey was to go to California, of which he had heard so many wonderful tales.

Fitzpatrick discouraged any talk of California. "There's no trail to follow there," he gruffly pronounced.

"But Thomas, you're a guide, a pathfinder. We hoped that you would be willing to blaze a new trail for us," Bidwell implored.

"Yes, I'm a guide, and so you should take guidance from me. From Fort Hall to Oregon is a safe and not too trying trip. We're late in the season, but you'll have no trouble making it to the Oregon Country before the weather turns foul. Between us and California, though, there are some mighty big mountains. I've trapped in 'em, so has William and we can tell you that there is no pass that will admit a wagon. If you go that way, you'll end up on foot, plodding through deep snow and arriving barely alive, if you make it at all."

The mountain man's wisdom was lost on Bidwell and the others, for whom California was a golden sun beckoning to them across a continent. They had endured the rigors of the trail for three months and they felt confident that they would be able to find a way to their promised land.

Bidwell quietly sought out William, and finding him alone, asked him, "Mr. Kennedy... you've travelled in these mountains, the Sierras that Thomas says are so fearful. Is he right? Can they not be conquered by perseverance and fortitude?"

William pondered the question and then replied, "I'll nae say they can niver be crossed. But Tom is richt when he says not with wagons. Unless there is some pass or valley that no one has seen before, there is nary a path for a wagon train across the Sierras. I masel hae found my way ower the crest of those mountains, but a trapper going alone or with an Indian friend is a far different thing than a wagon train."

Bidwell's ears perked up at William's words. "But you, yourself, have crossed the crest of the Sierras?"

"Aye, and mair than once. But afoot and travelling light."

"Mr. Kennedy," Bidwell implored once more, "if you were able to make that journey, I believe that we could. We can leave our wagons behind if we need to and cross on foot, but it would be so much harder without an experienced guide."

"But I tell you, John, I'm nae a guide for those mountains. I dinna ken any paths to travel, but only went following me nose, so to say. It wad be late in the year when we got to the high mountains, and the snaw comes early up there."

But nothing the mountain men said could sway Biddle and his friends. They determined to strike out for California, with no guide at all if need be.

"Tom," William said to his friend, "I'm thinkin' of going along with these fowk. I ken the danger and aw, but I believe they're goin' with or without us. And mebbe I could help them some. I canna watch them go aff alone to their deaths."

"You'll be as big a fool as them," Tom growled. "You can't save them, and you'll likely leave your own bones in the mountains."

William chewed on this for a moment. "Ye're a wise man, Thomas," he said at last. "I dinna doubt that ye're right." Then he gave a fatalistic chuckle. "But I hae always wanted to see California anyway, and I believe I will jyne the others in their folly."

Tom shook his head and put his big hand on William's shoulder. "There's no reasoning with a mountain man," he said. "That's the way of it, we're always going just a bit too far. If there's a man who could lead this bunch of tenderfeet to California, it would be you." William began to smile but was cut off. "But there is no such man!"

On August 11, with many tears, prayers, and well wishing, the party split in two. Fitzpatrick was to lead the Oregon-bound settlers as far as Fort Hall, from whence they could make their own way to the Oregon Country. William accompanied the thirty-four souls, including young Nancy Kelsey and her infant daughter, who were determined to brave the unknown road to their futures.

William had joined informally, not wishing to assume the responsibility of being their official guide. He was happy to contribute what skills he could to their venture, but when his advice wasn't followed, he simply shrugged and went along. They made good progress through the difficult terrain, arriving on the north shore of the Great Salt Lake on August 23rd. Running low on potable water, they searched urgently for a good source and found a fresh spring and lush grass on the 26th.

They soon found the headwaters of what was called Mary's River, which John C. Fremont would rename, the Humboldt a few years later. They followed this river for some distance, but the grueling journey was taking its toll on the draft animals. On September 12th, they had to abandon two wagons, making good on Thomas

Fitzpatrick's prediction that they would never be able to make the journey with their wagons. Gradually, as the days went by, more and more emigrants packed what goods they could onto their oxen and left their wagons to stand as forlorn sentinels in the salt, sand, and sagebrush.

By the time they arrived at the wide, marshy sink where the river disappears into the desert, they had abandoned all the wagons and were now on foot and horseback, with their goods piled high on the oxen. William, who had seen this swampy area many years before, took a few men and reconnoitered to the west. They found the seemingly impenetrable wall of the Sierra Nevada blocking their path. Upon hearing this report, many emigrants despaired of finishing their journey, or of even surviving in the remote wilderness. Many wanted to try to return to Fort Hall before the winter caught them, but to William's considerable surprise, a majority voted to continue.

They found a river, which in a few years would be named after William's old companion Kit Carson, coming down from the mountains. They followed this river to another and then, as he scouted ahead, William saw a river running west toward California! The group plodded on through the fantastically beautiful, rugged mountains until finally, on November 4th, they reached Rancho Los Mendanos, owned by the American John Marsh. They had made it to California, though they were emaciated and destitute. Miraculously, all thirty-four had survived the epic journey, making Nancy Kelsey the first woman to cross the Sierra Nevada into California.

As the party recuperated at the Rancho, William Kennedy said his goodbyes to the people with whom he had crossed the continent and set off to have a look at this fabled land of California.

CHAPTER ELEVEN

William liked what he saw in this new land of California. It was lush and green if a bit soggy in the winter. A good place for an old mountain man to settle down, maybe. Like all the Americans who found their way into northern California, he was drawn to John Sutter, the center of gravity for much of what was to happen in the next few years. Sutter had already lived an exotic life by the time he accepted Mexican citizenship and acquired a huge ranchero on the Sacramento River. Now he had built a rapidly growing, near-feudal empire centered on the sturdy fort he called New Helvetia, after his native Switzerland.

William, Bidwell, and the other members of the party who had transited the summit of the Sierras made their way to Sutter's fort and found a genial welcome and employment. John Bidwell soon became Sutter's right-hand man, assisting him in the various operations of the fort, including herds of cattle and horses, a flourmill and bakery, a distillery, a blacksmith shop, a carpenter shop, and a boat launch to carry freight and passengers between Sutter's Fort and the San Francisco Bay.

William also found plenty to do at the fort, and he came to know Sutter pretty well. The entrepreneur persuaded William to buy land in the valley, a tract with rich meadows and sunny hillsides. This could be the home he had never had before, a place of real substance where a man could build a life. His wages from Tom Fitzpatrick had been generous, and he was earning his keep at Sutter's Fort, but he didn't have enough to buy the parcel he coveted.

In the middle of the winter, though the cool, misty weather didn't feel like winter to William. He received a letter carried by a trapper who had been visiting Tom out in Fort Hall. The old mountain man had a thick but readable scrawl.

To William Kennedy

Fort Hall, January 15, 1842

I hope this finds you well, as I have heard that your party all made it through the Sierras, without their wagons as I foretold. To come to the point directly, I am contracted next summer to escort an emigrant party from Fort Laramie to this point. They have offered me $500 for this service, which as you know, is no dangerous route anymore. It appears that there will be more trains through next year than this past season. Would you consider joining me in this endeavor? I will arrange all details. If interested, make your way this point as soon as the weather allows.

Yours sincerely, from Ft Hall

Thomas Fitzpatrick

William saw at once that this was his path to buying the land from Sutter if he could arrange terms with him. He found Sutter on the veranda of his house inside the walls of the adobe fort.

"Good day, William," he said pleasantly as William approached his table. "Join me, won't you?"

"Thank ye, John," William replied as he took a seat opposite Sutter. "I do have a matter to discuss with ye."

"I thought as much, my friend."

"About that land we talked of."

"I assumed so."

"You know I don't hae aw the money right now, don't ye?"

"Of course, I know that" Sutter calmly answered.

William regarded his friend skeptically. "Do ye ken the entire purpose of my visit, then? Need I say more?"

Sutter laughed. "I might hazard a guess," he answered.

"Go aheed, then. What am I here aboot?"

"Why, I imagine that you want to arrange terms for the land so you can take the purchase of it now and finish paying over some time."

"Aye," William reluctantly replied. "Ye've certainly seen through me. Since ye seem to be a prophet, can ye also tell me what job I'm takin' the coming summer?"

Sutter started. "Job? No, I assumed if you bought this parcel, you would be settling here."

"Ay, I do want to settle here, but I need more money than I can make in California. I've had an offer to shepherd an emigrant train from Fort Laramie to Fort Hall. My old friend Tom Fitzpatrick offered me the job. But I'll be back in the fall and make a big payment on that land."

"I've heard a lot about Broken Hand," Sutter said, surprising William with his knowledge of Tom's nickname. "He'd be a good man for New Helvetia. Why don't you suggest it to him?"

William, a bit confused, asked, "Do we hae a deal, then? How much d'ye need now?"

"How about three hundred now? Can you manage that much?"

"Aye," William replied with a smile. "An there'll be another three next fall!"

Sutter pulled out a paper with simple terms for the sale sketched out, which the men both signed. As William happily walked away, Sutter softly muttered, "Three hundred next fall? A Scot indeed!"

William left New Helvetia in early April. He snow shoed across the crest of the Sierras and cached his shoes when he reached the lower elevations on the eastern slope. Twenty-five more days of walking brought him to Fort Hall and a joyous reunion with Tom Fitzpatrick.

"Tom," William shouted in the midst of a long series of toasts, "John Sutter told me to invite ye to come to California!"

"California!" Tom yelled in reply. "It's too damn rainy there in the winter. Give me the good old Rocky Mountains any time. Besides, this escort job is a license for printing money. I'll milk that cow as long as I'm able."

The two scouts rode to Fort Laramie in late June, where they awaited the party that had engaged Tom. William's group was about two weeks behind them.

Tom's clients showed up a day early, a good sign that it was a serious crew with the discipline to push ahead on schedule. They rested three days at Fort Laramie and then departed with Tom in the lead. William checked with the merchants to be sure there were enough supplies for his group, supposed to be fifteen wagons and seventy people, about the size of the train he had ridden with Tom the summer before, and then he had nothing to do. He played his fiddle, he sat on the rampart of the adobe walls, he played the fiddle some more, he tried to strike up conversations with the merchants, but as soon as they realized he wasn't buying, they lost interest.

Long before two weeks were up, William began haunting the ramparts, searching the southeast horizon for the first hint of a dust cloud or white glint of a covered wagon heralding the arrival of his party. On the fifteenth day without any sign of the emigrants, William decided to ride out to meet them. He rode two days, nearly forty miles, before he saw the telltale dust cloud raised by a wagon train.

His crew was not the energetic type that Tom had been blest with. There was dissention in the party that William was engaged for, and before they even arrived at Fort Laramie, William found it necessary to remove the elected captain and assume dictatorial control over the train. After the chaotic situation they had endured since departing from Sapling Grove, most of the emigrants welcomed the order and discipline William brought. They rested three days at Fort Laramie, during which time William ascertained which of the settlers had the strongest character and which would be most likely to defy his orders, and then they departed for the last leg of their long journey.

The trip was uneventful, as Tom had prophesied. William enjoyed the feeling of command, and the route was very familiar. "It's only a damned road now," he complained to Tom as they shared a drink after sending both their parties safely on the way to the Oregon Country. "Naw much for a scout to do."

"Oh, I had a couple episodes where they were glad, they had me along," Tom replied. "Some Sioux youngsters grabbed a couple men from the train. I went out and talked to them and gave them a few gifts and mentioned some of my friends in their tribe. They let the fellows go. Without a guide along who knew the Indians that might have been an ugly situation."

"Ay, they had the guid luck, then, to have you along. Meself, I just stood there like a statue and pointed the richt way to go." He took a deep draught from the mug of ale before him. "Still and aw, it's a bonnie life on the trail and an easy way to make a dollar. I'll be comin' back next summer sure. And won't ye come wi me to California? It's aye a fine country."

"No, Billy, I've got all I need right here at Fort Hall. I may visit you out there one of these days, but not this winter. Safe travels to you and I'll look for you in the spring."

William took his leave and retraced his steps to the mountains. There were a few emigrants determined to go to California, but William declined the offer to lead them. He gave what advice he could, mostly that they should go to Oregon, but he wanted to move faster than he could with a train of settlers.

He recovered his snowshoes where he had left them in the foothills and crossed the mountains, arriving at Sutter's Fort in early November. A fine mist was falling, and fog filled the lower valleys when William approached Sutter. "William! I'm glad you made it home safe. And looking no worse for wear I see. Come have a drink and tell me of your adventures."

William sat and said, "Nae, I've had naw adventures. The wilderness is being tamed, John, getting filled up with people, and aw the rough edges being made straight. It'll nae be long before there's no place left where a man can be alone. For masel, I'll make a home richt here in New Helvetia." He fumbled with the rawhide purse that hung at his belt and withdrew twelve $25 gold pieces and counted them out on the table.

"There's ye're next payment, John. If ye'll gie me one more year, I'll pay off in full."

Sutter looked at the coins and then swept them in with a broad wave of his hand. "Thank you, William. Of course, your credit still stands firm with me. What are your plans for the winter?"

"If ye hae any work for me here at the fort, that'll be a blessing. An I ought to be clearing some of... some of my land, mebbe start to big up a cabin, too."

Sutter was pleased to have a man like William Kennedy as a permanent resident of his little kingdom. He was dreaming of a utopia in New Helvetia, where people from all over the world could live in peace and prosperity, under his benevolent leadership, of course. He was seeking migrants from France, the U. S., and his native Switzerland to meld with the Hawaiians he had brought from the Sandwich Islands and the indigenous Maidu people with whom he had close relations. He was somehow able to harmonize these lofty ambitions with his enslavement of some native peoples, his firm commitment to white domination of other races, and his sexual predations on young Indian women.

William managed to clear enough timber to build a respectable cabin. "It's a wee modest thing," he said, "but I see it as a start to something grand. One more emigrant train to guide, and this will aw be mine, free and clear."

In April 1843, William again crested the lofty Sierras and made his way to Fort Hall.

"There are going to be more people than ever on the trail this summer," Tom told him as they sat together in the fort's dark saloon. "I've heard over a thousand settlers will be leaving Elm Grove this spring." The young trees that had given Sapling Grove its name had matured to the point that it was now called Elm Grove. "That means an unwieldy wagon train. My own guess is that they will split off one from the other, some going faster, some slower, others discontented with their leaders, still others wishing to try new cutoffs. I'm planning to go to Fort Laramie in July and see what shows up. I might even be able to escort two groups through – double the money!"

"None o' that for me, Tom. One train is aplenty. This'll be my last time on the trail. I'm settlin' in California."

Tom laughed softly. "I've heard that before, from you and others. You'll soon find the settled life chafes a bit, then you'll be back out in the wild again."

"I'm naw prophet, Tom. I won't make ye a promise. But I feel a bit weary in me bones, and I b'lieve that I'll bide on my ranch in New Helvetia."

"You'll need a wife for that, won't you Billy?"

William stared somberly at his old friend. He hadn't thought about a woman since the horrible day he found that his beautiful Annie was dead. He was forty-three now, not too late to start a family, if he could find the right woman to share his life with him. "A wifie," he mused. "Ay, Tom, that would be bonnie. But I've none in mind, an I fear I mus' leave all of that to fate."

Tom left early for Fort Laramie as he had planned, and William rode along with him for the company. By the middle of July, a few emigrants began to arrive at the fort. The stories they told again showed Tom to be an accurate prognosticator. There were well over a thousand people strung out on the trail between Elm Grove and Fort Laramie. They had elected a captain, Peter Burnett of Tennessee, but frustrations and responsibilities soon led him to shout to an angry group of settlers, "I throw down my job right here!" The captaincy devolved to William Martin, but the sheer size of the train made it ungovernable.

Those who had no, or few cattle moved faster and soon outdistanced the main body. Those with sizable herds made up the "cow train" that travelled more slowly. As Tom had foreseen, personality conflicts caused smaller groups to split off and seek their own way. As a result, people would be arriving at Fort Laramie in various contingents over a period of two months, and they all sought a guide to take them through the last stretch of wild country before they reached the well-worn route to Oregon.

Tom was hired by the first party to arrive. It was a lean group, mostly men, with few animals and lightly loaded wagons. They had made record speed on the first leg of the journey, and they wished to press on with all haste. That exactly suited Tom, since he wanted to return and escort another train before the winter arrived.

William planned to return to California as soon as he completed the trip to Fort Hall, so he was content to be picked up by one of the early arrivals. Besides, the later an emigrant band arrived at Fort Laramie, the greater the chance that they were troublesome, making more work and aggravation for their guide.

In the first week of August, a small, tidy group of wagons appeared outside the fort. William went out to greet them as they neared the palisade and found their captain was Rev. Benjamin Greider, a tall, thin-faced Unitarian minister whose pince-nez accentuated his stern aspect.

"We hail from New England," he explained to William. "I may as well tell you right away that we have in our company several families of free Negroes. Some of our fellow emigrants didn't care to share the trail with them, so we isolated ourselves and set out on our own. The trail wasn't difficult to follow – rather, it would be difficult to lose the path, beaten down as it is. By our persistence and good order, we far outdistanced those who disdained our company, and here we are. We are seeking a guide, and our prerequisite is that he not take offence at the company of colored people."

"Ye need naw worry on that account," William smiled, quoting his favorite poet: "'A man's a man for aw that.' What I expect is a train in good order with fowk as can follow a command when need arises. From the looks of your people, ye would fit that bill. If ye'll have me, we'll shake on it and make a bargain right now."

As was the usual practice, the party spent three days at Fort Laramie, resting their animals, buying supplies, and enjoying a short holiday from the rigors of their travels.

It soon became apparent to William that Greider and his fellows were abolitionists, anti-slavery crusaders who were nearly as unpopular in the North as in the South. They kept to themselves for the most part, especially the three black families. They relied on Greider for all the dealings with the merchants at the post and contented themselves tending to their cattle and enjoying a few days free from the jolting of the wagons. William made no effort to mingle with his clients. He would get to know them soon enough on the trail.

He never gave much thought to this intractable controversy that tore at his adopted country, slavery. When he first saw it in Baltimore, he hadn't understood it, and that led to his fight with Curry and his hasty escape to the West. In fact, that incident set the course of his life ever since. And he nursed a bitter hostility toward the slavers who destroyed his family. Still, he could see no way to eliminate it. The slaveholders would never give up their way of life or their "peculiar institution." William always subscribed to the maxim "to each his own," and tried to put the entire matter out of his mind.

The party left for Fort Hall on August 7th, considerably ahead of the usual departure date. As they settled back into the routines of the trail, William made a point of dropping back along the line of wagons to greet his new clients and reassure them that the next leg of their trip would be a challenge, but safe. About halfway to the rear of the train, he saw the first of the black families. There was a large, well-muscled man walking beside a shy-looking woman in a bonnet and a young man, perhaps their son. Driving the wagon was a teenaged girl, whose steady hand and calm demeanor told of the many miles she had piloted her prairie schooner.

The next wagon in line was driven by a handsome, light-skinned woman, while two youngsters, a boy, and a girl, walked alongside the oxen. "'Mornin'", he said to the pair on foot. He turned to the driver of the wagon and nodded. He was struck by some distant recognition, a feeling that he had seen this woman somewhere before. Her eyes locked in with his, and he could see she was experiencing the same mysterious feeling. He squinted at her, shook his head, and softly mouthed, "Lisbeth?"

Her head jerked back with sudden recognition. "No, it can't be. William? William Kennedy?"

The two stared in bewilderment at each other, seeking the faces of twenty years past. Lisbeth really didn't look so different. She was older, of course, and filled out a bit more, but her smooth features were still very attractive. William, on the other hand, had a face that was adorned with a grizzled beard and weathered from the years of exposure to sun and wind. It was harder for her to find in the mountain man's face the young fiddler she had briefly encountered so long ago. Though they had known each other for only a short time, he had changed her life when he inadvertently killed her master and thus gave her freedom.

Their interlude was rudely interrupted by a hostile shout from the young man walking alongside. "What have you got to do with my mother?"

As if awakened from a dream, William shook the cobwebs from his mind and said, "Why, son, I think we might have met once a long time ago. My name is William Kennedy, the guide for this outfit. And you are…?"

Lisbeth interjected, "This is my son Lloyd. Please forgive him for his abrupt manner. He feels he must protect me since his father died. And this is my daughter Sarah. Children, William is an old friend to whom I owe a great debt."

Sarah smiled pleasantly at William, but Lloyd retained the hard look in his face, acknowledging the introduction with a curt nod.

"So, your husband died?" William asked awkwardly.

"Yes, John died two years ago. It was his idea to go to Oregon, to start a new life away from slavery and prejudice. He passed before his dream could come to fruition, but we are carrying on in his memory. He was a good man, a strong man. I miss him so terribly."

"Ay," William said quietly. "We hae something in common there. My wife was killed three years ago. I keep it at arm's length when I can, but I hae ne'er got over it."

They continued a few minutes in silence and then William said, "I see we hae a few things to catch up on. I must be aboot my business now, but later if you like, I'll stop by, and we can share our stories."

Lisbeth looked softly toward him. "Yes, I'd like that. I'd love to know how you came to be a mountain man and what you've been up to all these years."

William tipped his hat to her and said to the children, "Guid to make ye're acquaintance," and slowed to slip back to the next wagon in line.

That evening, after the meals were over and the train made tidy and secure for the night, there was dancing and singing while William played several tunes on his fiddle. The night was mild and after the music, some sat and talked quietly while others got their children settled in bed. William made his way to Lisbeth's wagon where she was sitting with her two children.

"Evenin', Lloyd… Sarah. Evenin', Lisbeth."

Sarah nodded shyly and Lloyd looked at William cooly and nodded. "Good evening, William," Lisbeth said. "Sit a while and let's visit a little before bedtime."

William sat on an upturned water cask and asked, "Should I begin?"

Lisbeth laughed and said, "Yes, you first, and then I'll take my turn. But we better be brief, or we'll be up all the night."

William told his story of the past twenty years. The escape to St. Louis, the years as a mountain man, his marriage to Tsunnunk, his talented child Quaninch, the brutal slave raid that destroyed his family, and his new vocation as a trail guide. He choked up when he told of the awful day, he discovered his home in ashes and his family gone, and Lisbeth sadly shook her head and gently touched his arm.

"So that's me tale, Lisbeth. Is it too late to hear yours?"

Sarah had nodded off and Lloyd was struggling to keep his eyes open. "Let me put the children to bed and then I'll tell you, my story. It won't take as long as yours. Really there's not much of a story there." After settling her children in the wagon, she returned and quietly began to speak.

"Well, William, the last time I saw you, you were fleeing for your life from Curry's. I hated to see you go, but I knew that I didn't want the life of a fugitive especially since I knew I could be legally free if only I kept calm.

"The next morning, I awoke and 'discovered' Curry's body. I didn't have to pretend to be grief-stricken. No one expects a slave to mourn the loss of a master, but I did need to use all my acting skills to portray shock and hysteria. There seemed to be no mystery for the watchmen to unravel Curry's fiddle-playing boarder had robbed and killed him and fled into the night.

"I knew that Curry had a will that stipulated my emancipation, but I didn't trust his heirs to do me justice, so I sought out a free black lawyer in Baltimore. He represented me at the reading of the will, and from the looks on the faces of the others there, I knew I had been wise to retain him. I left the lawyer's office with my official manumission papers and a bequest of $200.

"I didn't want to stay in Baltimore, or any city where slavery was practiced. I simply didn't want to be at the mercy of a government that would as soon enslave me as protect me. So, I took passage on a ship to Boston. I didn't know anyone in that city, but I had heard the slaves talk about how many free blacks lived there and that there were whites who were working to end slavery altogether. Abolitionists, they were called, and among the white people they were more hated than the devil himself.

"Boston was quite a breath of fresh air," she continued. "I'm not saying it was a citadel of justice, but there was a large and prosperous black community there. They welcomed former slaves from the South, whether they had run away or had been freed by their owners. Some, who had a price on their heads for escaping, were helped to move on to Canada, a land where they could be truly safe from capture. Others, like me whose freedom was perfectly legal, they helped to settle in the city.

"I had the skills I needed to find work at a tavern, cooking and serving, but with the huge difference that I was getting paid." She stopped and with downturned face she whispered, "And I didn't have to warm anyone's bed."

The dark night hid William's flushed and guilty-looking face. She noticed his distress and gently chuckled. "I didn't mean anything about you, William. Please don't ever feel bad about that. You weren't responsible. It was just the way things were then.

"To finish this overlong and rather uninteresting story, I met a wonderful man in Boston. John Winston had been born free there. His mother had been a lady's maid and his father an escaped slave.

They raised a family and through hard work had achieved a very comfortable life in the city. Even though John had never been a slave, he felt the immeasurable suffering of his people. He worked with the African Society, a group that assisted the community with financial and legal aid and promoted education and hard work as the means to improve the lot of blacks."

She glanced around the quiet, dark wagon train and saw that no one was about except the night watch. "I must finish this, William. It's getting very late."

"I coud listen to ye the aw night through," he said softly.

She cast a curious look in his direction and said, "But we have another day of hard travel, and many more beyond that, so I'll bring this tale to its close. John and I were married, and we had the two wonderful children who are sleeping right now in this wagon. We named them after two friends who were working for the end of slavery.

"John felt that freedom wouldn't come in time for our children to see. And Boston, while the safest city for blacks, wasn't free of prejudice and discrimination. It was still a hard life there, with hatred and danger waiting around any corner. So, he decided that we should leave Boston, leave the United States, and make a new life where color wouldn't control every part of our lives; where our children could grow up and have the opportunities they deserved.

"Boston is a seafaring town, and John had heard stories from sailors, many of them black, about the wild, beautiful free Oregon Country. He determined to move us there and we began to plan, to save money, to learn the skills we would need as emigrants and homesteaders."

She stopped again, and with eyes closed, continued in a soft whisper, "But we didn't plan on John getting sick and dying. He took the cholera and was gone in a week. I was crushed, but we determined that his dream would not die with him." She lifted her head and William could see the bright tears in her eyes reflecting the dim firelight. "And so here we are."

"That's nae a dull tale, Lisbeth. It's a fine story and the ending is yet to be told. You get off abed now. I've a bit of work to be done before I sleep. That blamed bugle sounds michty early in the morning, don't it?"

The journey to Fort Hall took twenty-five days. They arrived in late August, well ahead of the inexorable deadline dictated by the approaching winter. William and Lisbeth had spent many more evenings talking. He enjoyed showing her landmarks along the route, Independence Rock and Devil's Gate. He delighted in her awe-struck face when she beheld the distant mountains crowned with early snow. They soon realized that they were falling in love and that maybe the new lives they were each beginning could become one life lived together.

"Lisbeth," William haltingly began, "Ye have your heart set on Oregon. An it's a pretty place, tis true. But, as ye ken, I have a place in California. Oh, lass, it's a fine country, and I've already built a solid cabin and with this summer's wages, the whole rancho will be mine free and clear."

Her mouth formed a small quizzical smile, but she remained silent. William groped on, "It'll be a new world there, lass. Do ye think... I mean, Lisbeth, I'm wondering if..."

Her smile grew and she shook her head. "William, you needn't say any more. Yes, I will come with you to California. I can't help but feel there is a reason why we've met again, after so long and in such a remote place. You and I both have our ghosts that we will always live with, and love, but that doesn't mean we should be alone the rest of our lives. Yes! I will go with you!"

"An does that mean ye'll marry me, Lisbeth?"

"Are you asking?" she laughed.

"Ay! Ay, I'm asking ye! Lisbeth, will ye be my bride?"

The Reverend Greider officiated at the ceremony outside the adobe walls of Fort Hall with the entire party of emigrants looking on. Sarah stood at her mother's side, though Lloyd wasn't completely sure that he approved. For a change, after the ceremony, someone else played the music and William danced, though he apologized more than once for his clumsy feet.

Joseph Walker, one of William's mountain man friends, was preparing to lead a small group of emigrants to California, and he welcomed William and his new family to join them. Some in the party might have been uncomfortable at the notion of travelling with a biracial couple, but that was no concern to the old timers who had lived in the wild for decades. Many of them had taken Indian wives, and they were used to sojourning and working with people of all colors. No one in their train was foolish enough to confront William Kennedy or Joseph Walker over the color of Lisbeth or her children.

The California-bound party left Fort Hall at the end of August. By 1843, the trail to California, while still challenging, was becoming less dangerous and unknown. William had walked over the Sierras with a small group two years earlier and crossed over several times by himself since then. Other parties had found their way there in 1842, and Walker had found a fairly low pass, which bore his name, just earlier this year.

It was still impassable for wagons though, so by the time they began their ascent of the towering range, they had transferred what belongings they could to their animals and formed a pack train. Luck was with them, and they arrived at Sutter's Fort just before the snows began to fill in the passes of the Sierra Nevada. Sutter's welcome was warm for William and his new brood. They settled in at William's cabin and immediately began the hard work of building, clearing timber, planting crops, and all the countless labors required to wrest a living from the wilderness.

New arrivals continued to pour into Sutter's remote paradise. Mostly they were Americans now, though the land was still part of Mexico. William prospered, and he had every reason to believe his wandering days were over. "Tis a bonny place, Beth," he said more than once, sitting on his veranda watching the sun setting over the valley. "Nae, I'll ne'ermore roam from here."

But the remote and sheltered settlement of New Helvetia was not free from the currents of history that flow into even the quietest places. The region had filled up with Americans, and their country was rushing toward war with Mexico. The very air was alive with dreams of conquest, and the newly minted phrase "Manifest Destiny" summed up the appetite of Americans for expansion. Plots, plans, and revolution swirled throughout Northern California in the mid-1840s. William tried to stay out of any adventures and keep to his own growing rancho, but in 1845, with war threatening and the arrival of John C. Fremont in the province, he found himself inexorably drawn away from his family and closer to the erupting conflict.

Fremont was nicknamed The Pathfinder for his explorations in the 1840s, though many of the paths he found had been blazed years before by Jedediah Smith, Kit Carson, and many others, including

William Kennedy. He came to California after a mysterious meeting with President Polk. What clandestine instructions he bore from the President were unknown to anyone but Fremont, but once in California, he busied himself in trying to separate the northern part of the province from Mexico.

William met Fremont at Sutter's Fort in December of 1845 and they swapped many yarns of adventures in the Great American Desert and reminisced about the mountain men they had met and travelled with. William noted with amusement how prominently Fremont promoted his own name and exploits over those of his companions. Before he left for Monterrey, Fremont took William aside and confided in him that war with Mexico was a certainty. "Bill, you mentioned that you know Steve Kearny?"

"Aye, we met out in the Yellowstone country back in the twenties. And he commanded the Jefferson Barracks in St. Louis in the days afore I moved west for guid. What of him?"

Fremont lowered his voice, although no one was near the two men. "He's going to be made a general and sent to take Santa Fe and then come on to California when the war starts."

William's eyes narrowed. "How do ye ken that war will come? Mayhap a way to keep the peace will still be found."

Fremont exuded an insider's smugness. "Oh, the war is coming, Billy, you needn't doubt that. But the reason I mention it to you is that a mutual friend of ours, Kit Carson, is joining Kearny as a guide and he asked me to persuade you to join them."

Seeing the frown on William's face, Fremont cut in before the mountain man could refuse. "The pay's very good, and Kit tells me you know the lands between Santa Fe and Las Vegas better than any other guide."

William sighed. "When are ye thinking this might happen?"

"We expect war to break out early next year, and Kearny will move west in June. You could meet him in Santa Fe at the end of the summer. We don't expect there will be any fighting. The Mexicans have only small forces anywhere in New Mexico and California, and Kearny's army, along with men I plan to raise here in the north, will join with our naval forces in the Pacific and it will be a walkover. You could leave here in August and I'm sure you could be back in your cozy rancho by Christmas."

When he broached the subject with Lisbeth, she wasn't pleased. "William, think of what you're doing. You're no youngster anymore. You're forty-five years old now, no age for playing at war. Besides, you're needed here to take care of this property and of me and the children."

"Ay, ye speak the truth. I'm nae thrilled aboot leaving. But a man has his duties, love. I may be needed here to look after the ranch, but what would that avail if the Mexicans come in here and evict us all from the land?"

"Do you really think that's likely?" she asked sharply.

He looked past her into the infinite distance. "Nae, that's not likely, is it? But there's no stopping what's afoot, lass, and we will be on one side or the other, no matter what we wish. The Americans hae taken Oregon and they'll be taking California, too. And besides, the pay is verra guid. We can use that money here on the ranch."

Lisbeth deeply searched her husband's eyes. "I can see that your mind is set, William, and I won't try to sway you any further. Only be safe and come back to us soon."

Fremont's promise that Kearny's campaign would be a walkover held true, at least in New Mexico. William arrived in Santa Fe just after Kearny had officially annexed it to the United States and appointed officials to govern it while he moved on to California. William's years in the canyon lands proved invaluable to the large, unwieldy army. The sights of the magnificent landscape made his heart ache bitterly for the loss he had suffered in this same locale six years earlier, but he remembered the terrain perfectly and had no trouble guiding the troops successfully on the difficult trail.

Kearny, flush with his unchallenged military supremacy, and encouraged by word that Los Angeles and San Diego were already occupied by American forces, sent two hundred troops back to Santa Fe, certain that he wouldn't need them in California.

He began to regret his confidence when he encountered Captain Gillespie and thirty of his men who had been expelled from Los Angeles by General Flores and the Californios. This news wasn't totally unwelcomed to Kearny, as it held out the promise of military conquest and glory for him.

Against the advice of his seasoned desert scouts, Kearny blundered into an ambush at San Pasqual and suffered a serious defeat with the loss of many men and officers. Kit Carson and

William Kennedy were sent on a perilous mission to notify the American forces in San Diego of the disaster, and they barely managed to make their way through enemy lines in the harsh desert winter.

The American forces regrouped, though, and on January 8, 1847, at the Battle of San Gabriel, William found himself watching two wounded Indian boys ride across the battlefield in front of the muskets of the Americans. He waved to his compatriots not to shoot, and the memory of his own lost child saved the lives of the badly hurt youngsters.

He stayed on in Southern California only a few days before heading back to his growing rancho in the foothills of the Sierras. As he neared his home, he passed a work party along the American River, where he met James Marshall who had just returned from service with Fremont in the war and had been contracted by Sutter to build a sawmill on the river.

Lisbeth rushed to greet him as he rode up to the log ranch house that he and his family had built. "Aye, Lisbeth," he said between the happy, frantic kisses she bestowed on him. "There's the end of all the huddy-wuddy. We'll be able to spend aw of our days here in New Helvetia, safe from all the turmoil and distourbance fro' the outwith world."

CHAPTER TWELVE

Quaninch and Diego plodded slowly away from the battle. Both boys had been hit by shards of hot, sharp metal from the canister shot that left them dotted with small bloody blotches. Quaninch had been deafened and his left side, from his face to his wrist, had been peppered with fragments. Diego, who had been closer to the blast, was more seriously wounded. He had a gash on his left temple that was bleeding profusely and, in addition to other small cuts, a piece of metal about three inches long was embedded in his left side under his arm.

The roar of the fighting was moving away from them, northwest toward the town of Los Angeles, while they crept away to the southeast. Diego drifted in and out of consciousness while Quaninch tried to staunch his friend's wound. They descended into a small gulley where a sluggish stream held some water pooled in the rocks.

Quaninch dismounted and removed his shirt. He could see that his injuries weren't mortal unless infection developed. He wet his shirt and washed the blood and sand from his body, wincing at the sting where he had been cut. Then he turned to Diego, who was unconscious on the horse's back. Quaninch reached up and wiped some of the blood from Diego's temple and then lifted the arm to inspect the chest wound. He was completely ignorant of such things, but he thought that he should try to remove the shrapnel that protruded from his friend's body.

He wrapped his wet, bloody shirt around his hands and grasped the sharp metal. It seemed to be solidly wedged between two ribs. Diego groaned when Quaninch touched it. Then, steeling himself, he tugged at the shrapnel with all his might. As it pulled free, Diego screamed in pain. Quaninch quickly held the shirt tightly against the gaping hole to try to stop the bleeding. He didn't think Diego could tolerate getting off and back on the horse, so he climbed back on and, keeping his left hand pressed against the wounded boy's side, he urged the horse forward with a kick. The bleeding slowed and then seemed to stop. Diego remained insensible as they slowly followed the little stream — to where, Quaninch had no idea.

Sometime later, Diego stirred and whimpered, slowly returning to awareness. "Where are we Jaime?" he weakly asked. Quaninch was relieved to realize his hearing had partly returned.

"I don't know, Diego," he answered. "We've just been following this stream because it's leading away from the battle."

"The battle," Diego murmured. "The battle! What happened, Jaime? Didn't we defeat the Americans?"

"I'm not sure. I only know there was a big explosion, and we were both hurt. I put us on this horse and headed upstream, trying to get as far away from the fighting as I could. I don't think our soldiers were getting the best of it, though. No one was left beside us on the bluff when we were hit."

Diego felt around on his left side and found the deep wound between his ribs. "I'm wounded!" he cried in dismay.

"Yes, we both were hit. I think we'll be all right, but we better get to somewhere we can rest and find some medicine. I'm afraid to go back to Los Angeles. If the Americans won the battle, they will have occupied the town."

Diego struggled to sit up. Grimacing, he looked around them at the distant mountains. "Jaime, I know this country. The village where I was born, Temal Wakhish, is not too far from here."

Quaninch remembered that Diego had told him he was a Cahuilla, but he didn't know where his people lived or how he had come to be a slave at the mission. "Do you think we could make it there, Diego? Would they give us help?"

"Yes, they can take care of us." He closed his eyes and gathered his strength. "I never told you my story, did I Jaime?"

"Not really. I was always afraid to ask too much. You didn't seem to want to talk about it."

"Let's get moving. I think I need help soon. Head toward that hill with the sharp peak. I'll tell you as we go."

Quaninch gently kicked the horse's side, and they resumed their slow journey.

"My real name is Nakai," he began. "The padre gave me my Christian name when my grandmother brought me to the mission."

"Brought you to the mission? Why?"

"My parents were both killed in a raid by the Luiseno, the ancient enemies of my people. My grandmother knew she couldn't take care of me, and besides, she worried that our village would be attacked again, and I might be killed, too. She had heard of the padre who took in boys and trained them to play music, so she took me there and Father Xavier agreed to buy me. The padre discouraged her from contacting me, since he wanted to wipe away all my Iviatim identity. I did see her just a few times when she travelled to the town and secretly visited me. The last time I saw her, just after Father Xavier died, she seemed very well in spite of her great age. Unless she has died since then I think she will be in the village, and she might have the knowledge to treat our wounds. We should be able to reach Temal Wakhish before nightfall. That's our only hope I think."

The effort of talking had exhausted him and he slumped forward. "Rest, now Diego," Quaninch whispered, "or should I say Nakai?"

Diego slept while they moved on through the desert. He awakened as the sun was sinking low behind them and peered around. "Yes," he said, "We are very near the village now. I'm surprised a sentinel hasn't picked us out already."

As if in response, they heard a voice shout, "Halt!" They couldn't see anyone, but they stopped their horse and waited, looking all around. They saw a man stepping cautiously out to confront them. They especially noted the musket he kept pointed in their general direction.

Diego roused himself and, making his voice as loud and strong as he could, shouted, "I am Nakai, son of Kunvachmal. My grandmother, Moki, lived in Temal Wakhish. Is she living still?"

The sentinel lowered his rifle and approached cautiously. "Yes, she lives and is here in the village. You are Nakai, the one who went to the mission to play music?" He walked closer and, seeing the blood on both boys, said, "You are injured."

"Yes, and we need help, right away. Can you guide us to my grandmother?"

"Who is this other one?" he asked suspiciously.

"This is Jai... uh, Quaninch. He is a Nuwuvi, a friend."

"I don't know this people," he said. "But if you vouch for him, I will call him friend also. I am Yuyuelkik. Follow me into the village."

The village of Temal Wakhish was well-situated, both for living and defense. There was a large spring of good water and the whole area was shielded by rock walls. The houses, called kish, were simple conical dwellings made of brush and reeds. The place strongly reminded Quaninch of his own village Mukuntuweap. As it was near the end of the day, the people were finished with the day's labors and were sitting and standing in small groups.

The arrival of these two bloodied young strangers attracted everyone's attention. Yuyuelkik took them directly to a kish near the center of the settlement. "Moki!" he called out. "See who has come to us needing help!"

A small elderly woman with a deeply wrinkled face stepped out from the doorway of the house and squinted at the young men on horseback in front of her door. For a moment she was puzzled, but then she recognized her grandson. "Nakai!" She cried out in dismay. "What has happened to you?"

"Oh Grandmother," Diego cried, "I'm hurt. I need you to save me."

Quaninch spoke up, "We were wounded in a battle. I'm not badly hurt, but I'm afraid Diego... Nakai... is in trouble."

"You are the one who played violin with my grandson, aren't you? I saw the two of you playing at Mass. You both made such beautiful music."

"Yes, my name is Quaninch, though I was known as Jaime at the mission, just as Nakai was called Diego."

Moki looked at Yuyuelkik and said, "Get some help and bring these two into my house. Be careful how you move them!" She went back into the house and began to assemble some herbs and powders. Yuyuelkik and two others carefully carried Diego into the dark, warm interior and placed him on a blanket. Quaninch walked in under his own power, but he was very unsteady on his feet. He sat down heavily next to his friend. "Boil some water," Moki instructed the men, and they went outside to obey her instructions.

Other women joined them, and they undressed the two boys and carefully cleaned their wounds. Moki was a skilled healer, and she determined at a glance that Quaninch was not in any danger. She told her helpers to put ointment on his cuts and bandage him while she turned her attention to her grandson.

She kept her face unexpressive, though in her heart she despaired of Nakai's recovery. The gash on his temple was not serious, it could be cleaned and treated with her herbal preparations. But the injury to his chest was something else. Despite Quaninch's efforts to clean it off, sand and gunpowder residue were visible within the two-inch-deep hole. Diego winced and cried out at her first gentle touch. How could he stand the agony of cleaning out this devastating wound?

She rummaged through her supplies and located a small brown vial. She had purchased it from an apothecary on one of her visits to Los Angeles. The druggist had called it laudanum, and it had the power to induce sleep and ease pain. She placed a few drops in a cup, added some of the hot water and blew on it until it was cool enough to drink. Then she brought it to Diego's lips, and he sipped at it.

"Ugh!" he said, trying to spit it out.

"No!" Moki admonished. "I know it is bitter, but you must take it. It is powerful medicine." He meekly drank the rest of the mixture, though he had to fight off a gagging reflex.

She placed her grandson's head in her lap and gently stroked his hair as he drifted off into a deep sleep. Then she laid him on his side and exposed the gaping wound. One of the other women sat next to her, and they began to slowly, tenderly remove the small pieces of debris from the injured area. Diego slept fitfully, occasionally whimpering in pain. They worked first on the surface of the skin, but as they got nearer to the opening, he cried out more often, even muttering, "Stop! Ow, that hurts!" Then Moki would give him another sip of the laudanum and he would sink deeper into sleep.

The cleaning process went on through the night, with other women coming in to take a turn at the exacting task, though Moki stayed at his side the entire time. By the time sky lightened, they had done all that they could. Moki knew that there was still dirt in the wound, and she feared that it would fester, but all she could do was to apply her healing herbs and place a bandage over the injured flesh.

"It is in Mukat's hands now," she sighed.

Quaninch, who had slept through most of the long night, heard her and asked, "Who?"

"Mukat," she answered. "That is the name we give to the spirit that rules over us in this world."

"My people call him Thuwipu Unipugant," he said.

"There are many names, my son, but the Spirit is the same. He is the one who made us, and we look to him to deliver us from all the evils that these times bring us."

"They taught us at the mission that there was only one true God and that our people's gods were demons."

Moki smiled ruefully. "I know that is their teaching. I know they also call us savages and devil-worshipers. For that reason, I hesitated to take Nakai to the padre. But I worried that he would be killed by the Luiseno or captured by Mexican slavers, and I knew that our little village was no longer strong enough to protect him. So I took him to the mission and I prayed that he would always remember that his people are not savages and that the gods we pray to are not demons."

Quaninch pondered this for a moment and then asked, "Moki... may I call you Grandmother?"

Moki's smile broadened and she said, "Of course, my son. I can see that you are a true friend to Nakai and so I am happy to have you as a grandson also."

Talking to this wise, kind woman seemed to ease Quaninch's pain and lighten his heart. "Tell me then, Grandmother, which is the true God?"

"I cannot answer that for you, Quaninch, but I tell you what I have come to believe. There is only one God, but he has many names and attributes. The Iviatim call him Mukat; your people call him... how do you say his name?"

"Thuwipu Unipugant."

"Yes, Thuwipu Unipugant. I must remember that name. The Mexicans call him Dios; the Americanos simply call him God. And all the tribes have their own names for the Great Spirit, but it seems to me that any god big enough to create the earth and all that lives on it is big enough to have many names, and yet he is one God. Now you must rest, Quaninch, my new grandson. You will heal quickly, I know. As for Nakai," she cast a worried glance at her sleeping grandson, "only time will tell if he survives this terrible injury."

When Quaninch next awoke, the sun was high in the sky. He was stiff and sore and very hungry. Diego still slept beside him; his face tensed as if in pain. No one else was in the room, so Quaninch gingerly tried to stand. He made it to his feet with some pain and difficulty, but he felt so lightheaded that he sat right back down. He would have to wait until someone checked on them before he could get something to ease his hunger and thirst.

He lay there thinking, wondering what would befall him now. He was confident that he would recover from his injuries, but what then? His fiddle, his beloved king's head fiddle, was gone. He had left it with his few belongings at the army headquarters. Some American soldier had surely picked it up and sold it, or maybe thoughtlessly destroyed it. The army he had served was defeated and probably disbanded; his only friend was grievously wounded. The town he had lived in was in enemy hands. There didn't seem to be any hope for his future. He should have gone to sea with Jack, he thought. He might be lying on a beach in the Sandwich Islands at this moment.

His gloomy reverie was interrupted when Moki entered. "Quaninch," she said, "You are awake, I see."

"And I'm hungry, Grandmother."

Moki laughed. "That is a very good sign," she said, as she handed him two mesquite cakes and a small bit of rabbit meat. "Eat slowly," she cautioned and handing him a cup of water she said, "And drink even more slowly."

She turned her attention to the still-sleeping Nakai. Quaninch asked through a mouthful of cake, "How is he this morning?"

Moki tenderly lifted the dressing from Diego's wound and inspected it. "I am praying that our medicine will be powerful and that Nakai has great strength for recovery. Prayers are all we have now." She applied more herbs and covered the wound with a clean bandage.

Quaninch finished his food and water and then, feeling a great weariness come over him, he fell back asleep. When he next awoke, it was night again, and Diego was groaning and muttering. "No, Padre, I didn't take it. Oh, Father Julio, please don't hit me. I don't know, I promise, I don't know where he is." Moki cradled his head in her lap and gently wiped perspiration from Diego's feverish face.

"How is Nakai, Grandmother?" he asked.

She raised her eyes to look at Quaninch with a sad, knowing expression. "He is in the fever," she said. "If he survives until it breaks, he will live. But his face is hot, and his wound is very angry." She shook her head. "I fear he will not make it."

Quaninch was chilled at Moki's solemn words. He knew she was an experienced healer and if she despaired of Diego's life, it was because she knew the seriousness of his wound. "Is there anything I can do?" he asked plaintively.

A wan smile crossed Moki's lips. "You must heal from your own injuries, my grandson. The best thing you can do now is to rest, eat, drink, and grow strong. And pray that Nakai's life will be spared."

Quaninch soon slipped back into sleep, and when the morning light filled the room, he awoke to find Moki in the same position she had been in when they spoke during the night.

"Grandmother," he sleepily asked, "Haven't you slept all night?"

She looked at him with sorrowful eyes and softly shook her head. Quaninch looked at his friend, his head still in Moki's lap. His face was no longer flushed, though he was still covered in sweat. His skin was pale and drawn, his eyes clenched tight. Quaninch felt a sharp constriction in his belly as fear pulsed through him. "Is he... dying?"

Moki burst into tears, unable to speak. Quaninch had his answer. Nakai did not live out the day. He breathed his last without ever regaining consciousness.

In the old days, the Cahuilla – Iviatim in their own tongue – cremated their dead, but the Spanish priests who visited them hundreds of years before had persuaded them that they should bury them instead. And so, after a night of singing the traditional funeral songs, the body of Nakai was placed in a simple coffin and buried a short distance from the village.

Quaninch didn't know the funeral songs, and Moki told him he must not rise from his bed to accompany his friend to the burial grounds. "You can mourn for him when you regain your health," she told him. "For now, the best thing you can do for Nakai is to get better and to take his place as my grandson." Not for the first time in his young life, Quaninch wept bitter tears of despair and loss.

Nakai's death cast a pall over the village, but his was not the only death they had mourned lately; the Luiseno had raided them often, usually stealing horses and food, but sometimes killing or capturing one of the Iviatim. As the war had raged between the Californios and Americanos, the Luiseno had allied themselves with the Americans and, using the new weapons their allies provided, had attacked Mexican troops as well as Cahuillas and their close allies, the Gabrielinos.

The few young men in the village had to devote themselves to defending their people from these powerful enemies, and as Quaninch quickly regained his strength and health, he gladly joined with Yuyuelkik and the others in training, drilling, and manning the lookout posts. Quaninch was angry with the Americans for killing his friend, but he also blamed the Luiseno, since it was their ambush of General Pico's troops that made Diego so eager to join in the fighting.

The village of Temal Wakhish was a poor remnant of what it had been in ages past. The constant warfare had taken a great toll of warriors, and many others had been captured by slavers or had left to seek opportunity in the neighboring missions. Life there was hard, with the women endlessly searching the desert for acorns and nuts and grinding them into flour, while the men had to leave their outposts to hunt rabbits and other small game. There were deer in the region but stalking them took the men too far away from the village. These were perilous times, and the men couldn't take the chance of leaving their homes and families undefended.

Quaninch was now sixteen years old. He was strong and graceful, and the crises of his life had hardened his body and mind. Yuyuelkik was happily surprised at how quickly this new arrival learned to handle a musket, a knife, and a bow. As the winter wore on, the people of Temal Wakhish rapidly came to rely on his strength and sharp eyes to help protect them. And Quaninch in turn relished his role as a warrior and guardian of the Iviatim.

He missed his fiddle terribly. The Iviatim had music, of course; they sang "bird songs," accompanied by flutes, whistles, and rattles made of turtle shells, or gourds. This hardly filled the void left by the loss of his beloved instrument. As time went by, he also became restless at the harsh and primitive living conditions. Though Quaninch had never known luxury in his life, he wasn't used to the limited diet and constricted life of the village. He longed for the pleasure of playing his fiddle before excited crowds who threw coins and applauded him. Nevertheless, he was determined to remain with his newly adopted grandmother and take the place of his missing comrade Nakai.

Winter turned to spring, with only the lengthening days to mark the change of seasons. The weather remained warm and dry, as it did throughout the year. Late one night near the spring equinox, Quaninch was shaken awake by Yuyuelkik. "Get up!" he whispered harshly. "There are people moving in the desert. I think it's a raid by the Luiseno."

Quaninch shook himself awake and glanced around the kish and saw Moki fast asleep on her pile of blankets. He quietly rose and dressed, picked up his musket and long knife, and followed Yuyuelkik to the hill outside the village where they maintained their lookout. Quaninch peered through the moonless darkness, at first seeing nothing. Then Yuyuelkik pointed and whispered "There. In that gully."

Quaninch strained his eyes to see if there was any movement there, and shortly he caught a glimpse of a man furtively creeping in the dry watercourse. "I see one," he whispered.

"Yes, and there are others," Yuyuelkik replied. The other men of the village also been awakened, and they were arriving one by one on the hillside.

"Do you have any idea how many of them there are?" Quaninch asked.

"I have counted only three," Yuyuelkik whispered back, "but the Luiseno usually don't dare to attack us unless they have greater numbers. I think we should turn the tables on them and attack them while they gather in the arroyo."

Quaninch quickly took in the lay of the land and saw that there was no good place to defend against an attack from the gully. "Yes, you're right," he said.

Yuyuelkik scampered from man to man, whispering a hasty battle plan to each. Next to Yuyuelkik and Quaninch, the best warrior was Yukaipat, a young man of great strength, if not possessed of the strongest mind. He moved close to Quaninch and at a silent gesture from Yuyuelkik, they began to creep forward into the darkness.

In all, the Iviatim could muster only fourteen fighters, each armed with a musket and a sharp knife. They moved over the stony ground as softly as a spring breeze, communicating only with gestures visible by starlight.

As they neared the lip of the arroyo, confident that they had turned the tables on their enemies and achieved total surprise, the night was rent by a piercing war scream and Luiseno warriors began to leap up from the steep sides of the gully. Musket fire erupted and after each man had fired his weapon, he ran toward his enemy with drawn knife in hand, since there was no time to reload. Men on both sides dropped from the initial fusillade and war yells mingled with screams of pain as the melee turned into a series of hand-to-hand combats.

Yukaipat dropped heavily at the first exchange of gunfire. Quaninch had no time to see what had befallen his comrade as he fired off his musket and then ran with a savage whoop toward his enemies. He collided with a Luiseno warrior and the two fell to the ground in mortal struggle. All the world narrowed to the face of the man he fought with.

"Morir, cabrón," shouted the Luiseno as he thrust his long knife toward Quaninch's face. Quaninch caught the wrist and held it fast while he brought his knee up hard into his enemy's crotch. The man screamed and Quaninch pushed him over onto his back. He raised his knife high to plunge it into the writhing body beneath him. He smelled the scent of terror and could see by the flickering starlight the dreadful fear on his face. Then he rammed the knife home, directly into the heaving chest. The man's death scream was drowned in the outflow of blood that gushed from his mouth. His body tensed and jerked and then collapsed into the languor of death.

Quaninch, gasping for breath, rose and looked around him. Yuyuelkik was struggling with an enemy warrior just a few feet away. He moved to help his friend when abruptly the night exploded into violet light, and he felt his legs give way underneath him. As he collapsed on the ground, he maintained enough consciousness to quickly roll to his left, avoiding a death blow from the rock-wielding fighter who had slammed a large stone into the back of Quaninch's head.

He saw the grinning face of his opponent preparing to bring his knife down on Quaninch with his full force. Then a musket roared in his ears and his attacker's grin changed to a look of horrified surprise. He clutched at the gaping hole that had opened up just below his chin and crumpled to the ground.

He recognized Yukaipat standing near him, a grim smile on his face. His shirt was covered in blood pouring from a vicious wound in his brawny chest and in his hands was a smoking musket. Yukaipat lurched toward the spot where Yuyuelkik was struggling with his attacker. He turned his weapon around and savagely clubbed the Luiseno warrior's head with the butt of the musket, killing him instantly. Yuyuelkik pushed the dead man off his body and shakily stood up. For a moment the three of them stood looking at each other in the bewilderment of battle, stunned by their close brushes with death.

Yukaipat looked from Quaninch to Yuyuelkik with a dignified, sorrowful expression. Then his knees buckled, and he collapsed on the ground.

Around them, the sounds of battle had faded into the scrambling of the Luiseno warriors hurrying back into the arroyo and the groans of the wounded. The first traces of dawn revealed six bodies lying on the ground near them. The man Quaninch had stabbed, the two that Yukaipat had killed, two Luiseno who had been shot in the first volley, and the big Iviatim warrior who had staved off his own death long enough to save his two friends.

The village had awakened with the first volley of musket fire. Now they crept out to survey the results of the battle. They were saved, but at the cost of one more irreplaceable fighter. They took Yukaipat's body to be prepared for the funeral rites and burial. That afternoon, the three dead Luisano warriors were cremated on the field of battle. Two other Iviatim fighters were wounded by musket balls, but the healing powers of Moki would return them to health soon enough.

They sang the funeral chants that night for Yukaipat and took him to the burial ground the next morning. The village mourned his loss and feared the next revenge attack that would surely come their way.

Moki and Quaninch sat outside their kish in silence that afternoon, each lost in thought. Finally, Moki broke the quiet. "My grandson," she began, "we can no longer stay here in Temal Wakhish. We have dwindled in these evil days and our warriors cannot protect us forever. We must take our people and move away, south, to join the rest of our tribe in safety."

Quaninch looked at her quizzically. "As you say, Grandmother," he murmured.

She shook her head at him. "But not you, Quaninch. You have a different destiny than the Iviatim."

"No, Grandmother," Quaninch instinctively began, but she cut his words short.

"You must not argue with me," she said, wagging her forefinger at him. "You have tried to take Nakai's place, and you have been a very good grandson to me." She looked around the village. "And you have defended the village at the risk of your own life. We will always be grateful to you for that. But you have a different fate, my grandson. I cannot see it clearly, but I know that you will walk another path, far away from the Iviatim, and from the Nuwuvi, too."

Closing her eyes, she reached out and touched his temples. "You are a man of two peoples," she said as if in a trance. "You will go from here to learn of your other people, your father's people. You have lost your music, and you will take it up again. You must, for it is deep within your soul."

They sat in silence, frozen in that pose for some time. Then Moki took her hands away from his face and said, "We will gather our things and go to the south as soon as we can. You must go back to life that beckons you." She saw Quaninch's eyes filling with tears and continued, "We will always live in your heart, and your name will be recited in our songs for as long as the Iviatim exist and, in spite of these troubles we now face, I believe that will still be a very long time to come."

She reached into a leather bag, pulled out three small gold coins, and placed them in Quaninch's hands. "No, Grandmother!" he exclaimed. "You mustn't give me your money. You'll need it."

"I have saved these coins for many years," she softly said, "for just this purpose. I am going to be with my people. My brothers and sisters will take care of me. I have no need for these coins. But you are going to the world of the white men, a world where money is very important. You must listen to me in this."

Quaninch reluctantly took the coins and slipped them into his pocket. "Thank you, Grandmother," he said, throwing his arms around her. "I will try to use them in ways that would make you proud of me."

It took only two days for the people to pack their goods and prepare for the journey to their cousins in the south. Quaninch stood watching as they slowly wended off through the desert. Then, with a mixture of great sorrow and excitement, he turned his face to the west and began his journey back to the world of the white men.

CHAPTER THIRTEEN

The village of Los Angeles had changed since Quaninch had seen it last. The sleepy Mexican mission town was in the process of becoming American. There were soldiers in the streets and the same flag Quaninch had sailed under on the *Abigail* floated above the town hall. There also seemed to be more Americans in the streets— sailors, soldiers, and civilians.

Quaninch's first task was to find some means of supporting himself, and the first thing he thought of was to resume his fiddle playing on street corners for whatever coins he could gather. But of course, he had no fiddle. That obstacle would have to be overcome before he could do anything else.

He went straightaway to the violin shop of Gabriel Ortez. The world had turned upside down since the time when he feared that Ortiz would report him to Father Julio and send him back into slavery. The man held no terrors for him now, and if he intended to get a violin to play, he must find one at Gabriel's shop.

He entered the dark, musty shop where the walls hung full of violins of all kinds. Quaninch knew he couldn't afford a very good one, but he fingered the coins Moki had given him and figured he could buy a serviceable instrument with one of them.

Gabriel Ortiz had heard the shop bell ring and he brusquely came into the front room. He stopped short when he saw that it was Quaninch, who somehow looked older and very much more dangerous than he had the previous summer when he was a runaway slave. "You!" he said. "What do you want here?"

"Why do people usually come into your store, Senor Ortez? To buy a violin, I would suppose. At any rate, that is why I have come. What do you have to show me?"

The shopkeeper looked curiously at Quaninch. "Of course, it takes money, Jaime," he said nervously. "Do you have any?"

"I have. Let's get on with it, then. May I look over your violins?"

Before Gabriel could answer, Quaninch began to look over the instruments hanging on the walls. He was looking for one that would play well but not be too expensive. He gave each one a quick glance and then suddenly his eyes opened wide, and he gasped in surprise.

"My fiddle!" he shouted as he laid eyes upon the ornate headstock with the king's head carved into it. He whirled on Ortez. "How did you get it?" he demanded.

Gabriel stepped back toward the doorway. "Your fiddle?" he chirped in a suddenly high voice. "I think not, Jaime. I bought that violin from an American soldier. I have a copy of the bill of sale in my records."

"But it's mine. You know it is. It was my father's, and he gave it to me!"

"I don't know anything about the history of this instrument," he responded icily. "But I do know that it is mine, legally purchased from its former owner. I also know that you once stole this very violin from the mission and I warn you, it would be very dangerous to try the same trick with me!"

"How much do you want for it?" Quaninch asked sullenly.

Gabriel stroked his neatly trimmed beard and said, "I could probably get more, but since you claim to have an attachment to the instrument, I would sell it to you for, say… twenty dollars."

The coins in his pocket didn't amount to half of that. "I can't pay that," he said angrily.

"Well, perhaps we could find a suitable violin that you could afford," Ortez said.

He picked several violins from the wall and let Quaninch examine them. He sighted down the neck, peered inside the f-holes, plucked the strings. "Do you have a bow also?" he asked dryly.

The merchant procured one and Quaninch played a tune on each of the fiddles. He selected one that he felt was the best of the bunch and haggled with Gabriel until they arrived at a price he could afford.

He took his new purchase out of the store, but as he left, he vowed silently that he would return and buy his father's fiddle back. He had to earn enough money before anyone else beat him to it.

He knew he needed to get a room in town. Hopefully it was very cheap one. He made his way to the part of town where his friend Jack had roomed at Bella's Saloon. He gave one of his precious coins to the seedy bartender at Bella's for a week's stay. The room was much like the one Jack had rented, shabby and dark, but an hour's cleaning made it habitable, and at least he had a roof over his head.

He hadn't touched a fiddle since the terrible day of the Battle of San Gabriel, the fight that took his friend's life and sent him off to live with the Cauhilla people in the desert, so his fingers were a little stiff. He found a quiet spot just outside the town and spent the afternoon practicing. After a few hours, though, his fingers were a little sore and his right hand felt crampy. He was confident that he could play well enough to garner some tips.

The spring evening was mild when Quaninch strolled through the area of bars and burdels where he and Jack had played the previous summer. The crowds weren't nearly as big and boisterous as they had been then, when the American soldiers had been greeted as liberators and the Californios caroused late into the night to celebrate. Still, there were people on the streets, and Quaninch found a suitable spot close to the milling crowds and began to play. He got a few glances, mostly friendly, and a few meager contributions in his bowl, but the mood of the people on the streets was somewhat suppressed. The best reactions he got were from American soldiers and sailors out to blow off steam and spend their money.

The streets emptied before midnight, and Quaninch looked forlornly at the pittance he had collected for his night's work. "At this rate, I'll be an old man with gnarled fingers before I can buy back my fiddle," he thought.

Waking the next morning to the dingy reality of his surroundings, he was gripped by despair. He was lonely and depressed. Maybe Moki had been wrong, maybe this was not the world for him. Perhaps he should return to the desert and find the Cauhilla to share their ancient way of life. But first, he wanted to recover his father's fiddle. If he could only buy that back, he could take it to Moki's village and live happily there.

He could think of no other way to make the money he needed than to play in the street though, and so it was that he returned that night to try again. His luck took a turn for the better. The *USS Cyane* was in port and her crew had shore leave. They were an ebullient crew, still celebrating their role in the recent American victories at San Diego and in the Gulf of California. Quaninch noticed that the Californios didn't mingle with the American sailors. Perhaps they felt that they were being dispossessed of the land their ancestors had inhabited for two centuries, and the Americanos were the new heirs.

In any event, the sailors liked Quaninch's playing, and they tipped him generously and insisted he drink with them. He had rarely tried strong drink, but there was no refusing the importunities of the happy seamen. "Drink it up, fiddler boy," they shouted as Quaninch quickly swallowed a shot of rum. They howled with laughter when he coughed and spat, his face turning crimson.

He played some of the current favorites, "Old Dan Tucker," "Walk Along John," and "The Boatman's Dance." When he tried out his newest piece, "Columbia, the Gem of the Ocean," the sailors went mad with joy, clapping him on the back and filling his bowl with coins, and refilling his glass with rum.

Quaninch was quite unsteady when he arrived at his room late that night and fell into bed with the room spinning uncontrollably. He awoke late the next morning, eyes encrusted and head pounding. The taste in his mouth was much worse than any nasty thing he had ever eaten in the desert and his stomach was complaining loudly of the abuse it had endured the night before. His thirst couldn't be quenched no matter how much water he drank.

The small pile of bright coins on his table did wonders to cheer him, though. Perhaps he had been too easily discouraged on that first night, this might just work out well after all. He vowed to avoid drinking so much in the future, though. The happiness it brought was no match for the misery of the morning after.

His luck was inconsistent as he continued to play for passers-by in the streets. By far his best audiences were American sailors and soldiers. They had money to spend and were in a celebratory mood, while the Californios sullenly ceded the night to their conquerors.

Quaninch anticipated that Saturday night would be a good one, and he wasn't disappointed. Noisy partiers swayed through the streets, one hand clutching a bottle and the other wrapped around a pretty puta. The street stayed alive very late, and by the time Quaninch returned to Bella's, he was exhausted and just a little drunk. He hadn't been able to completely avoid the drinks he was offered, but he did manage to slow down the pace of the drinking.

The next morning, for the first time in months, he thought about church. He didn't know if there was a priest in town or if so, when and where Mass was being said, but he wished he could go. He would ask around and maybe by the next Sunday he could go to confession and receive Holy Communion. Everything was closed on Sundays, so he spent the day resting up from the wild Saturday night. He counted the money he had earned that week and was pleasantly surprised. He had enough to pay for another week at Bella's and was well on the way to being able to reclaim his precious fiddle.

He sat at a table on Bella's porch, enjoying the warm, sunny morning and sipping strong black coffee when he saw a familiar form taking a seat at a nearby table. "Jack!" he shouted in amazement. "Jack! I thought you would be in China by now!"

The ginger-haired youth turned a bleary eye to Quaninch and then jolted upright when he recognized his old friend. "Jaime!" he shouted back. "How is it possible? I heard you were dead, killed in the war!"

The two young men embraced joyously and then Jack took Quaninch by the shoulders and stared intently at his friend's face. He gently traced the small scars that wandered down the left side of his chin and neck, shaking his head slowly. "I can see that you've got a tale to tell. Sit down and let's hear it."

Quaninch's smile turned rueful. "Yes, Jack, I've had a few things happen to me since we last met. But before I begin, you must tell me how it is that you're here in Los Angeles and not sailing in the Indies."

Laughing, Jack said, "There's not much to tell. Right after you left the ship, with the war breaking out and all, Captain Truxhall offered the services of old *Abigail* to the army. They needed plenty of boats to ferry men and supplies from Yerba Buena, San Francisco they're calling it now, to Monterrey and San Diego, and here, to Los Angeles. So all this time, we've just been skimming the coast, south to north and back again. We heard you'd joined the Mexican army and that you'd been killed at San Gabriel. Of course, I felt terrible about that, but I must admit, we all joined in the celebration of that victory. Why, it marked the end of the war and put Los Angeles right smack in the good old USA." He saw that his words had troubled his friend and he said, "So that's it, all in all. It's your turn to tell a story, make it a good one!"

Quaninch began by telling of his reunion with Diego and how they came to be attached to the headquarters of Commandante Pico. When he got to the part where Diego died of his wounds, he had to stop, his eyes brimming with tears. Jack placed his hand on his friend's shoulder and silently commiserated with him.

As he finished his story with his arrival in Los Angeles and the discovery of his fiddle, Jack smiled broadly. "Why, listen here Jaime. I've got plenty of money. We've been getting paid regularly, and I don't spend all that much. I'll give you what you need to go get that fiddle, then we can take up where we left off, banjo and fiddle. At least until I ship off for the Far East... which actually should be pretty soon now, since the war is over, and our ferrying days are finished."

They both seemed to run out of things to say at that point until Jack brightened. "Say," he smiled, "why don't you ship with us when we go. You said your grandmother told you that you'd find your father's people. Well, that's where we'll be headed, after a year's cruise across the Pacific and around the Cape to London. That's not far from Scotland, your father's native land."

Quaninch mulled this offer over and was just ready to politely decline when he realized that he had no reason to stay in California. He had almost been ready to return to the Cauhilla and their hardscrabble way of life in the desert. But here was a chance, an opportunity, not only to see the world, but to go to the land of his father's people, Scotland. How many times his father had told him of the misty glens and stark highlands of his native land? And how many fiddle tunes from Scotland had he learned at his da's knee?

"All right," he said. "I'll do it, if Captain Truxhall will have me back."

Jack grinned and slapped Quaninch heartily on the back. "Why Truxhall has remarked every day since you left how much he misses that fiddle, and how tired he is of hearing my poor old banjo all by itself. The old man'll be ashore today, it's Sunday – and we'd best not disturb him in a delicate situation. But tomorrow we'll go out to the ship and get you signed up on the *Abigail* again. After we pry your fiddle loose from that old miser, that is. Now let's celebrate! I'll get the banjo and you fire up that fiddle and we'll make some noise!"

The next morning, Jack asked Quaninch how much he had saved toward the purchase of his fiddle. "I have about fifteen dollars, total," he replied, "but I don't want to spend every last cent, I need something to live on, too. And even if I were willing to part with all of it, it's not what Ortez is asking."

"Give me ten," Jack said breezily.

"But he wants twenty. I can't let you pay half the price."

Jack smiled confidently. "Just give me the money and we'll see what we can do."

Quaninch reluctantly handed over several of his small cache of coins and Jack headed off to the violin shop of Gabriel Ortez.

Gabriel was in the store when Jack casually walked in, looking with displeasure at the fiddles hanging on the wall.

"Good morning, sir," Ortez called to him. "How may I assist you today?"

Jack frowned. "Is this all the stock you have? Don't you have any banjos in this place?"

"Banjos? Oh, no sir, I deal only in good quality instruments here, such as may be used in an orchestra or string ensemble."

"And I understand that you have the only instrument shop in the town. Is that right?"

Ortez nodded deferentially and replied, "Yes sir, that is true. I'm sorry to say that this banjo you speak of is not known in California. I myself have heard of it only as a novelty in the American minstrel shows, an instrument primarily played by African slaves, I believe."

"Yes, but don't forget, California is part of America now, and I think you'll find that Americans like the banjo!"

Gabriel smiled wanly and said, "Be that as it may, sir, I have no banjos in stock, and I don't know where one might be obtained anywhere in the province."

"Anywhere in the territory, don't you mean?"

"As you say," Ortez nodded and turned to the paperwork in front of him. Jack remained in the store and continued to peer at different violins. When he saw the King's head, he spoke up. "Say, here's something a bit different, isn't it?"

Ortez looked up and, seeing the fiddle that attracted Jack's interest, said, "Yes, it's a unique piece. I got it from a soldier after the recent battles. I don't know anything of its origins, but it does play well enough, though the carving on the headstock is quite garish."

"Can you take it down for me?" Jack asked. The proprietor obliged and Jack held the fiddle in his hands, inspecting it closely. "Myself, I sort of fancy the carving. How much?"

Ortez had taken stock of his potential customer and, taking him as a seaman who might have some coins in his pockets, pronounced, "I have priced it at twenty, but I could bargain a bit for it. Are you interested?"

"Well, I don't rightly play the fiddle, I was hoping to get a banjo because I hear that it's an easy instrument to learn. Still and all, this fiddle is an interesting piece. I can't pay twenty, I only brought ten with me. You couldn't come down that low could you?"

"I'm afraid that's out of the question. I have to make something on it, after all. Perhaps we could agree on… say, fifteen dollars."

Jack stroked his chin and made a show of pondering the offer. Then he reached in his pockets and took out thirteen dollars. He counted it in his palm and said, "This is all I have along, and I'm shipping out this afternoon. I don't have time to go back to the ship to get any more. It's thirteen or no sale," and he started to slip the coins back into his pockets.

Ortez thought quickly. He had only paid the soldier five dollars for the thing, and, except for the thieving slave Quaninch, he hadn't found anyone interested in the odd piece. Perhaps he should take this deal, at least he wouldn't have to worry that Quaninch would try to steal it from him. "It's a hard bargain, but all right, it's yours for thirteen."

Jack paid him the coins, waited for a bill of sale, and hurried off to find his friend. Quaninch was still sitting on the patio of Bella's softly playing the violin he had purchased from Ortez the previous day. "I don't think you're ever going to make that old piece of furniture sound worth a peso," Jack called. "Why don't you try playing a real fiddle?" and he lifted the king's head triumphantly.

Quaninch was speechless. He gaped at the apparition and finally was able to say, "Jack! What? How in the world?" Then he stopped short. "Did you put up ten dollars of your own money? I told you…"

"Only three!" Jack laughed, "And you can pay me that if you want to. Here, it's yours once more."

Quaninch lovingly cradled his lost treasure. "Three times now, I believed that I would never see this again. I can only think that something… or someone wants me to have it. And I expect to keep it the rest of my days. I can't thank you enough, Jack. Now, get your banjo and let's play!"

"We can play a few tunes, enough to try it out and make sure it still works, but we must be on our way to the ship to get you signed on."

The fiddle had lost none of its musical prowess, and after they played a few favorites, they gathered their possessions and made their way to the port of San Pedro, where the brigantine *Abigail* was moored. "Ahoy, Warren," Jack shouted to the sailor who stood by the launch tied to the pier. "Is the old man aboard?"

"Aye," he answered. "He arrived very early this morning, not in the best of humor, I perceived. He appeared to have somewhat of a headache."

Jack smiled and nodded. "I expected as much. Can you take us out there?"

Warren glanced at Jack's companion. "Why, Jaime!" he exclaimed. "Is it really you? We heard you was dead."

"I came pretty near it, Warren, but as you see, I outfoxed the old grim one this time."

"Are you shipping out with us? We surely missed you and your fiddlin'. All we've heard for months is this one's infernal banjo."

"If the Cap'n will have me," Quaninch laughed. "And you shouldn't be so hard on Jack's playing. He's gotten a good deal better since the last time I saw him."

The two piled into the boat and with the three of them pulling at the oars arrived at the ship in no time. Clambering aboard, they saluted the ensign and asked the watch where the captain could be found.

"In his quarters," the sailor answered, "But I advise you to knock softly."

Jack heeded this advice and gently tapped on the captain's door. Receiving no answer, he tried again a bit more forcefully. This provoked a response. "What is it? " Came an angry shout from within. "I left orders that I was not to be disturbed!"

"It's Jack, sir. I brought someone I think you'll want to see."

The boys heard muffled thumps from inside the cabin and then the door opened abruptly. The angry look faded into one of pleasant surprise when he saw that Quaninch was standing in front of him.

"By the Almighty," he said in wonder. "We heard…"

"Yes, sir, that I was dead. But I'm not, as you see, and I would be very grateful if you will see your way to signing me on."

Truxhall pretended to think about it for a moment before saying, "We hated to see you go the first time. I wonder if you don't wish you had stayed aboard then."

Quaninch nodded and Truxhall continued. "And we are glad to have you back, you and your fiddle," he said, casting a rueful look at Jack. "Come on in and sign your papers. We're weighing anchor tomorrow morning bound for the Sandwich Islands at last."

When Quaninch took the pen in hand, he paused and then announced, "Since I'm now an American, and sailing on an American ship, I'll no longer be Jaime." Nor Quaninch, he thought. And he signed the ship's log with his new name, James Kennedy.

CHAPTER FOURTEEN

James quickly recovered his sea legs and the skills he had learned on his voyage along California's coast. After a few days at sea, his memories of being wounded at San Gabriel, of losing his friend Nakai, and of the battle with the Luiseno seemed to become dream-like episodes from a different life.

Instead, his days were now full of the endless chores of the sailor, swabbing, painting, repairing rigging, furling, and reefing sails, and a hundred other jobs. Like all ships, the *Abigail* was an extension of the captain's personality. Captain Truxhall was a man who brooked no incompetency or malingering and who insisted upon hard work well done. Yet he was no tyrant, he justly compensated the men for their labors with free time, good food, and music in the evenings. He maintained a gruff exterior, but his men felt affection for him that had been earned by his consistent reasonableness and fairness.

They were at sea, beyond the sight of any land, for over three weeks. Shortly after the new year of 1848 arrived, they caught sight of the fabled Sandwich Islands, increasingly being known as Hawaii, after the name of the largest island in the chain. The pleasant climate and beautiful views of the mountainous shoreline were a welcome relief from the unchanging prospect of endless grey Pacific waves they had seen ever since their departure from California.

"Jamey, you are going to love this place," Jack sighed as the two friends leaned on the railing overlooking the harbor at Honolulu. King Kamehameha III had just moved his capital from Lahaina to this bustling, growing city, and the harbor was filled with ships, mostly whalers from New England, though there were also merchant vessels from all over the world.

"It's a very musical place, too," Jack said dreamily. "And, of course, the girls... they're not like the girls back home."

James knew very little about girls, next to nothing, really. He had grown up in the all-male mission and he hadn't had much chance to meet women in the year and a half since he had run away from Father Julio. The streets of Los Angeles had been full of girls, many of them putas, or prostitutes. James had been too busy playing the fiddle for tips to think much of them, and to tell the truth, he was more than a little afraid of the pretty, painted-up women who laughingly clung to the arms of sailors and soldiers.

"How do you mean, Jack? What's so different about them?"

Jack blushed a bit and cleared his throat uncomfortably. "Well, they're friendlier, you might say. They aren't so stand-offish around men as the girls back home are."

This made no sense to James. None of the women he had seen in Los Angeles had seemed to avoid contact with men, just the opposite. "I don't understand what you mean, Jack," James said plaintively.

"Confound it, Jim, it's a hard thing to explain. Now, back home in Massachusetts, the girls are shy. They cover up in layers of clothes, big hoop skirts and shawls, and they only talk to a fellow if they've been properly introduced. And they won't give a man a kiss until he proposes marriage to them!"

He looked hopefully at James but saw only a blank and confused expression.

Jack took a big breath and tried another approach. "I know you've never been to Massachusetts, of course. And in Los Angles, things are a bit different. You've seen all the girls in the saloons and on the street, haven't you? A lot of them are... are ladies of the town, you might say. They'll lie with a man for money."

James was trying his best to follow his friend's drift. "And is that like the girls here?" he asked.

"No, not exactly. I mean, there are them as want gifts and money for their favors, but they look at things a whole different way than we do. For one thing, they don't wear much in the way of clothes. In fact, you'll see some of them bare naked, right out in the town!"

This thought was highly disturbing, though strangely appealing, to James. "I guess I'll just have to see when we get ashore," he said. "And what did you say about the music?"

"They're wonderful singers and dancers. The instruments they play are mostly local – drums and flutes and such, but they're quick to pick up the music that has come here with the sailors and merchants. You'll hear Hawaiians strumming on guitars that the vaqueros brought over from Mexico, and I've even heard a fiddle or two. I tell you when I was here last, they went wild about my banjo, too, even though I had barely learned to play it then."

James continued to stare at the hazy tropical shoreline with majestic mountains rising over the blazing white beaches, wondering what would befall him in these magical isles.

Anchoring in harbor after a lengthy ocean voyage calls for a great deal of work. Although Truxhall demanded that the men keep the ship in good order while at sea, there was still much to be done to prepare for time in port. Clothes were washed and spread on the deck to dry; decks were scrubbed afresh, and ropes were tarred. Sails were mended, and the men were busy with their razors and scissors.

After two busy days fitting the vessel for port, the captain called all the men to assemble on the quarterdeck. "So, men," Truxhall began, "as you are all aware, we are anchored off the beautiful island of Oowhayoo, one of the famous Sandwich Islands. I know a few of you have been here before, and I also know that you have filled the heads of your friends with stories of tropical nights in the arms of the fair island goddesses." This brought forth guffaws and playful shoves among the crew. "And you may be on to something there, after all," he continued, provoking whoops of approval.

"I have no desire to impede your pleasures on our brief," — this word elicited groans —"sojourn on the island. But men, I ask you to harken carefully to my words." The murmur and jostling abruptly ceased as the captain went on. "These are no longer the days of Captain Cook, when the natives had never seen white men and were generous with their food, drink, hospitality... and women. No, the locals you will encounter have made a good living for years now catering to the desires of visiting seamen like yourselves. It's a harsher world than it used to be. You may be lying with a local beauty in the bushes while her compatriot steals all your money and leaves you with a knock on the noggin. You may pay good coins for the favors of a pretty wahine and have a fine time, only to find yourself a few days later scratching your privates raw from the crabs, or worse, pissing fire and dripping pus!"

Truxhall looked over the crew's faces and saw some that he knew had experienced these very maladies. "But I know that none of my words will keep a lusty lad from his fun, so enjoy your liberty ashore and heed my warnings to be careful, stick with a friend or two, leave your valuables on the ship, and be sure to show up when the boat comes back. We'll have no deserters on the *Abigail!* Bos'n, set the watch, and for the rest, dismissed!"

James and Jack were not in the section whose turn it was to stand watch while the others went ashore, so they hurriedly made preparations for their visit. "What did the captain mean about crabs and pissing fire, Jack?" James asked his companion.

Jack shook his head in awe of his friend's innocence, and ignorance. "You see, some of the ladies ashore have been with so many men that they've picked up some pests. The crabs are a kind of little lice that travel from her private parts to yours and itch ungodly bad. And the other is the clap; I've heard strong men scream and cuss from the pain of peeing once they got the clap."

"But how do you avoid the crabs and the clap?"

Jack chuckled. "Of course, you can just keep your distance from the girls, that's the surest way, if it is no fun. Or what I plan to do is get out in the country where there haven't been so many sailors yet, where the girls are likely to be cleaner. None of the whorehouses in Honolulu for me."

"And the captain said to leave your valuables here. Are you taking your banjo? Should I leave my fiddle on board?"

Jack pondered a moment and then replied, "We've got today, tonight, and tomorrow morning ashore. Even if we find some girls, we'll want to do some other things than just cozy up with them. I tell you, the people here love music. We'll listen to their own kind, but we should play some of our tunes, too."

"But aren't you worried about someone stealing them? The captain said to be very cautious."

Jack looked thoughtful. "Here's what we should do. When one of us finds a little wahine to spend some time with, the other will guard the instruments. We can take turns, kind of. That way, we can safeguard our fiddle and banjo and keep a lookout that no harm will come to us, either."

So, the boys joined the other crew in the boat heading to the shore that morning carrying a change of clothes, a few dollars, and their beloved instruments. The beach where they landed was in the middle of a bustling, polyglot community. They didn't know anything about the shifting forces that were contending over the fate of Hawaii or about the western diseases that had shrunk the native Hawaiian population by half since the days when Captain Cook visited the islands, but they could see at once that there were more outsiders than Hawaiians in the city. Portuguese, Chinese, English, American, French, Mexican, and other nationalities thronged the port area.

The boys immediately saw some of the girls they had been fantasizing about, but they seemed a little bedraggled and bored as they performed a listless hula in front of the saloons and the shacks where they could repair with clients under the baleful gaze of the men who acted as their procurers. The visitors crowded around the dancers in a thick line, waiting their chance to put down a few dollars and disappear into a shanty with one of the dark-haired, bare-breasted women.

"See, Jim," Jack whispered, "This is what I mean. We don't want to stand in line for a few minutes in a dirty shack with one of these poor souls. Let's head for the back country where people will be more natural-like."

In spite of the tawdry setting, James was stunned by the sight of the women, nude to the waist and wearing only a grass skirt, swaying sensuously. "I don't know, Jack," he said thickly, "Maybe we should stay here for a bit."

"Come on, Jimmy, remember what the captain said, you don't want to catch any of them diseases, do you? Out in the country we'll find clean girls who haven't been with a hundred sailor-men."

Jack tugged at his reluctant friend, and they turned away from the beach to walk inland, James casting more than one backward glance at the naked dancers.

They walked through large plantations of sugar cane and open areas with cattle grazing, but they encountered few people. The small villages they came to were sparsely populated and seemed shabby and impoverished. The only people they passed walking on the road were foreigners like themselves, very likely on the same quixotic mission that Jack and James were on, to find the original, unspoiled Hawaii. But they were too late by many years.

They returned to Honolulu disillusioned and depressed. Even their raging interest in the girls of Hawaii had faded, and they turned their attention to their old standby, music. They heard the sounds of the islands everywhere, accompanying the hula dancers, emanating from the saloons along the waterfront, and rising from knots of men sitting in the shade of palm trees along the brilliant sandy beach.

Jack and James found a nice spot a ways away from the crowded saloon district and began to play. Their music caught the ear of several passers-by, and before long, they had acquired a small audience. The sun was sinking in the west and several fires were burning on the sand, surrounded by drummers and dancers. A young Hawaiian man with a guitar shyly approached the boys as they played, and they invited him to join in.

They played several songs, and the young man, who introduced himself as Kalei, strummed along with them on his guitar. Then Kalei asked if he could sing a song. They eagerly agreed and he began to sing an airy melody that spoke of soft sea breezes and rustling palm, though they didn't understand any of the words.

"Your guitar sounds different than others I've heard," James commented after the song was done.

"Yes, and I notice that your chords are more like the ones I play on the banjo. Can I see it?" Jack asked.

Smiling, Kalei handed the instrument to Jack. "It's tuned in an open key," he said. "Maybe it's a little easier to play that way."

Jack was able to use his banjo chords on the guitar, though he couldn't duplicate the clear melody and haunting drone notes that Kalei had played. He returned the guitar and the three continued to play and sing. James found that he could not keep his eyes off a lovely young girl who swayed to the music in the deepening twilight.

Like many of the girls in the area, she wore nothing but a grass skirt, and James found that his interest in women had rekindled.

As Kalei sang another song, James stood and walked over to her. "Hello," he hesitantly said.

"Aloha," she replied with a seductive smile.

"My name is James," he said, gesturing to himself as if she couldn't understand him.

"I speak English, James," she replied condescendingly. "And my name is Hokulani. I was listening to you play your fiddle. You have a very different style from most of the sailors I've heard."

"Yes," he answered, relieved to have something he could talk about. "I learned from my father, who was a Scot, but I also have learned to play many of the songs of my people on the fiddle. That may account for the difference in my music."

She noticed that he couldn't keep from staring at her bare breasts, and with a smile, she said, "Would you like to sit over there under the palm trees?"

Speechless, he nodded his head and swallowed. "Just a moment," he gulped. He walked back to where Jack was lightly accompanying Kalei. "Watch my fiddle for a while," he whispered. Jack looked at him knowingly and nodded.

Hokulani took his arm and they walked down the beach until they found a secluded spot beneath some palms. They sat in soft grass and listened to the surf rolling in and the fading sounds of distant music. "You said you play your people's music," she said as she laid her head on his shoulder. "Who are your people?"

James felt his head spinning, even though he hadn't touched any strong drink. "My people are called Nuwuvi. They live in the desert and the canyon lands of America."

"And how did you come to be on a ship here visiting our islands."

James chuckled. "That's a very long story, I'm afraid."

She snuggled closer to him and said, "I'm in no hurry. Tell me."

He told her how he had been kidnapped as a small boy and raised at the mission, how he had run away from a cruel priest, how he had made his way with his fiddle on to an American ship, and then fought with the Californios' army and was wounded in a battle... and how his best friend had died of his wounds.

"And when I met up with Jack again in Los Angeles, I decided to try the sailor's life," he finished.

At that, Hokulani turned his face toward hers and kissed him deeply. His hands found her breasts and they embraced passionately. They fumbled with his sailor's clothes and awkwardly managed to strip them off, and then they rolled onto the ground with his body on top of hers. She led him inside her and James gasped with an intensity of pleasure he had never experienced. Suddenly he stiffened and lost all awareness of anything but the lovely girl beneath him and the shuddering waves of pleasure that coursed through his body.

As he gradually returned to his senses, he rolled off her and said apologetically, "That happened too quickly, didn't it?"

Hokulani laughed gently and pushed him onto his back, lying close beside him. She ran her soft fingers over his face and on his chest. "Was that your first time?" she asked in wonder.

James's blush was concealed by the tropical night. "Yes, it was. I'm sorry that I..."

She placed her finger on his lips and said, "Don't worry. You were fine. And we've got nothing else to do right now, do we?"

He lay on his back and lost himself in the soft sounds of the night. Hokulani stroked his face and traced invisible lines on his chest. Soon her hand slipped lower, and she found that he was ready again. She rolled over on top of him and began slowly rocking her hips. James wasn't frenetic this time; he relaxed and allowed her to control their lovemaking. Again, the entire world shrank to this one point of a man and woman sharing their bodies.

Later, as the breeze turned cool on their sweaty skin, James dressed, and they slowly walked back to the fire where they had left Jack and Kalei. The music had stopped and most of the people had drifted away. Jack was sitting away from the ebbing fire with his banjo and James's fiddle close at his side. On his other side was a Hawaiian girl nibbling on his ear. When he saw James and Hokulani return, he desperately caught James's eye. "Your turn to keep watch," he hoarsely whispered, and he disappeared into the night with his companion.

James and Hokulani sat close together, wordlessly enjoying the tropical evening. "This would be a lovely place to live," James finally said.

Hokulani nodded against his shoulder and said, "Yes, it has its beauties. But it's not perfect. These missionaries and planters have gotten control of the king, and nothing is as it was in the old days.

They take all the best of everything, leaving the scraps to us Hawaiians. There are so few of us anymore, so many have died from the new diseases, the ones the Haoles brought."

"I noticed when we walked inland how unhappy the people seem to be, living in this earthly paradise, yet poor and shabby."

"The outsiders come here in the big ships with their guns and Bibles and want to 'save' us from our primitive ways. But all they really want is power and money, and they don't care about the damage they do."

"It makes me ashamed to be one of them," he mumbled.

She turned her laughing face to his. "You're not one of them, James. You may sail on their ship, but you are like us, one whose home was shattered by the greedy clutch of outsiders."

"Yes, you are right... partly. But I also am one of them. My father was white, though he was a good man, not a destroyer."

They remained silent for some time. Then James spoke: "Hokulani? You know I have to leave tomorrow morning?"

She sat up and leaned on her elbow facing him. "Yes, I know."

He faced her earnestly. "But I'll never see you again. After what you've been to me..."

She touched his face and sighed, "Oh, James. You are so sweet. But to us, lovemaking is a great pleasure, and with you it has been very great, James, not the forbidden, earth-shaking event your missionaries seem to think it is. We have had an evening of joy, and I will surely always remember it. I think you will, too," she smiled. "But tomorrow you will go off to sea and I will go on with my life here. It has been a great gift to us both, let us cherish it forever and not ruin it with regrets."

They had both fallen asleep by the glowing embers when Jack and his partner came back. He noted that their instruments were secure and then the two of them joined James and Hokulani in slumber beneath the island stars.

When James awoke, Hokulani was gone. Jack, who was still sleeping, was also alone. James awakened his friend and they sat for a while looking at the sea, thinking their private thoughts.

"Well, Jamie," Jack said at length, "didn't I tell you Hawaii was a grand place?"

James was thoughtful. "Yes," he mused, "it's wonderful. And last night was... well, I can't put it into words. But there is something deeply sad, too. It reminds me of what happened to my people. They had their way of life, with all of its good and bad sides, but then when outsiders arrived, everything deteriorated. It seems to me that the native people of the world can't survive the arrival of newcomers who bring better weapons and machines. And what they leave behind is kind of a corrupted way of living, with most of the good things lost."

Jack looked puzzled. "I must say, Jimmy my lad, that you're the only man I've ever known who would turn a nice roll in the hay – or sand – into a treatise on the sad condition of the Indians. But as it may be," he said as he rose and brushed the sand from his pants, "let's find some breakfast and make ready to return to the dear old *Abigail*, after our one night of liberty with many a day ahead of us at sea."

They found some strong coffee, "locally grown," the man behind the counter assured them, and some eggs and ham too. They walked around the town idly for an hour, James hoping in vain that he would catch sight of Hokulani, but by noon they found themselves in the launch headed back to the ship. Most of their shipmates were hung over and several bemoaned the loss of their money to gambling, drink, and women.

"You all knew what you were about," Truxhall roared as they stumbled on to the deck. "You'll get no sympathy from me, you drunkards. Now clean yourselves up! We sail at four bells."

James watched the lovely islands sink below the horizon as they sailed on a southwesterly course. "Whatever else will follow," he thought, "I will always remember her – Hokulani – and that magical night."

Their lives returned to the timeless routine of sea duty, standing watches, going aloft, mending and cleaning, and the respite of music and dancing in the evening. James had learned many new songs from Jack like "Blue-Tailed Fly," "My Pretty Yaller Gal," and "The Old Grey Goose." They hadn't heard enough Hawaiian music to become familiar with it, but Jack had learned a few songs that Kalei had played, "While you were busy doing something else!" Jack teased.

The days and nights passed as they sailed southwest across the vast, featureless sea. Only the long, regular rollers gave texture to the unbroken sheet of blue. The weather was mild, with a fair breeze in the southeast quarter that propelled them along with minimal adjustments to the sails.

On the twenty-third day out from Hawaii, February 2, 1848, the wind shifted around to the southwest, sending the men aloft to change the rigging and set the sails. Dark clouds appeared on the southern horizon, the wind picked up in intensity, and whitecaps began to appear on the surface of the sea around them.

"All hands aloft" cried the first mate, and the men scrambled to their positions in the rigging. Rain began to pelt them as they frantically pulled in sail. Jack and James were reefing the topsail when a sudden gust smacked the ship with a hard broadside. James was reaching out to grasp the edge of the sail and pull it toward him when the unexpected jolt shook the mast, and his feet lost their purchase on the rope ladder. He swung out over the surging water below him, desperately holding on to the spar. "Jamie!" Jack called to him, but James's hands slipped on the wet rigging and with a strangled shout, he plunged straight down twenty feet into the ocean.

James had been born in the desert and had lived his entire life in a dry country. He had never learned to swim. He crashed into a rising swell and shot immediately to a depth of ten feet. In his terror, he flailed wildly, though that only seemed to push him ever deeper into the dark, swirling water. Through the shock and panic, he realized the hopelessness of his predicament. "So, this is it," he thought. Struggle was useless, he knew. They would never reach him before he drowned. "Too soon... can it really be over so soon? Mother... oh, Mother, I'm coming to be with you."

His stoic acceptance of death was rudely shaken by a heavy thump on his shoulder, followed by a strong tug upward. The dark water danced with air bubbles as he was dragged closer to the surface. Suddenly, he heard the roar of the wind as he broke the surface. He sucked in a huge gasp of air and coughed up seawater. "Stay still, you fool!" he heard a voice scream in his ear. He realized that he had been thrashing wildly and he tried to overcome his mindless terror and let his rescuer guide him.

He saw that Jack was in the water with him, holding tightly to his collar and pulling him toward the ship towering over them in the stormy waves. Several ropes were thrown from the deck to the men in the water; Jack grabbed one and pushed another one to James, who clutched it tightly in both hands. The men aboard quickly pulled their comrades from the raging surf and lifted them to the deck, both completely exhausted. The captain stood above them.

"Well, I figured we'd lost the music for the rest of this voyage," he said gruffly, hands on hips as he surveyed the two nearly drowned men collapsed listlessly on the deck. "But I'm glad to be wrong in this case." He frowned toward Jack. "Though that was a damned foolish thing to do, sailor. It was all for the best this time, but it was much more likely that we'd have lost the both of you. Don't think that you're a hero, my boy. You could just have well been shark food."

The storm continued to build despite the excitement on board, and the men had to return to their work immediately. Jack and James had to help themselves crawl across the deck to the hatch and down to their quarters, where they got dry clothes on and were given hot tea and a piece of biscuit. They sat dazedly trying to piece together what exactly had occurred.

"You saved, me, Jack. I can never thank you enough for that," James said quietly between sips. "Why was the captain so mad at you?"

"I didn't follow the drill, Jimmy. When a man falls in the sea, we're to shout, 'Man overboard!' Then the captain will back off the ship and put out a boat to try to recover the poor soul. But Jamie, I knew you would never last until we got a boat after you. You'd have never even broken the surface, just sunk on down to the bottom. So, I dove after you without thinking much. I'm a strong swimmer. We swim all the summer long in Massachusetts and I thought I had a good chance to find you if I acted quick." He looked at his friend hunched over his tea and wrapped in blankets and smiled. "And I'm mighty glad I did."

By the time they recovered from their shock, the boys were needed back on deck to fight off the storm. With its sails tightly furled and reefed, the *Abigail* plowed through the high swells and slid down the steep sides of the waves like a sled on a snowy slope.

The wind and rain continued unabated for two days. When on deck, the men had to be always tied to safety lines to avoid being washed overboard by the black breakers that soaked the deck. When below, they curled in the hammocks trying to catch some snatches of sleep during the howling wind and tossing ship. Dry clothes quickly became a thing of the past and food was salt pork and biscuit, no cooking fire was lit for the duration of the blow.

James was in his hammock when he noticed that the rocking of the ship was decreasing and the howling of the wind began to abate. By the time his watch was called on deck, the sky in the east was clear and growing in brightness as the sun began to rise. The waves were still high but diminishing and the dark clouds were moving off top. To the north were calm and blue seas in their path. They unfurled the sails and caught a fresh breeze, which didn't leave them for the next two weeks as they headed toward the East Indies.

Life on board returned to the routine they knew so well. James knew they still had many months at sea before them, but he was beginning to tire of the sailor's life. In spite of the good friends and music, and pleasant enough life aboard, his thoughts turned to Scotland. What would he find when he reached the home of his father's people?

The remainder of their run to the East Indies was uneventful. The days grew hotter and the nights balmier as they sailed south. They dropped anchor in the bustling Dutch colonial city of Batavia and Captain Truxhall supervised the loading of spices, the most valuable portion of their cargo, and certainly the most aromatic. Jack and James drew the watch during this stopover, so they only saw the exotic harbor from their anchorage. The roadstead was crowded with vessels of all kinds. European warships and merchants, Chinese junks, and local vessels with brightly colored rectangular sails. All was motion and color in the harbor as the boats all sped to their destinations and returned.

James found himself standing next to the captain as he peered over the railing at his ship's boats ferrying their valuable cargo. "Captain," he asked, pointing to the mighty men o' wars in the harbor, "whose are these warships with all the guns?"

"Those are the Dutch," Truxhall replied. "They've been expanding their colony here for a couple hundred years, I guess, and it's still going on. Right now, they're fighting to subdue the big island of Bali. And only a few years ago, the natives here on Java rose up in rebellion, and the Dutch had to put that down as well. Didn't do the locals any good. They're little more than slaves now in their own land."

James had another question, but he was afraid to ask it of the captain. Finally, he blurted out, "Why do the white men have to have rule everywhere? To replace the local ways of doing things with their own ways?"

Truxall looked puzzled at the question. Then he nodded with a knowing smile. "Well, that's right, isn't it? You're half Indian yourself. I've been thinking of you as a white man all along. That's why your question sounded sort of funny." The captain stared directly at James, peering closely at his face. "Yes, I can see that you've got some Indian in you," he said, "but with those blue eyes and your hair cut short, and your skin's no darker than any of the lads who've been in the tropical sun so long. You pass easy for a full-blooded white.

"But to your question. The white man has the civilization, James. They have the science and the weapons, the ability to build boats and cannon such as those yonder. They have a hankering to travel, to see the world. Take the Italian Marco Polo, back in the Dark Ages going clear to China. And wherever the white man goes, he sees riches. Riches that are being unused, or misused, they decide to take a piece of that for themselves.

"And then there's religion. The white man has the true religion, though I'm not too sure which one that is. You were raised up Catholic, weren't you?"

James nodded silently.

"Well, they think they have the one true faith, and the Spanish, Portuguese, and Italians have made sure that folks living in their colonies get the straight deal. The English the same with their own church, and the Dutch with whatever is theirs. It's just normal, James, that the stronger rule the weaker, that the more advanced look after the backward."

James remained silent for a moment. "Did that answer your question or cloud it up more?" Truxhall asked.

"Thank you, Captain, yes. There's certainly a lot to know about this old world, isn't there?"

Truxhall watched as James returned below deck. "Yes, lad," he muttered under his breath, "a powerful lot to know. And I don't know as we ever learn all that much."

Even though James was becoming a little bored with the life of a sailor, he still had many months at sea before him. The trip from

Batavia to Cape Town was the longest leg of their journey, six thousand miles across the vast Indian Ocean. It was summer in the Southern Hemisphere, and the ocean was calm and predictable as one could desire. After fifty days of sailing, they were nearing the end of summer and the autumnal storms were not too far off. They hoped to make it to Cape Town before the weather turned, and they arrived in the stunning harbor nestled beneath the towering heights of Table Mountain in the brilliant sunshine of May 1848 – mid-autumn in the southern hemisphere.

Truxhall planned to stay a week in port. They had been a long while at sea and they needed to replenish their water, foodstuffs, and other essentials like gin and tobacco. The men also needed to stretch their legs and have some time away from the ship and from each other. They had little trading to do. Their holds were topped off with the tallow and hides from California and the aromatic spices, so the crew was granted liberty on a rotating basis. Two days ashore and one on watch.

Jack and James lolled along the wharf, idly glancing into the interiors of the dark, shabby structures on the waterfront. Some were smoke-filled and loud, while others seemed to be nearly deserted. Aromas vile and succulent wafted on the sea breeze, weaving a unique tapestry of harbor scents. Then they heard the unmistakable sound of a fiddle drifting out of an open door of The Ferryman, a pleasant-looking inn facing Table Bay.

Inside, they easily found a table in the close, smoky darkness. About twenty people were scattered in through the interior, more than half filling the place. Standing beside the bar was a young man vigorously sawing on a fiddle. James recognized the tune as a version of "Haste to the Wedding." When he finished, the fiddler received a polite round of applause. Jack and James, knowing from experience how much audience approval meant to a performer, clapped louder and longer than the others.

The fiddler sat down and another man holding a fiddle and bow rose and tuned his instrument. "My name is Harold Winsell," he stated, "and the tune I'm playing is 'Bonnets So Blue.'" At that, he began sawing away, not nearly as skillfully as the first performer.

"Is it a contest?" Jack whispered to James.

"I'm not sure. It sure looks like it, though."

"Jimmy! You've got to enter!"

"Yes, but I don't know what the rules are. Maybe you have to sign up in advance or be invited or something."

"I'll find out," Jack said, and before James could stop him, he walked toward the bar and was talking to the barmaid. James saw him gesture in his direction and the barmaid nodded. Jack made his way back to the table.

"It's all right," Jack said as he sat down. "There's one more to play; four, including this one, have played so far. You'll be the last. Then the judges pick who wins the prize."

"Which is?"

"The prize is only a free pint of ale, but the fame that goes with it is considered the real award." James nodded. "This next fellow is supposed to be pretty good. The barmaid says he's won several weeks in a row. Few are willing to challenge him. That's why the crowd is a bit thin tonight."

The next contestant rose and plucked some notes on his fiddle. He was a middle-aged man, rather stout, with salt and pepper hair and beard. "My name is Johnny Guiteaux," he softly announced to the small crowd, "and the tune I will play is "Granny Does Your Dog Bite.""

With that, he began to saw furiously at the fiddle. James recognized the tune, though he had never played it. He turned to Jack and whispered, "This fellow is pretty good. Should I take a turn?"

Jack looked in surprise at his friend. "He may be all right, Jimmy, but I don't think he's any match for you."

"But all his friends are here," James answered, pointing out the enthusiastic clapping that accompanied the music.

Jack shook his head with a wry smile. "I will clap along with you, Jim. Does that ease your mind?"

"All right, I'll play. But what should I do? I better have a catchy one or I'll lose them sure."

"If only I could play the banjo along with you, but I don't think they'll have that in a contest like this. Go ahead and do your old 'Soldiers' Joy.' It's a common one, but maybe it hasn't been heard much here in Cape Town."

Johnny Guiteaux finished his piece to a sustained shout from the crowd. As the clapping and hooting died down, James gathered his courage and stepped forward with his violin in hand. The crowd quieted to a low murmur as they sized up this youngster in their midst.

James walked to the center of the room and, calling forth his deepest, most confident voice, said, "My name is James Kennedy. I'm from the American brigantine *Abigail* and I'd like to play 'Soldiers' Joy' for you." He lifted the fiddle to his chin and began to play the familiar, beloved melody that he had learned from his father.

The song didn't have any fireworks or trick fiddling in it, it was merely a catchy tune that folks couldn't quit humming or whistling once they'd heard it. James played the melody with a strong, rich tone, in contrast to the fast, but scratchy style of Guiteaux. When he got to the" B" part, he launched into double stops and picked up the volume.

As promised, Jack clapped along in time, and soon the crowd was joining in, stomping their feet, and shouting. When James finished with a flourish, the place erupted in applause and yells. Johnny Guiteaux walked over to James, confronting him face to face. Then he reached out his right hand and heartily shook James's hand with a wide grin spreading across his face. "I say you are tonight's champion," he roared. "And I'm proud to be beaten by such a fiddler!" The crowd cried their approval louder than ever.

"Peace!" Johnny called as he raised his hands high over his head. "The contest is over, but the music don't have to stop. I want to play some tunes with this talented youngster. Are you game?" he asked James.

"Oh, yes sir," James responded, "and my friend here, Jack," Jack shyly acknowledged the people with a little wave, "plays the banjo. Can he join in as well?"

Jack pulled his banjo from its case and moved next to James and Johnny and the three began to play. Soon the other fiddlers who had entered the contest joined in and the small tavern filled with music. James noticed that it had also filled with people, as word of the impromptu concert had spread along the waterfront.

The music went on and on, encouraged by generous helpings of ale that appeared at the elbows of the musicians as if by magic. After midnight, the crowd began to thin, and Johnny put down his fiddle. "Well, lads, that was as fine a time as I've ever had. You both have quite the gift for music, I say, and the *Abigail* is a lucky ship to have you aboard. How long will you be here at the Cape?"

"Not long, I fear," Jack answered. We have liberty tonight and tomorrow, and then our watch is called for the next day. And then we're off for London."

"I'm going on to Scotland," James interjected. "That's where my father is from and I hope to find some of his people, my people."

"Boys, I wish you all the best luck. You have made this a memorable night for me and for all the folk who had the good fortune to be here at the Ferryman this evening." He shook their hands and walked out into the street. By this time, the place was nearly empty. They drained their last pint of ale, packed up their instruments, and walked back to the wharf. The night was mild, and they lay back to wonder at the brilliant stars shining over the placid bay.

James remembered some of the constellations that his mother had taught him, but he couldn't find any of those. In their place were mysterious fuzzy spots and many bright stars, some placed very close to each other. Jack knew a few of the stars of the northern sky. He could find the Great Bear and knew how to follow the pointer stars to the North Star, but these were nowhere to be seen.

"See those four bright ones close together?" Jack asked. "I think that's what they call the Southern Cross. You can see how they make a cross, can't you?"

"What are these fuzzy patches over there?" James asked, pointing to the Magellenic Clouds.

Jack shook his head. "I've no idea," he answered. "Maybe some of the men on board will know. They've sailed the Southern Seas many a time."

They lay awake for some time, staring at the unfamiliar sky and talking softly until they both fell asleep on the wharf, leaning on some cotton bales for pillows.

CHAPTER FIFTEEN

London! In 1848 there was no competitor for title of the greatest city in the world. Not only the largest in population and size, but the capital of the planet-girdling British Empire. The only cities James had ever seen were Los Angeles, Yerba Buena, Honolulu, Batavia, and Cape Town, all mere villages by comparison.

The *Abigail* docked at the Port of London after a day's sail up the Thames in which they encountered a steady increase of development until they reached the city itself. There, the river front was packed solid with docks, warehouses, storefronts, taverns, and people. Everywhere enormous crowds were going about their business at a frenetic pace.

James didn't have the leisure of standing at the rail and watching the immense city as it glided by. He, along with Jack and the rest of the crew were absorbed in the many urgent tasks necessary to make port and prepare to disgorge their cargo.

Here in London, they would empty the ship of its hides and tallow from California and the spices they brought from the Dutch East Indies, replacing them with manufactured goods to be taken to New England on the final leg of *Abigail's* circumnavigation. They were hard at work clearing and cleaning the holds and performing the myriad repairs that were required after their long sea voyage.

When James was able to steal a quick glance at the massive city before him, he was filled with anxiety. How could he ever find his way around such a metropolis? Perhaps he should stay with his ship when it crossed the Atlantic to its homeport of Boston. That was a big city, too, he knew, but nothing like this inconceivable mass of humanity. And he would have Jack, who knew the city so well, with him in Boston to guide him and help him to find his way.

But what would he do there? His only purpose since he had left the village of Temal Wakhish eight months earlier had been to go to Scotland to learn about his father's people. Now he was only a short train ride away from his goal and he realized he had no idea how to proceed.

The captain had told the men there would be no liberty in London, even though this decision was most unwelcome to the crew. "Men," Truxhall had announced as they neared the broad estuary of the Thames, "Most of you have never been to London before. You will soon see that it is much larger than any place we have seen in our voyage thus far. In fact, it is the largest city in the world. And it is dangerous! We are only six weeks from home, God willing, and I would hate to lose any of you able seamen to a British press gang or a knife between the ribs in a London whorehouse."

The crew looked sullen but knew better than to grumble audibly. "We have a great deal of work ahead of us to offload our cargo and to take on new goods, not to mention the attention we must pay to the upkeep of our old *Abigail*. And so, I am not granting shore liberty to anyone here in London."

This pronouncement did provoke a disgruntled murmur. Truxhall snapped his head erect and shouted, "None of that, now men! I tell you that this city is crawling with them as would knock you on the head and sell you to an outbound ship and you'd never be heard from again. This is not Oowhayoo nor Cape Town, in this city you are all tenderfeet and greenhorns. I want to see you all going ashore in Boston with money safe in your pocket and your bodies whole. We've been on a long voyage, men, and we're near to the end of it. Look lively and do your jobs, and we'll be back on good old New England soil before you know it."

But James had only signed on as far as London, and he alone of the crew would be taking the barge ashore when the *Abigail* next weighed anchor.

"Jack," he sighed as they lay in their hammocks, "I'm afraid."

"Of London?" Jack asked.

"Yes, and of what comes next. What am I to do in a strange land with no friends or family to help me?"

"I just don't know what to tell you, Jim," Jack said. "I'd love to ask you to stay on, to sail with us to Boston, and to strike out for a new life there. But I know you want to find something of your father and his people. And Scotland is the only place you'll do that."

"Jack?" James asked diffidently. "Why don't you come with me? We could have a fine time playing music and roaming England and Scotland."

Jack was silent for a minute. "No, Jim, I must be going home. I've a mother and family there who I haven't seen now in two years. I don't know what the future holds for me, either. I've had enough of the sailor's life, though what I can do ashore to make my way, I don't know. But I must be off for my home, much as I will miss you and your fiddle."

The *Abigail* stood to anchor for only one week while its holds were emptied and refilled, and its crew made all repairs. The captain shook James's hand solemnly as he bid goodbye to the young seaman. "James," he softly said, "You have been a great blessing to this ship, for your music, of course, but also for the good, cheerful lad that you are. We wish you were continuing with us, but I know where your heart is leading you, and besides, we've only another six weeks and the whole crew will be broken up. That's the way of the sea," he mused, "and of life, too." He proffered his hand and James shook it heartily.

"Thank you, Captain," James said, "for all your kindnesses. I hope we will meet again someday."

"As it may be, James. God's blessings be on you."

Jack and two other crewmen joined James in the barge as it pulled away from the ship toward the dock. James, his sea bag slung over his shoulder and fiddle case in hand, stepped out onto the pier. Jack followed him.

"I won't say goodbye, Jim. We thought we had parted forever once before. It's a big world, but it's a small one, too, if you get my meaning."

James struggled to hold back tears. "Yes, I will look for the day when I hear that banjo twang again. Good luck to you, Jack, and thank you for everything, including saving my life!"

The waterfront looked blurry to James's eyes as he turned his face away from the water and his departing friends. He had been given directions to the newly opened Waterloo Station and he had every intention of proceeding directly there. He plunged into the jostling crowds, nervously clutching his fiddle and frequently tapping his breast to ascertain that the wallet containing his pay for the entire voyage was still safely tucked away under his seaman's coat.

He passed by the famous Tower of London, crossed the London Bridge, and wended along the boisterous, noisy streets toward the newly opened Waterloo Station. Following the detailed instructions that Captain Truxhall had carefully given him, he found a ticket window and ordered a coach seat for Edinburgh, the only Scottish city whose name he knew.

He avoided the temptation to save a few pennies by purchasing a third-class ticket; that would entail standing or sitting on luggage for the entire twelve-hour journey. He bought a second-class seat and quickly moved to the railway carriage. The conductor examined his ticket and showed him to his seat, one of eight in the compartment.

He was quite nervous about travelling by rail. This was the first railroad car and locomotive he had ever seen, and he had heard that they raced on their tracks at breakneck speeds of over thirty miles an hour. But he saw the seats filling with ordinary people who seemed completely calm about the journey, even women and children. James felt he could do no less than his fellow passengers, so he settled his belongings and quietly awaited the departure.

They were soon rolling through the city and into the suburbs, stopping often for passengers to exit and enter. James noticed that even though he could see from the window, they were moving at great speed, inside the coach, he had no sensation of forward movement except when they slowed or sped up. In all his travels, he had either walked, rode a horse, or sailed on a ship; this was his first experience of smooth, effortless transportation.

He was nervous and self-conscious sitting in the compartment until the man directly across from him noticed the fiddle case at James's feet. "I assume you play the violin?" the man asked.

"Yes, sir," he replied. "I've been playing it just about all my life."

"Would you care to give us a taste of your music to help pass the time?"

The other passengers looked with interest at James, and several nodded their encouragement.

"Certainly, if no one minds," he said, glancing at the others' faces. Seeing no disapproval there, he opened his case and brought forth his beloved fiddle with the face and crown carved into the headstock.

He quickly tuned and rosined his bow. He wondered what kind of music this group of English travelers would like. He could play several classical pieces as well as his large repertoire of fiddle tunes from Scotland, Ireland, and America. He decided to begin with the organ sonata by Soler that Father Xavier had arranged for the violin. At the first notes, the passengers looked surprised and pleased; several of them swayed or waved their hands in time with the music. He finished to sincere applause and compliments.

A small old man sitting in the corner on James's side of the carriage leaned out to get a view of the musician. "That's very fine, son. Do you know anything a bit more lively?"

James smiled. "Why, yes, I do. Here's one of my favorites," and he launched into "Ol' Zip Coon," an American minstrel song he had learned from Jack. His fellow travelers clapped and tapped their toes in time to the sprightly melody. He finished to laughter and applause.

"That sounds like an American song. Is that where you come from?" asked a lady sitting opposite James.

"Yes, from California. It used to be part of Mexico, but it's American now."

"Did you ever see any redskins?" a small boy sitting next to the woman excitedly asked.

James was taken aback, but he quickly realized that with his sailor's coat and trousers and his hair cut short, he didn't look like an Indian. "Why, yes," he replied with a secretive smile. "Yes, I saw quite a few in California. Perhaps not the kind you've read about in all the stories, though."

They pulled into Euston Station to take on more passengers. With the train stopped and the window open, James continued to play. Since he was on his way to Scotland, he played a waltz he had learned at his father's knee — "Scots O'er the Border. "The crowd jostling along the railway platform heard him, and many glanced his way with pleased smiles.

The last one to board was a very thin man with dark hair, accompanied by a woman at each elbow who appeared to be helping him to stay on his feet and slowly walk to the waiting train car. He heard the music coming from James's car and he indicated with a nod of his head that he wanted to approach. He stood near the open carriage window and listened intently as James finished his performance.

As the riders in James's coach applauded, the frail man smiled and softly touched his hands together in an inaudible salute. Then he reached into his pocket and handed James a small card along with a sixpence coin. "Thank you, sir," James blurted out.

"Dobry. Très bien," the man said, and he went on his way with his helpers on either side of him walking feebly toward the first-class coach at the head of the train.

James pocketed the coin and looked at the card: "Frederic Chopin," he read aloud.

"Chopin!" the man across from him exclaimed. "Why, you should be very flattered, young man. He's the greatest composer and pianist of the age. I saw him perform last spring at Stafford House. The Queen and Prince Albert were there!"

James had heard of Chopin, though Father Xavier had rejected all the Romantic composers as modernists and atheists. He was immensely proud of receiving a compliment from such a renowned musician. The warmth of that feeling kept his anxieties at bay for the rest of the long ride to Edinburgh.

When the train pulled into Princes Station, though, his dilemma returned: he was alone in a place he had never been and where he knew no one. He hadn't been able to plan much beyond the moment of his arrival. His purpose was to discover something of his roots on his father's side of his family, but how does one go about that?

He had a small amount of money with him, his pay from the long voyage on the *Abigail* along with a few of the coins that Moki had given him. He could live for a time on that, though he would have to find a livelihood soon. As he walked out of the station with his pack slung over his shoulder and his fiddle case tucked protectively under his arm, he saw a line of hansom cabs awaiting fares, their drivers standing on the station side of the street.

He approached one who had a friendly expression and asked him, "Pardon me, sir, but I'm new in Edinburgh. Could you give me some idea as to where I could find decent lodging? I can pay," he added in response to the skeptical look on the cabby's face.

"Aye, lad, I ken aw the hostels in the city." He looked James up and down again and added, "Ride wi' me on the top. Ye'll get a view of the city an' I'll point out some of the points of interest. Let's just wait a bit till I get a few more fares an' we'll be off."

James stood in silence while the cabby sought passengers. A young couple climbed in, followed by two well-dressed gentlemen. The cabby shut the door and effortlessly swung himself up onto his high perch, beckoning James to join him. The ease of the driver's ascent was deceptive. James struggled to scale the seat without dropping his fiddle or bag but managed to pull himself awkwardly to the cabby's level and arrange himself and his belongings as the driver snapped his whip and the cab rolled forward.

"Mah nam is Alick," he said, turning to James.

"And I'm James," he replied. "James Kennedy."

Alick beetled his brow in thought. "Ye dinna sound like a Scot," he mused. "Nor Irish neither. Where do ye hark from?"

"I come from California – part of America, now – but my father was from Scotland, and I've come to find if any of his family is here."

As they rattled along the cobblestone streets, Alick pointed out the famous landmarks of the city. Edinburgh castle standing high above the town, the hump of Arthur's Seat, and the many gardens, churches, and galleries. It was a fair city, and still huge to James's mind. It was nothing like the megalopolis of London, but vastly larger than the small villages James had lived in and visited. He had no way of knowing that his father had walked these streets, seen these sights, and worked at these docks thirty years ago as he saved up enough money for his passage to Baltimore.

He still had no idea of how to begin his search for the Kennedy family. He started to ask Alick if he had any advice when the cab stopped in front of a pleasant-looking two-story sandstone house.

There was a low wall along the street and the house itself was set back from the road with a well-tended garden in the front.

"Here be the Widow Campbell's rooming house," Alick said. "She's a braw lady, her place is clean, and rates are affordable. You can mention that Alick brought ye."

James grabbed his bag and fiddle and turned to Alick before descending from the high driver's seat. "I wanted to ask for some advice about how to find my father's family and where to look for work," he began, but Alick waved him to silence.

"I've naw time right now, lad, mah other fares hae places to go, too. Get yer room settled and ask Mairi Campbell yer questions. She's like to help ye somewhat. Good luck to ye," Alick said as James tentatively climbed down to the street. The hansom cab pulled away with a jingle and left James staring at the pleasant house and yard before him.

The home was modest and respectable, but to James's eyes, it seemed a mansion. He had lived in a bark teepee, an adobe mission, a Cahuilla kish, and on the *Abigail*, but never had he stayed in so grand a place. His feet seemed rooted to the pavement for several minutes. Finally, he mustered his courage and advanced to the door.

A very attractive young woman opened the door. "Hello," she smiled. "How may I help you?"

James struggled to spit out, "Alick told me I might find a room here. Are you the Widow Campbell?"

To James, her laughter sounded like beautiful music. "Nay, that's my mother, Mairi. I'm her daughter Flora. Please come in and I'll fetch her."

He stepped into a small foyer with a marble floor. On a stand near the wall stood a large vase full of fresh-cut flowers that filled the air with the scent of a summer garden. Flora slipped away through the door to his left. He stood there taking in the curved stairway that led upstairs and the old portraits that adorned the walls. Soon the door opened and a pleasant-looking woman in her mid-forties emerged.

"My daughter tells me you are seeking lodging?" she asked in a smooth, melodic voice.

"Yes'm," James answered with a nervous nod, "Alick recommended you to me."

She shook her head with a kindly smile. "Yes, good Alick. He is a dear man if a bit on the rough side. He has a gift of sizing up people, though, and if he brought you here, I will gladly take his opinion. And with my own eyes, too, I see that you are a fine young man."

James hoped his blush wasn't too obvious. Mairi's face betrayed some discomfort as she said, "Of course, there's the matter of the rent. I ask for two weeks' payment in advance. Are you employed?"

"Only just arrived, ma'am," he replied, "but I have some money and I'll be looking for work right away."

"What brings you to Scotland?" Flora asked.

James smiled. "That's quite a long story, miss," he began, but Mairi interrupted.

"Let's not stand here in the foyer talking. I'll pour some tea and we'll sit in the parlor and make our acquaintances."

She pulled a bell rope and the three adjourned to a small, rather cluttered parlor and took seats around a small table. A woman wearing a cap and apron leaned into the room. "Yes'm?" she asked.

"Some tea for us, please, Davina," Mairi said, and the maid ducked back out of the door.

Mairi turned to James and said, "First things first. I am Mairi Campbell, and this is my daughter Flora." She couldn't help but notice the suppressed excitement on the two young people's faces. She wasn't totally pleased by it.

James spoke up, "I'm James Kennedy," he began. Mairi and Flora exchanged a private glance. "My story is a long one and I won't bore you with all the details. I'm from California, and I've only just arrived here by way of the Cape of Good Hope on the brigantine *Abigail* out of Boston. I've come to Scotland in hopes of learning something about my father's people. He was from Scotland, and we were parted at an early age."

He paused, unsure of how much of his history to reveal. He decided not to mention his Indian identity just yet.

"Go on, dear," Mairi gently prompted.

"It's not a pretty story," James continued. "My mother was killed, and I was captured by an outlaw band when I was not quite ten years old."

The women's faces showed expressions of pity.

"Oh, dear," Mairi said, "How simply awful. And what happened to you?"

Trying to stay one step ahead of his fictionalized story, he replied, "I was taken in by a priest at the mission in Los Angeles." The word "priest" was not a welcome word in the Campbell household. They were staunch Presbyterians and held no love for Catholics.

Sensing this, James resumed his tale before they could interrupt. "You see, my father was a fiddler and he taught me how to play, even at my young age. The priest, Father Xavier, was a musician himself and he encouraged my musical education." He patted the fiddle case at his feet. "And this fiddle has been my boon companion ever since. It's been with me through war, rebellion, and a stormy sea voyage."

Davina entered the room and placed a large tea service on the table and then quietly left. "Thank you, Davina," Mairi said, and she poured the tea for the three of them.

Mairi was still concerned about their guest's religion. "And so, James, you were raised a Papist?"

James didn't fully grasp the import of the question, but his instincts told him to be wary. "Yes, the priest gave us religious instruction, and I played in the church regularly. That was the only religion in California in those days when it was part of Mexico. But since I left the mission during the war with the Americanos, I haven't been back to church. Captain Truxhall conducted services on board the *Abigail,* and he was a Congregationalist, I believe. The whole of it is I'm not really churched at all at the present."

Flora broke the short silence that followed. "Perhaps you'd like to come to church with us!"

"Why, that sounds fine," James eagerly replied.

"Yes, that would be lovely if you would care to join us on Sunday next," Mairi said somewhat primly. "It's apparent that you have quite a colorful history, and we will look forward to hearing more of it in coming days. But what of the present? What are your plans?"

James furrowed his brow in thought. "I can't say that I have planned anything out. I really know nothing of this country except that my father, William Kennedy, emigrated from Scotland and became a mountain man in America. I hope I can find some relatives, or at least learn something of my father and the place he came from. In the meantime, I must find some kind of work to keep body and soul together."

"What kind of work have you done?" Flora asked.

"Oh, I've worked with cattle and crops on a California rancho, been a seaman on a trading vessel, worked as a longshoreman on the docks... and of course, played the fiddle." He patted his case again.

"Perhaps you wouldn't mind playing a little tune for us," Flora said.

James fumbled for his fiddle case. "Of course, I'd be very happy to play for you." He lifted the fiddle from its case and quickly tuned it. He rosined the bow and placed the instrument under his chin. As he put bow to string, he noticed that Mairi and Flora were staring at the carved headstock of his fiddle. He took the fiddle away from his chin and held it out toward them. "It was my father's. I don't know how old it is or what the carving represents, but it's been my only possession for many years."

Mairi reached for it. "May I?" she asked.

"Surely," James replied and handed the fiddle to her.

She looked closely at the king's head carved into the headstock. "I see he's wearing a crown so it can't be a carving of the Pretender, Charles."

"Oh, Bonnie Prince Charlie," Flora piped up.

"He was neither bonnie nor a prince nor a King," Mairi snapped. "Our own Campbell ancestors fought against him and beat him, too, at the Battle of Culloden. And your folk, too, the Kennedys, they also stood up for the Crown, and the Protestants. So, who could this be"?

James was completely bewildered, never having heard of Bonnie Prince Charlie, though unbeknownst to him, he played several fiddle tunes, like "Johnnie Cope" and "The Skye Boat Song" that were inspired by the Stuart claimant to the throne.

"I'm sure he meant no disrespect, Mother," Flora said meekly. "It's just what you hear about in the songs and tales, you know."

James chuckled. "And I must confess that I don't understand a single thing you are talking about."

Mairi, calming herself, handed the fiddle back to James. "I realize that the history of Scotland may not have been taught at your mission in California. Perhaps you'd like to learn something more about it, and we can certainly share with you the story of the Scots, your own ancestors, you know. But for now, let's hear you play."

"California," Flora said dreamily. "Such an exotic name."

Mairi gave her a sharp, disapproving glance and then turned, smiling, to face James. He began with his oldest standby, "Soldiers' Joy." Mother and daughter were surprised and pleased at his virtuosity. "That's wonderful," Flora gushed.

"Yes," her mother chimed in, "It's delightful. I recognize that melody as 'King's Head.' Do play more."

James reddened slightly and played a waltz he had learned from his father, "Scots O'er the Border." He played a classical piece that Father Xavier had taught him and one of the American minstrel songs he had done with Jack.

"You have quite a large range of styles," Mairi said.

"And you play beautifully," Flora added.

"Very well," said Mairi abruptly. "I'll have Davina show you to your room. We dine at six."

James said, "I'm afraid all I have in my pack are sailors' clothes. Perhaps I can buy something more appropriate tomorrow."

"Yes, you'll want something other than these for your job-hunting. What kind of employment do you think you'll be seeking?"

"Well, as I said, I've worked on docks, loading and off-loading ships. Maybe I could find some quick pay at the wharf. And there's always a way to make a penny with a fiddle."

"I'll go with you tomorrow to help you get some attire," Mairi said.

"I'll come, too," Flora added.

They went to a few shops the next morning to find him some clothes. James thought his sailor gear would be fine for manual labor, the only work he thought he might find, but Mairi and Flora helped him select what he needed for social occasions. His purchases, along with payment for two weeks' lodging, drastically reduced his means. He would need to find a job quickly.

After returning to his new lodgings, he modelled his new clothes for Mairi and Flora, who both approved. Then he donned his work clothes and headed for the wharf area. He had plenty of experience loading and unloading ships from the many ports he had visited while on the *Abigail,* and he thought that working as a stevedore would be the quickest way to replenish his dwindling resources.

The busy waterfront seemed chaotic at first, but he asked around and soon found himself signed on as a longshoreman. The work was hard, but as he approached his eighteenth birthday, he was strong and fit, and he had no trouble hoisting the heavy crates and stacking the piles of every conceivable type of merchandise.

In a few weeks of looking over the bustling city, he spotted the places where he might try to earn a bit extra playing the fiddle. There were contests and festivals where he was able to show off his abilities on the instrument. But Scotland was a nation of fiddlers, and his own skills, while superb, did not yet match the virtuosity of the best of them. Still, with his youth and good looks, and his extensive repertoire, he won many an audience over and earned some coins in the process.

In this way, James occupied the remainder of the year 1848. He became an accepted member of Mrs. Campbell's household and enjoyed many evenings around their hearth, playing the fiddle and hearing stories of the history of Scotland. Mairi was able to tell him a great deal about Clan Kennedy and their associations with the Campbells.

"Of course, there are many Kennedys in this city," she told him, "And I believe you might have the best chance of locating your father's people by placing a notice in the paper. Perhaps something like, 'Desire information about the family of William Kennedy, who emigrated to America around 1820.' You may very well find what you seek as easily as that."

"What a wonderful idea," James said excitedly. "I couldn't come up with any plan to find my father's kin. I think this may very well do the trick." Mairi nodded pleasantly and looked very pleased.

James placed the advertisement in *The Scotsman* the next morning. The next issue appeared two days later, and the day after that, a letter arrived at Mrs. Campbell's home addressed to James Kennedy.

It read, "In response to the notice in *The Scotsman* this date, my brother William left these shores in 1822. We had a letter from him after he arrived in America, at Baltimore, but after that, we have no word. If this could be the William Kennedy about whom you ask, send word to 43 North Princes Street. Your servant, Alan Kennedy."

"How exciting!" Flora cried as James read the letter aloud to her and Mairi. "Do you think this could be your father's brother? Your uncle?"

"I suppose it could be," James replied tentatively. "My father never talked about where he arrived in America, only that he came from Scotland."

"We must reply to this Alan Kennedy at once," Mairi stated. "But there are many Kennedys and William is a common name. Do you have any other details about your father that could help establish a connection?"

"Well, of course, he was a fiddler and a very good one at that. He also told me once that he was the third son and that there was no opportunity for him in Scotland, so he came to America. And if this man is kin to my father, there may be a resemblance. Even though it's been almost ten years since I last saw him, I remember his face very well."

James wrote to Alan Kennedy that same day inviting him to come to Mrs. Campbell's home to delve more deeply into the matter. Alan's acceptance came the next day and James prepared to meet the man who might be his uncle.

Alan arrived promptly at three in the afternoon on a blustery November day. Davina greeted him at the door and showed him into the parlor, where James, Flora, and Mairi waited expectantly. James and Alan stared intently at each other's face as they shook hands, searching for traces of William Kennedy in the features.

"I think I do espy somewhat o' William in your face," Alan said. "The hair and complexion are a good deal darker, but the eyes and face are Kennedy sure."

James nodded and smiled, still grasping Alan's hand. "And I think I see a bit of my Da in you, sir," he said.

Introductions were made and Mairi gestured for Alan to be seated. "Bring us some tea, please," she said to Davina, who scurried off to fetch it. Soon they were comfortably seated with their tea and scones.

"I wonder how to begin," James said. "I last saw my father in 1840 when he left for the summer's fur trapping and trading in the mountains. Before he returned, our village was destroyed by marauders. My mother was killed, and I was taken away by the bandits."

Flora and Mairi exchanged glances. This was a bit different than the tale James had told them.

James noticed their confusion but continued. "All I know of my father's history is that he was the third son, he came to America seeking opportunity, and he was a very fine fiddler. He never talked much about his history before he married my mother and settled down in our village."

Alan nodded, oblivious to the growing consternation of the ladies. "Ay, that fits like a glove," he said. "William was the youngest and he always felt that he nae had a chance to rise in Scotland, where the eldest son, my brother Donald inherited all the property. Aw we lads played at the fiddle a bit, but William was head and shoulders abune us. Our da gave him the Kennedy fiddle to take with him when he left for America. He thought it might keep his thoughts on Scotland and his kin."

James stood and fetched his fiddle. He opened the case and showed it to Alan, who gaped in wonder at the instrument.

"Ay, that's it! The very one it is! Tis King Robert the Bruce's head carved on it just as it was when our great grandfather, Ewan Kennedy, took it for a prize after the Battle of Culloden. This is the fiddle that William took with him to America!" He stood and with a voice filled with emotion said, "And you must then be William's bairn, and my very 'un nephew!"

Alan took James by the shoulders and stared deeply into James's eyes. "Ay, there can be no doubt. You are my own kin, and well met, too. But can you tell me naethin' else of my long-lost brother?"

"I'm sorry, sir," James said softly. "I know he was a mountain man, a trapper and trader, but the path of my life has been such that I never heard anything more about him. I had hoped to find out something from his family here in Scotland."

They sat again and Alan shook his head. "Nae, only that he arrived in Baltimore and had found a place to play his fiddle. He said the people there were very fond of him and his music. And then naethin'. For nearly thirty years there's been naw word. We came to believe that he was deid. But you turning up here, that shows that he yet lived only eight years ago and may well be alive still." Alan left with the promise to tell all his kin of the news and to arrange a gathering so that James could meet his new-found family.

After she showed Alan out, Mairi turned to James and said sternly, "Perhaps you would like to tell us the details of your life story again, and this time tell us the truth."

James looked sheepishly from Mairi to Flora and said, "I'm very sorry to have misled you. I just wasn't sure of how to explain to you the events, which brought me to your door. Part of what I told you were true. My mother was killed by a band of ruthless cutthroats. But they weren't robbers, only they were slavers."

"Slavers?!" Flora exclaimed. "But I thought they only went after Africans."

James took a deep breath and reluctantly continued. "In California, they enslave Indians, not blacks." The women looked at him in bewilderment. "You see, my mother was a Nuwuvi, an Indian. My father traded for furs in the mountains with my grandfather Bobby Jack Qweets and he and my mother, Tsunnunk, fell in love and were married. It was a wonderful life for me," he continued, "surrounded by my friends and relatives in a beautiful village at the mouth of a mighty canyon. My father taught me to play the fiddle when I was very young, and in the winters when he was home from the mountains, we played music together."

Mairi and Flora were too stunned to make any comment. "When I was nine, as we were awaiting my father's return from the mountains, a band of Mexican slavers destroyed our village. They killed my mother and took me to Los Angeles to sell. A priest named Father Xavier bought me and allowed me to continue studying music – though he wouldn't allow me to play any of the songs my father had taught me."

He paused and the three sat in silence for a moment. "The rest of the story I told you is true, though. The war and sailing on the *Abigail* and coming here in search of my father's people. I'm sorry I lied to you. I was afraid you wouldn't have anything to do with me if you knew I was part Indian."

Flora finally found her voice. "Oh James, it doesn't matter to us at all," she said, though the expression on her mother's face told a different story. "We've come to know you as a good man, in fact, this explains why your hair and skin are a bit darker than most. It certainly doesn't make us think any less of you. And you've found your father's people! Your journey has been a success!"

Mairi didn't say anything.

CHAPTER SIXTEEN

Clan Kennedy held it's gathering to welcome their newest member from across the sea at the old family homestead at Christmastime. Donald, the eldest brother who had inherited the estate, had died and the farm was now in the hands of his son, Ewan. Donald's widow, Barabal, and his youngest son William still lived on the property.

James met many cousins, aunts, and uncles, and there were more than a few fiddle players in evidence. The drinking, eating, and fiddling started upon the arrival of James and his guests, Mairi and Flora Campbell, and it continued well into the night. Some of the fiddlers matched James in speed and technique, but none could touch the variety of his repertoire. He even found the courage, after several glasses of peaty whiskey, to play one of his interpretations of Nuwuvi music, and it was very well received by his Celtic relations.

He heard many stories of his father's youth; of the wild and improbable adventures he had had. Tears for his absence were shed and prayers offered that he would be found alive and well. By the time James was assisted into the coach with many good wishes, he had enjoyed his fill of the music, talk, food, and revelry. In fact, before the carriage reached Mrs. Campbell's door, he was fast asleep and snoring loudly.

For some days after the party, as he worked on the Edinburgh docks, James thought about his life and his future. He had made his journey to Scotland and had found his father's, and his own people. He also had found another, unexpected family in the Campbells, though Mairi had seemed somewhat distant to him since he had told her his true-life story. But there was Flora, what a lovely girl, and he was sure she had real feelings for him as well.

All those things were on one side. On the other, he really didn't like the cool, damp, cloudy weather of the Scottish winter; he had no love for the exhausting, repetitive job he had on the wharfs; and he had a nagging sense of restlessness, of the need to be moving on, to where or what he didn't know.

The news in the evening paper seemed to arrive in response to his malaise. "Gold Discovered in California" blared from the top headline. The story related that American President James K. Polk had confirmed the rumors that had been swirling around the country all year. Gold had been found at Sutter's Mill in Northern California.

"Did you see the news from California?" he excitedly asked Mairi and Flora as they sat in the parlor that evening. "Gold! What a prospect! To find oneself a rich man for just the picking up of gold nuggets from the stream beds where they lie."

Mairi gave him a skeptical look and, shaking her head, said, "I wouldn't believe everything I read in the paper, James."

"But the President confirms it!" he answered. He looked at Flora as he said, "I know California, I've been in this town they call San Francisco. I could find my way to the gold fields. I could make a fortune. And then I could marry you, Flora!"

Mairi sat bolt upright. "Marry?" she sputtered. "What are you talking about, James?" She snapped her head to face her daughter and saw by the blush on Flora's face that the topic was neither new nor unappealing to her.

"Mairi," James quickly interjected, "we've only lightly talked of it. We would surely broach the matter with you before we proceeded seriously."

"And I would surely forbid it!" Mairi replied stiffly.

"Mother! But why?" Flora cried.

She looked first at Flora and then at James. "Surely you both realize the impracticality. James, you have no education, no prospects."

"That's why this discovery is so important. It's my chance to make good, to be able to provide for Flora in the way she deserves."

"Oh, James," Mairi sighed. "Please don't be so foolish. Gold in California! Why you might as well talk of returning to the savage redskins!"

The insult was so unexpected, even to Mairi who uttered it, that the three sat in awkward silence for a moment. Then Flora spoke. "Mother, you seem to overlook what may be the most important factor, my feelings for James." She turned her gaze to meet his full on. "And I love him, Mother. I want to spend my life with him, wherever he goes."

Mairi also turned to face James. "So, this is how you repay the kindnesses I've shown you, by alienating my own daughter's affections, by trying to steal her away from me and take her to the other side of the world!"

"Please, Mairi, listen to me," James begged.

"I'll not listen! You may go off on your wild goose chase if you please, but you'll not marry my daughter nor take her away from her home to the savage wilderness!" And she stormed out of the room.

James and Flora sat in shocked silence for a long moment. Then James asked, "What shall we do, Flora?"

She smiled weakly at him and said, "Please don't worry. I know my mother well, and I believe I can help her to see reason. Be patient and give me a little time with her."

"But we don't have much time to waste," he replied. "Everyday people from all over the world are flocking to the gold fields. If we get there too late, there will only be the leavings."

She rose and walked to him. Putting her hand gently on his cheek, she said, "I will talk to her tomorrow after she has calmed a bit. Let's see what she has to say then. For now, good night, my love. Don't lose your hopes."

James had a solitary and gloomy breakfast the next morning, with only Davina stirring in the house. He was distracted throughout his day at work, nearly dropping a load of cargo into the water. As he made his way home that afternoon, he was filled with dread at the prospect of confronting Mairi's wrath.

She was waiting for him as he entered the foyer. "Hello, James," she said quietly. "Please come into the parlor. We need to talk."

They seated themselves and Davina brought tea. "James," she began, "I want to apologize for any hurtful words I spoke last night. You surely understand my deep concern for my daughter and her happiness. I have the highest regard for you, and I have appreciated the countless ways you have made our lives better. It is only my concern for Flora that led me to the unseemly outburst of last night."

James began to reply, but Mairi waved him to silence. "Please let me have my say. Flora and I have spoken all day of this matter, and I have come to understand that if I maintain my intransigence, there are two possible outcomes: first that she will defy me and elope with you. She is of legal age, as she reminded me of that many times. Or that she will reluctantly obey my wishes and remain here while you go off on your own. In that event, we would be left here with a household full of tears and recriminations, perhaps that would last our lifetimes."

James maintained his silence until she continued. "The other course is that I consent to your marriage. If I do that, the two of you will leave me and go to California to seek your wealth. Flora has pointed out to me that I have had some small number of suitors that I have rejected out of concern for my daughter's happiness. If she goes away with you, there may be a chance for me to find my own happiness. She also swears that once you have attained your fortune, you will come back, either for extended visits or perhaps to live here, and your improved prospects will be of common benefit."

James sat upright and said, "Of course, Mairi, we will return, and you will never be out of our thoughts and prayers while we are separated."

She managed a wan smile. Then she asked Davina to fetch Flora. James stood as she entered the room and walked to her side, taking her hand in his. Mairi also stood and said, "While this is not what I had always pictured when I thought of Flora's marriage, she has led me to see that it is the best outcome for us all, in the circumstances. Therefore, I do give my consent to your marriage, and my blessings."

To accommodate James's desire for an early departure for California, the wedding was set for the middle of February, on St. Valentine's Day. The event called forth Campbells and Kennedys from all around the city and the outlying areas. These two huge, fractious clans had a complex relationship, often hostile, but usually friendly, and many previous unions had joined the two families through marriage. The joyful gathering was long and very musical, taking on the aspect of family reunion and bon voyage party as well as nuptial celebration.

James promised his Kennedy kin that he would make every attempt to seek out his father, and if he be found alive, to report his history to the clan. Flora equally promised her mother and relatives that she would write faithfully, would observe every precaution for her safety, and would, indeed, return to Scotland, hopefully laden with riches. With many toasts, heaps of sumptuous foods, and myriad fiddle tunes, the festivities wound on into the night.

James knew of three ways to travel to the gold fields. One would be to take ship for America, Boston, New York, or Baltimore, and then go overland. That would involve a cro ssing of the North Atlantic in winter, travel by newly laid rail and by stagecoach over variously improved roadways and would culminate with two months in a wagon across the open prairie and the perilous crossing of the High Sierra. Another choice would be to take passage on a ship bound around Cape Horn to California. James had heard many tales from his mates on the Abigail about the terrors of those seas. The icy mountains of grey water threatening to engulf them, the days spent shivering in a rocky harbor awaiting favorable winds, and he had no wish to expose his new bride to the vicissitudes of that dangerous journey. The third choice, the one James picked, was to cross in the more southerly seas to the Isthmus of Panama. There, by boat and mule train, one could traverse the narrow neck of land to the Pacific side and there take ship for San Francisco.

While this third route seemed the most favorable to James and his new wife, it did entail some worrisome aspects. The sea voyages should be safe enough, but the days spent traversing the Isthmus carried the risk of disease. Yellow fever and cholera were endemic in the moist, hot jungles of Panama, and many a traveler endured debilitating bouts of ague and death from these sicknesses.

James and Flora bid their tearful farewells to Mairi, Davina, and Alan Kennedy and boarded the Fortitude bound for Panama with some 134 passengers, most of them gold-seekers. After a week of sailing southward through cold and rainy weather, they encountered the milder weather of the lower latitudes. It felt odd to James to be a passenger and to watch the labors of the seamen. He, more than most of the passengers, knew what tasks the crew had to perform and understood the risks that they ran when they went aloft to trim the sails.

As newlyweds, they were frequent guests of Captain Adrian Cole at his table. When the captain learned that James was a former seaman and an outstanding fiddler, he arranged for several concerts on the forecastle for the passengers and crew. The air turned balmy as they entered the Caribbean Sea and approached landfall on the Isthmus. It had been a most pleasant crossing, but they now faced a less pleasing prospect of overland travel.

Had they arrived one year later, they would have had a much easier crossing. Efforts to build a railroad across the narrow neck of land had been underway for several years, and the evidence of false starts and unfinished construction was clearly evident as they came ashore at Colon. As it was, they had to make the journey as it had been for centuries. First by boat and then by mule train over poorly maintained paths.

Flora endured the hardships of the trek with good cheer and high spirits, even though she had never experienced anything like the omnipresent heat, humidity, and insects. After four days of travel, they arrived at Panama City, a dilapidated town overrun by gold seekers from around the world. For the first time, James and Flora began to realize that their adventure to the gold fields of California was going to be crowded with thousands of others who had the same dreams of easy wealth.

Lodging was extremely difficult to find, and transportation to San Francisco proved to be a great challenge. The SS California, a new side-wheel steamship, was in port, but with a capacity of only four hundred passengers, she was already fully booked by the time James and Flora attempted to buy their passage.

James approached an officer in the crowded ticket office and asked, "Do you have your full complement of crew?"

The man looked James up and down and asked skeptically, "Are you an able seaman?"

"Aye, sir. I've sailed on the brigantine Abigail from San Francisco to London, around the Cape of Good Hope."

The officer glanced at the fiddle case in James's hand. "And do you play that as well?" he asked.

"Oh, yes sir. Would you like to hear a tune?"

The officer glanced at the throng clamoring for tickets and shrugged. "All right," he sighed, "Let's hear a piece. If you're good enough, we can find a place for you in the crew."

216

James quickly produced his fiddle and began playing the most spirited melodies he could think of. The mob at the counter momentarily forgot their frantic efforts and listened, tapping toes, and clapping along.

"That'll do," said the officer. "If you're as good a seaman as you are a fiddler, we'll make good use of you. I'm Miles Fletcher, first mate of the California. Our skipper is Thomas Bunn. Step into the office to sign the papers."

James hesitated. "Mr. Fletcher, sir," he said.

The officer turned. "What is it?"

"My wife, my new wife is travelling with me. I'll have to have her aboard as well."

Fletcher looked at Flora standing forlornly by herself in the bustling crowd. "Oh, I see," he said. "My, she's a beauty too, you're a lucky man." He bit his lip and thought for a minute. "Well, it's only a three week's sail up the coast. I guess for that time, I can have some midshipmen bunk with the crew and give you, their quarters. But you'll have to pay us back with hard work in the day and good music at night."

"I'll do my best, sir. And thank you!"

The cruise from Panama to San Francisco evoked familiar memories of his trips up and down the California coast in the Abigail. He hadn't lost any of his seaman's skills and the passengers, nearly four hundred souls, delighted in the fiddle music James played for them in the warm, enchanted nights at sea. They stopped for fuel in San Diego, the California was designed to burn either coal or wood, and again in Monterrey, where the offshore breeze brought James the familiar smells of California.

As they neared their destination of San Francisco, James, and Flora, along with all the other passengers, grew more excited. He recalled very well the picturesque village of Yerba Buena where he had loaded tallow and hides and enjoyed the fresh air and scenic views of ocean and bay. It had been renamed San Francisco after the Americans had taken over California from the Mexican government.

He was unprepared for the sprawling chaos that met their gaze as they passed through the Golden Gate and made anchor. Everywhere were tents of all colors and fabrics, unpainted ramshackle buildings, muddy streets, and foul odors of fires and offal. Storefronts advertised mining supplies; merchants dealt goods from their temporary stores made of flapping canvas; prostitutes, gamblers, and desperados rubbed shoulders with men of all races and nationalities. Chinese, African, Hawaiian, Mexican, British, American, and others. People in various forms of attire crowded every establishment and thoroughfare.

With a sinking heart, James began to doubt the wisdom of their journey. They were arriving too late he feared. If San Francisco was this crowded with gold-seekers, what must the actual gold fields be like? How could there be any gold left to find after being picked over by this throng?

Still, he gathered his courage. He had a wife to care for and protect. If all their effort and expense were to come to nothing, then he would have to be a man and find some other way to provide for Flora. Perhaps they could return to Scotland, his tail between his legs, and make a life there. But for now, they had to seek shelter in this seething cauldron of humanity.

He tried to protect Flora from the jostling crowds as they pushed through the streets looking for rooms. The boarding houses had "No Vacancy" signs prominently featured near their doors. Some tents were advertised as rooming houses, but they too, were all filled up.

Their spirits were low as they surveyed the bleak scene and walked aimlessly through the packed dirt streets. They had heard music flowing out of many of the drinking and gambling halls, mostly out-of-tune pianos and wheezy pump organs. James caught the sound of a well-played fiddle coming from a plain but well-kept storefront. Above the busy door, inscribed in neat paint, was the name "The Mountain Man." Below, in smaller print, he read "William Kennedy, prop."

Flora saw it simultaneously. "James! Could that be your father?"

His knees weakened. "I don't know, Flora. I suppose it could be, but there are many William Kennedys in the world, I'm sure. How likely is it that we should find my Da in this uproar?"

They stood in shocked silence for a moment. Then Flora said, "There may be many William Kennedys, but how many of them can play the fiddle like that?"

James was transfixed as he tried to make out the music over the roar of the customers. "Oh, dear God," he said. "It's been long years since I heard my father play but that does sound like it could be him. Let's go in!"

They shoved through the boisterous mob and into the crowded tavern. Men stood three deep at the bar and all the tables were filled with men and their women, most of whom were clearly barroom girls. Two burly men stood along the walls, keeping a watchful eye out for any disturbance that might arise. Behind the bar were two light-skinned black women filling mugs and shot glasses and collecting money as fast as they could. Through the din, James could hear a very well played fiddle. He looked around to see who was playing it, and he saw a small stage in the corner, wreathed in thick smoke and surrounded by clapping cheering patrons.

One of the big men stepped away from the wall and approached them. "Would the lady like a seat?" he asked gruffly.

"I don't see one available, sir," Flora responded.

The man put his hand on the shoulder of a customer seated near them and whispered in his ear. Instantly the man jumped up from his seat and motioned for his companion to rise as well. The burly man then held a chair for Flora and helped her to her seat. James tentatively sat in the other empty chair and thanked the man.

"You're welcome, sir. We don't get many ladies like this in here and we want to treat them right."

The fiddler on the stage was a big man with buckskin clothes, a salt-and-pepper beard, and long grey hair falling to his shoulders. He held his fiddle low on his chest and clutched the bow as he would a knife. James leaned to Flora and whispered, "That's him! That must be him. That's the way he held his fiddle. He's more grizzled than he used to be, but I'm sure that's my father."

They listened to another tune and James told Flora to make a request. "Shout it out loud so he can hear you."

When the fiddler stopped to great applause, Flora half rose and yelled as loud as she could, "Soldiers' Joy!"

The fiddler searched to see who had shouted the request, and catching sight of Flora, said, "Ay, I'm not one to deny a pretty lass. This is one of my oldest tunes, a special one to me. You may know it as 'King's Head'." And he began to play the familiar melody.

James quietly opened his fiddle case under the table and removed the instrument. Without bothering to tune, he began to play along, quietly at first, but then he stood and played louder. The man on the stage heard the second fiddle joining in and beckoned with his fiddle for him to come up and join him. As James moved toward the stage, William's broad smile suddenly froze as he saw the king's head carving on the stranger's fiddle.

William stopped playing and stood on stage, mouth agape, while James continued the tune and stepped up onto the riser. "Quaninch?" William mouthed.

James continued playing and said, "Come on, Da, we must finish the song for the people!"

In complete shock, William joined in and played the tune, the first one he had taught to his son Quaninch in the bark teepee in the village of Mukuntuweap at the mouth of the beautiful canyon. Tears rolled down his cheeks and when at last they finished the song, they embraced to the deafening cheers of the audience.

"This is my son!" William shouted. "My son Quaninch who has been lost these ten years!"

The crowd yelled even louder. There would be time, now, time for each to tell the stories that had led them to this spot, this moment. Time to introduce Lisbeth and Sarah and Flora and Lloyd, time to explain how the onrush of gold seekers had inundated their quiet rancho and how they had discovered real gold in providing food and drink and music to the would-be prospectors as they arrived in San Francisco. There would be time for all of that, but for this moment, it was time to play music. And the twin fiddles soared joyously into the night.

The End

ABOUT THE AUTHORS

Arvel Bird is a Professional Violinist, a storyteller, and an aficionado of Shamanic Practice. This story had its origins in the playing of the violin. After studying classical violin for 11 years Arvel realized that he knew how to play the violin and decided to expand and move beyond reading music and evolve into playing by ear and finding his own style of playing.

After stopping the violin lessons and reading music he would go into his practice room and just sit and listen for music to come to him, but after hearing nothing but the traffic outside he picked up the violin and played just one note, and from that one note came an 8 movement concerto, for violin, the Native American flute, a symphony orchestra, and pow wow drums and singers. Not only did the music come but also a full-length movie of a journey of a Paiute.

This process took 35 years of contemplation, composition, and a year and a half of recording, from Boulder, CO, to Nashville, TN, to Tucson, AZ. This is the Journey of a Paiute and also the journey of Arvel Bird and the unfolding of his Lotus Blossom into who he was destined to be and become if he would but learn the lessons life gave him by following his heart, taking responsibility, accountability, building integrity through the art of persistence, determination and dedication.

This music is healing not only for Arvel but also for his Ancestral people, the Nuwuvi Indians now known as the Shivwit Tribe of the five Bands of Southern Paiutes of Utah. From the music of a violin came a powerful vision of a past life experience, or a parallel life experience starting back in 1829. It brought together the same elements of his past life heritage and his present life heritage, Scottish and American Indian, and, oddly, the one thing that tied them together was the violin. It was brought from Scotland and carried across the land of America and then sailed around the world to Scotland, and back across America again, to California where it would reunite father and son.

My musical singing partner on guitar, banjo, and piano from Ft Wayne, IN, Fred Rothert, expanded the story and brought my epic tale to a fuller, heartwarming historical novel. It's complete with the history of the time about the Old Spanish Trail, the early trappers and traders like Jedediah Smith, General Ashley's Hundred, Rocky Mtn Fur Company, Rafael Rivera, Antonio Armijo, the land of Mukuntuweap, and the Indigenous Nuwuvi Indians.

Fred Rothert is a musician and retired English teacher. He and Arvel Bird played music together in Indiana during the 1970s and 80s. They have maintained their friendship and collaborations over the years as each has pursued different life paths. Both are now living in Arizona and they have united their efforts to create this novel that is based on Arvel's *Journey of a Paiute*. Fred lives in Sun City, Arizona, with Bonnie, his wife of 43  years, and where he continues to be very active in the music scene.

An audio book is coming soon with music and the warm voice of Fred Rothert speaking the written words.

This CD had its origins in the playing of the violin. After studying classical violin for 11 years Arvel realized that he knew how to play the violin and decided to expand and move beyond reading music and evolve into playing by ear and finding his own style of playing. After stopping the violin lessons and reading music he would go into his practice room and just sit and listen for music to come to him, but after hearing nothing but the traffic outside he picked up the violin and played just one note, and from that one note came an eight movement concerto, for violin, the Native American flute, a symphony orchestra, and pow wow drums and singers. Not only did the music come but also a full-length movie in his mind of the journey of a Paiute.

This practice took 35 years to complete and a year and a half to record starting in Boulder, CO, then Nashville, TN, and finally Tucson, AZ. Those 35 years had to be lived before the meaning of this story could be understood.

This is the Journey of a Paiute, but it is also the journey of Arvel Bird and the unfolding of his Lotus Blossom into who he was destined to be, and become if he would but learn the lessons life gave him by following his heart, taking responsibility, accountability, building integrity through the art of persistence, determination and dedication.

This music is healing not only for Arvel but also for his Ancestral people, the Nuwuvi Indians now known as the Shivwitwhat iaw Tribe of the 5 Bands of Southern Paiutes of Utah. From the music of a violin came a powerful vision of a past life experience, or a parallel life experience starting back in 1829. It brought together the same elements of his past life heritage and his present life heritage, Scottish and American Indian, and, oddly, the one thing that tied them together was the violin. It was brought from Scotland and carried across the land of America and then sailed around the world to Scotland, and back across America again, to California where it would reunite father and son.

Visit arvelbird.com to purchase the book and CD online.

www.ingramcontent.com/pod-product-compliance
Lightning Source LLC
Chambersburg PA
CBHW031059020726
47495CB00007B/1959